Two brand-ne[w]
by popular auth[or]

GAVIN TEMP[LETON'S JOURNAL] ENTRY

Well, this is anoth[er . . .] [br]other, Trey, has gotten into. This livin[g-on-the-]edge stuff is getting to be too much—and all be[ca]use of this family "curse" he's convinced we have. Imagine believing that all men in the family die at thirty-seven! I mean, do I look worried? Of course, I'm only thirty-two.

Still, I think having a beautiful physical therapist around could be just what the doctor ordered—and maybe convince him, once and for all, that he's got a lot of living to do. And he shouldn't do it alone. . . .

❤ ❤ ❤

TREY TEMPLETON'S JOURNAL ENTRY

Well, now that I'm happily married, I think it's time to see old Gavin settle down. If only he'd meet the right woman. Of course, since he's married to his job, what are the chances of that happening? Still, he has this beautiful new temporary assistant. Hmmm. Maybe he can find a better use for all those hours in the office than just work?

Dear Reader,

Spring is a time for new beginnings. And as you step out to enjoy the spring sunshine, I'd like to introduce a new author to Silhouette Special Edition. Her name is Judy Duarte, and her novel *Cowboy Courage* tells the heartwarming story of a runaway heiress who finds shelter in the strong arms of a handsome—yet guarded—cowboy. Don't miss this brilliant debut!

Next, we have the new installment in Susan Mallery's DESERT ROGUES miniseries. In *The Sheik & the Virgin Princess*, a beautiful princess goes in search of her long-lost royal father, and on her quest falls in love with her heart-meltingly gorgeous bodyguard! And love proves to be the irresistible icing in this adorable tale by Patricia Coughlin, *The Cupcake Queen*. Here, a lovable heroine turns her hero's life into a virtual beehive. But Cupid's arrow does get the final—er—sting!

I'm delighted to bring you Crystal Green's *His Arch Enemy's Daughter*, the next story in her poignant miniseries KANE'S CROSSING. When a rugged sheriff falls for the wrong woman, he has to choose between revenge and love. Add to the month Pat Warren's exciting new two-in-one, *My Very Own Millionaire*— two fabulous romances in one novel about confirmed bachelors who finally find the women of their dreams! Lastly, there is no shortage of gripping emotion (or tears!) in Lois Faye Dyer's *Cattleman's Bride-To-Be*, where long-lost lovers must reunite to save the life of a little girl. As they fight the medical odds, this hero and heroine find that passion—and soul-searing love—never die....

I'm so happy to present these first fruits of spring. I hope you enjoy this month's lineup and come back for next month's moving stories about life, love and family!

Best,

Karen Taylor Richman
Senior Editor

Please address questions and book requests to:
Silhouette Reader Service
U.S.: 3010 Walden Ave., P.O. Box 1325, Buffalo, NY 14269
Canadian: P.O. Box 609, Fort Erie, Ont. L2A 5X3

My Very Own Millionaire

PAT WARREN

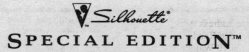

SPECIAL EDITION™

Published by Silhouette Books

America's Publisher of Contemporary Romance

This book is dedicated to Mike and Bob and Irene and all the great physical therapists at Southwest Sports Medicine, with special thanks to Dr. Angelo Mattalino and his assistant, Cheryl —thanks, guys, for helping me to walk again.

 SILHOUETTE BOOKS

ISBN 0-373-24456-8

MY VERY OWN MILLIONAIRE

Copyright © 2002 by Harlequin Books S.A.

The publisher acknowledges the copyright holder of the individual works as follows:

PRISCILLA AND THE PLAYBOY
Copyright © 2002 by Pat Warren

MILLIE AND THE MILLIONAIRE
Copyright © 2002 by Pat Warren

Visit Silhouette at www.eHarlequin.com

Printed in U.S.A.

CONTENTS

PAT WARREN,

mother of four, lives in Arizona with her travel agent husband and a lazy white cat. She's a former newspaper columnist whose lifetime dream was to become a novelist. A strong romantic streak, a sense of humor and a keen interest in developing relationships led her to try romance novels, with which she feels very much at home.

Priscilla and the Playboy

Prologue

Gavin Templeton exited the elevator and hurried along the hospital corridor of the orthopedic floor at San Diego General Hospital. A tall man with serious, brown eyes, he wore a beautifully tailored gray suit, white shirt with a muted-red tie and an impatient frown. He'd been called out of an important meeting by his friend, Dr. Jim Gordon, the orthopedic surgeon who'd recently operated on Gavin's brother Trey yet again.

Trey was being difficult, Jim had told him.

What else was new? Gavin thought, checking the room numbers as he walked along the hallway. He tried to remember how many bones Terence Templeton III had broken in his thirty-six years. At least a dozen. Maybe he should put Jim on retainer as his services were needed so often. Trey, as he was called, was older than Gavin by three years, a daredevil who enjoyed climbing mountains, skiing down the highest slopes, skydiving and racing sail-boats, to name a few of his reckless pursuits.

Gavin was running out of patience with him.

The two brothers had jointly operated the family business of Templeton Enterprises after college, running the huge conglomerate side by side because their father had died and left it to them in trust. They'd gotten along well until suddenly, four years ago, Trey had quit, leaving Gavin solely responsible, while he became the playboy of the Western world and the darling of the paparazzi.

Gavin loved his brother; they'd been through a lot together. But he was getting weary of waiting for Trey to grow up.

This latest fiasco had Trey indulging his passion for speed by racing a stock car, careening out of control on the last turn, flipping and crashing, injuring his shoulder and all but crushing his right knee. Jim had patched him up yet again, but ten days in the hospital and Trey was antsy and insisting on being released.

At the end of his rope with his impatient patient, Jim had called Gavin.

Reaching Room 304, Gavin stopped in the doorway. Wearing an L.A. Lakers basketball jersey and denim shorts, Trey was sitting up in bed while a nurse rebandaged his knee.

Dr. Jim Gordon, his usually amiable expression replaced by a look of exasperation, glanced up from making notes on a chart. "Gavin. I'm glad you're here. Maybe you can talk some sense into your brother. I'm about ready to give up."

Gavin walked in as the nurse finished and left the room. "What's the problem?" he asked, his serious gaze going from one to the other. He'd had to reschedule negotiations for a ten-million-dollar deal and he was not happy.

''Hey, little brother,'' Trey called out, his wide smile crinkling the corners of his green eyes. ''I hope you're here to spring me from this torture chamber.''

Not for the first time Gavin wondered why Trey never took anything seriously, not even his broken bones. Ignoring his brother, he turned to Jim, waiting for an explanation.

''He wants to be released, to go home, and he's had a little over a week of physical therapy sessions. He needs at least another month on that knee, several weeks on the shoulder.'' Jim ran a hand through his sandy hair. ''I can't be responsible if he doesn't do as I say.''

They'd been over this ground before. To cover his annoyance, Gavin shoved his hands into his pants pockets and rattled his change as he moved closer to his brother's side. ''Are you trying to kill yourself or do you just want to wind up in a wheelchair or worse?''

Trey put on his innocently shocked expression. ''Who, me? Hell, no. I'm trying to have fun. You remember fun, Gavin? The pursuit of pleasure, laughter, merriment. *F-u-n.* Ever hear of it?'' He watched his brother's brown eyes turn even more serious.

'''Fun' is hurtling around a track in a souped-up piece of tin at a hundred-plus miles an hour and seeing how quickly you can mangle another part of your body?'' Gavin was having trouble hanging on to his temper. Why would a man with everything to live for constantly try to cheat death? ''One day, you know, you're not going to make it.''

Trey shrugged, then winced as a pain sliced through his shoulder. ''We all have to go sometime, bro,'' he answered, but the humor had left his eyes.

''It's too soon to release you, Trey,'' Jim said firmly.

''I heal fast, Doc. You know that. Besides, I've got a

state-of-the-art gym in my house. Mats, machines, tables. Tell me what else I need and I'll get it. And I've got Connie to coddle me.''

Gavin shook his head. ''Your housekeeper isn't qualified as a physical therapist.''

''Then I'll hire one who is.'' He decided he'd get further with his doctor than his steely-eyed brother. ''Come on, Jim. You own a physical therapy clinic. There must be someone there who'd like to make some extra money.''

Jim stroked his chin, thoughtfully. ''I don't know....''

Trey saw him weakening and moved in. ''He can live in, have his own room, Connie's great meals, swim in the Pacific. Name his own price. What do you say?''

With a tired sigh, Jim turned to Gavin. ''What do you think?''

What Gavin thought was that Trey wasn't going to stop until he got his way. It had always been like that, even when they'd been kids. Trey the charmer, who kept getting into one jam after another and Gavin, despite being younger and smaller, bailing him out. Even in his mid-thirties, Trey still had that boyish appeal with his mop of sun-bleached blond hair and a lean, surfer's perpetually tanned body. Although he knew he wasn't hard on the eyes, still, alongside Trey, Gavin often felt like second choice.

He checked his watch. This was taking entirely too much time. ''Do you have a therapist who'd be willing to stay in his La Jolla place for a month or two?'' Gavin asked Jim.

''Not that long,'' Trey insisted. ''A couple of weeks and I'll be just like new.''

''No, you won't,'' Jim insisted. ''You forget that that's the third hit on that knee. How many times do you think I can keep putting it back together? I'm a doctor, not a miracle worker. You've got to change your ways, Trey. You're not getting any younger. Bones that have been broken before heal more slowly.''

''Yeah, yeah,'' Trey muttered. He'd agree to most anything in order to get out of this place. Hospitals smelled like death, he thought, shivering.

''I do have someone in mind who would probably do it,'' Jim told them. ''She heads my San Diego Physical Therapy Clinic.'' He eyed Trey. ''She's especially good with difficult patients.''

''A woman, eh?'' Trey grinned. ''Things just got better. Is she gorgeous?''

''She weighs three hundred pounds, shaves her head and has a big hairy wart on the end of her nose.'' By his shocked expression, Jim knew Trey didn't know whether or not to believe him. ''All right, so she's attractive, but I wouldn't go messing around with her. She's got a couple of really big brothers.''

Trey resumed his innocent face. ''She'll be as safe as if she were in a convent.''

At Jim's skeptical look, Gavin said, ''Don't worry. Connie's a terrific watchdog as well as a great cook.''

''Actually, I think Priscilla Kovacs can take care of herself,'' Jim acknowledged. ''She's a very dedicated therapist. Now, Trey, I'm going to make out a list of things I want you to do and another that you're *not* to do, understand?'' At Trey's docile nod, he went on. ''I'll go over your injuries and work out a program with Cilla— that's what we all call her. She'll report to me daily. And, Trey, I want you to do *exactly* as she instructs.''

''Okay, sure.'' Anything would be better than this hospital with its antiseptic smells and a two-hundred-pound therapist from Sweden with hands like pork chops.

''Are you sure this Cilla will agree?'' Gavin asked Jim.

Jim nodded. ''She comes from a big Hungarian family, and she helps them out whenever she can, so she can use the extra money. I'll call her, then put through the paperwork.''

''Thanks a lot, Jim,'' Trey said.

''Just don't overdo, you hear? I'll be out to check on you.'' He pushed his glasses higher on his thin nose. ''I could use a swim in the Pacific myself.''

''You're welcome, anytime.''

Gavin shook hands with Jim, then turned back to his brother. He paused, hands in his pockets again, studying the floor, searching for the right words, a man who wasn't used to expressing his emotions. ''Look, I know we don't always agree on everything...''

That was an understatement, Trey thought, wondering where this was going. Gavin was always too busy for more than a quick word or two, running off to some meeting, flying off to some appointment, letting life pass him by. Yeah, they didn't agree on a whole bunch of things.

''...but you're my brother and...and, well, we're all the family we have. I don't want anything more to happen to you.'' He raised his eyes, saw that Trey was looking serious for a change. ''Will you please cut out all this living-on-the-edge stuff? You don't have to come back to the firm if you don't want to. But all those reckless adventures, those friends of yours who risk their lives unnecessarily for the thrill of it.'' Gavin shook his head, truly perplexed. ''I don't understand. You're getting too old for all that nonsense.''

Trey leaned back against his pillows, wondering if he could ever make his brother see how he felt. ''We've talked about this. I told you why I want to try new things. As I've said before, life is short. Too damn short for some of us. There's such a big world out there, Gavin. So much to see and do. I don't want to die sitting at a desk in some ivory tower, making more money to add to an already-huge pile, wishing I'd have done more when the Grim Reaper comes calling. You like the business world, and I have no quarrel with it, but it's not for me. I want to taste life, see everything, do everything before…before they bring down the curtain. And that time's not far away.''

Gavin frowned. ''You're not going to give me that bull about the family curse again, are you? Because I don't believe any of it, and you're too smart to live your life ruled by happenstance.''

''Four male members of our family, all dying in their thirty-seventh year. Do you really think that's coincidence? I don't, maybe because I have six months to go before I turn the magic number.''

''I do call it coincidence, certainly not fate or pre-destination.'' Gavin's expression became beseeching. ''Please, don't throw your life away on a crazy superstition.''

This conversation was depressing Trey, and he knew they'd never agree on the subject. ''All right, I'll be careful.''

Gavin let out a long breath. They both knew he'd gotten nowhere in convincing his brother to quit his rash ways.

He glanced at his watch again. ''I've got to run. I'll come by and meet your new therapist in a day or two.''

''Yeah, okay. See you then.'' Trey watched Gavin walk away in that hurried, determined way he had. No two brothers could be less alike, except maybe in their looks, he thought. Gavin had blond hair like his own, but while Trey's was often wild and untamed, Gavin's was ruthlessly trimmed to a sedate cut every week. Gavin was six feet on the nose and Trey a couple of inches taller, but they had the same physical build. Trey was a natural athlete and Gavin ran every morning religiously, rain or shine, and worked out at the gym in his building twice a week. But there the similarity ended.

Actually, they both resembled their father, not their mothers. Trey's mother, Carolyn, had been small and dark and frail, and had died of complications giving birth to him. Gavin's mother, Cynthia, had been tall with dark hair and a womanly figure. She'd also had no interest in raising someone else's son, nor her own, for that matter. One fine day she'd walked out on both of them and their father when Trey had been thirteen and Gavin only ten.

Perhaps that was why they were so different, Trey thought, because they didn't have the same mother. He cared about his brother, too, well aware that it had been just the two of them against the world for a long time now. But their philosophies on life and how to live it were often miles apart, and that kept them from being really close. Maybe one day…

A nurse came in with Trey's discharge papers, quickly dispelling his gloomy introspective mood. He smiled as he signed his name with a flourish. After two weeks in this medicinal hellhole, it was going to feel great to be home.

Chapter One

Pacing while on crutches wasn't easy, Trey decided on his second turn around the marble foyer of his home. He'd nearly stumbled when one rubber tip caught on the oval oriental rug near the double doors. Annoyed, he used a crutch to shove it aside. That would be all he needed, to fall right now.

Stopping, he leaned against the balustrade of the winding stairway leading up to the second floor. Where was she?

All the arrangements had been made, and Jim had called last night to confirm that Priscilla Kovacs would be arriving this morning at nine. Trey glanced at his left wrist and realized he'd forgotten to put on his watch. It was upstairs in his room. Everything he wanted, it seemed, was either on the other level or several rooms away. Frustration had him gritting his teeth.

He hoped this therapist, the one Jim said was in charge

of his clinic because she was the best, would be able to hurry things along. Yesterday the equipment Jim had ordered had been delivered and set up in his exercise room across the hall from his bedroom. He already had a rowing machine, a stair-stepper, a treadmill and assorted weights, but Jim had told him to leave those alone, for now. The stationary bicycle, the padded massage table, an ice machine and a steamer for hot packs were all that he'd need in the beginning.

Trey was skeptical.

He wasn't afraid of hard work. Anything to get his body in shape quickly. He didn't mind pain because he felt the end justified the means. After all, he had places to go, things to do. He was not an old man who needed to heal slowly. He'd convince Cilla to use an accelerated program and keep it between the two of them so Jim and Gavin wouldn't go ballistic. He'd use his charm on her, Trey decided, smiling. That rarely failed him.

Carefully he hobbled to one of the two long, narrow windows flanking the double doors and gazed out. A beautiful May day, a little overcast, but the clouds would burn off in another hour or so. A great day to go sailing or maybe catch some waves. Soon, he promised himself.

Trey glanced down at the thick bandages covering his left knee and frowned. Why did this have to happen now? He hadn't had an accident since last June, nearly a year ago. He'd been waterskiing when a hard wave had upended him. Not unusual but one of his skis had come off and smacked his right wrist. Only two small bones broken, yet they'd taken weeks to heal.

He wasn't really a stock car racer, but a friend had asked him to sub for him. The challenge had been too enticing to resist. He'd been going along great, the finish line in sight. But that last turn on the track had done him in. All right, so he would use some care after his knee mended. Maybe buy some time.

His green eyes narrowed as he stared out again. Damn, where was she?

Priscilla Kovacs was having a bad morning.

She'd gotten up in plenty of time, had her bags packed and ready to go by eight. But her roommate, Jan Ellis, an oceanographer who'd been called out early by the Department of the Navy for a special run, had taken the last of the coffee in her thermos. So Cilla hadn't had her usual caffeine fix. Next she couldn't find her keys because Smokey had hidden them again. The short-haired gray cat was notorious for running off with things and stashing them all over the condo.

It had taken Cilla fifteen minutes to check all of Smokey's favorite places, finally locating her keys in a back corner of the hall closet. Hurrying, she thought she'd have time to grab a Starbucks-to-go before realizing she needed gas. Exasperated, she stopped to fill up, one eye on the time.

Cilla hated being late for anything.

Then, even though she was familiar with the streets of La Jolla, in her haste she'd made a wrong turn onto a one-way street and had to follow it all the way around. She checked the directions Jim had scribbled down for her before aiming her white Jeep Wrangler in the opposite direction. Glancing at the nearest street sign, she saw that she was finally on the right track.

Cilla had been to several homes in the posh suburb as part of her job, but never on this winding boulevard street. This was an area of huge houses, their fronts facing the Pacific Ocean, with manicured lawns and tall trees and shrubs to conceal the owners from the prying eyes of passersby. Mustn't have the riffraff peeking over the bushes. Money could buy a lot of things, and privacy was one of them.

She wasn't looking forward to this particular job, not after Jim had told her about Terrence Templeton III. Cilla and Jim had known each other for a long time, and she trusted him to tell her the truth about the patients she handled. He'd told her that Trey was difficult, obstinate, impatient. Careless and reckless, too, if the number of injuries he'd sustained through the years was any indication. He'd broken more bones than most pro athletes, yet he kept going back for more.

What drove a wealthy man in the prime of life to keep risking his neck for thrills? she wondered, as she maneuvered around a curve in the road. Jim had also said Trey was self-assured, charming and generous. Certainly the salary he'd offered her was more than ample, which was a major factor in Cilla agreeing to the job. She ran the clinic and worked with recovering bone injuries. Occasionally she had accepted a few wealthy private patients on Jim's recommendation. He knew her circumstances, that she needed every dollar she could scrape together.

Finally she spotted a large, sprawling home painted a dazzling white sitting on top of the highest hill. Checking the discreet numbers along the way, she decided that had to be it because the road dead-ended just ahead. Slowing, she turned onto the narrow tree-lined lane leading to the house.

Mansion was a better word. Three stories high with a gabled roof and wings on each side, it was larger than the La Jolla library and less inviting. How many rooms must there be in there? Cilla wondered as she cruised closer. Jim had mentioned that Trey lived alone with only a housekeeper. Pity the poor woman who had to clean such a big place. She counted sixteen windows on this back side, framed by black shutters that seemed too austere. She would have chosen a forest green to blend in with the environment.

What kind of man would want to live in this mausoleum-like structure?

Casual, Jim had said in describing Trey. He'd known both Templeton brothers since their college days, adding that Trey was very informal and had an irreverent sense of humor. One would need that to live in this place, Cilla decided as she circled around to the front and came to a stop near the double doors which had to be twenty-feet high. Gothic columns supported a wide overhang that shaded the flagstone walk leading to the porch where twin wrought-iron benches faced each other.

Climbing out, she took a moment to admire the emerald-green lawn that sloped down toward steps leading to the sandy beach and the clear blue sea. A row of purple jacaranda trees added a profusion of color to the hibiscus, oleander and poinsettia bushes artfully planted in beds along the recently mowed grass, their scents mingling with the salty sea air. Cilla drew in a deep breath as she retrieved her bag from the back of her Jeep, enjoying a light breeze that whipped her shoulder-length hair about.

Someone definitely tended these gardens unless the millionaire playboy himself liked to get his hands dirty. No, that picture wouldn't compute from what she'd heard of Trey's playboy lifestyle, she decided as she hurried up the three stone steps, hoping she wasn't late.

She pressed the doorbell and stepped back.

Inside, the chimes rang out, but Trey had moved back to the bottom of the staircase, knowing Connie would answer the door. He wasn't sure he could manage the heavy door on his crutches. Sprawling onto the floor at her feet was no way to meet his new therapist. Although he'd been practicing, he still wasn't very good at walking with crutches, mostly because his left shoulder was still painful. Besides, this way he could size her up before she noticed him.

Wiping her hands on a kitchen towel, Consuela Ortega came bustling from the kitchen, her clogs noisy on the bare floor. As usual, her salt-and-pepper hair was pulled tightly back, the length knotted at her nape with an ornate turquoise clasp. Noticing the rug tossed into a heap, she frowned as she turned to Trey, hands on her ample hips.

"What is this?" she demanded, as only someone who has worked for a family for over a quarter of a century can do.

"I almost tripped on it," Trey explained. He wasn't sure why, but Connie could make him feel contrite with just a look, much less words. He often wondered who worked for whom.

Tsk-tsking under her breath, Connie picked up the rug and folded it neatly. "You should tell me. I would remove it." The chimes sounded again and she put the rug aside and swung open the heavy right-hand door.

"You must be the new therapist," Connie said, stepping back invitingly and smiling at the young woman.

"Yes. Cilla Kovacs."

"I'm Connie, the housekeeper. Come in, please."

Carrying her large shoulder bag, Cilla picked up her leather case and stepped in from the humid morning into the coolness of the foyer. She couldn't help noticing that this anteroom was bigger than the two largest rooms in the house she'd grown up in. Marble floor, old-fashioned, dark wallpaper, an enormous chandelier and what looked like an ornately hand-carved railing on the staircase going up.

Her scrutiny stopped there when a tall man on crutches, wearing gray shorts and a football jersey, stepped out of the shadows. Her new patient, Cilla thought as her practiced gaze traveled from his bare feet up his well-toned physique and ended at green eyes that were studying her intently. He needed a haircut, or perhaps he liked to wear his hair all tousled, and he needed a shave, which gave him an edgy look. Then he smiled, revealing strong, white teeth with one eyetooth slightly crooked. She was relieved to see the slight imperfection, for she'd been thinking that, all healed and cleaned up, Terrence Templeton III would make a woman's mouth water.

Which might prove to be a huge and unwelcome distraction.

Trey knew he was staring, but he couldn't seem to help himself. He'd worked with a string of physical therapists over the years and none had looked like this one… certainly not the Swedish therapist with pork-chop hands. Her auburn hair was windblown and her cheeks slightly flushed. She was wearing light-blue sweatpants and shirt, concealing her slender figure. But it was her dark-blue eyes that captured his attention. They were an intriguing mixture of wary and curious.

Attractive, Jim had said. Yeah, in spades.

"Hi. I'm Trey, and you're late." His smile widened, intending to take the bite out of his slight rebuke.

Cilla pushed up her sleeve to check her watch. "Oh, I…" Just then, the grandfather's clock on the side wall of the foyer chimed the hour of nine. She smiled as the last bong sounded with a slight echo. *Gotcha!* "I try to be punctual," she said, her lips twitching.

Trey cleared his throat as he took a step, using his crutches. Attractive and smart, too. He'd have to keep things strictly business or they'd never make progress. "I'd like to get started as soon as possible."

"Trey," Connie admonished, "will you let the lady settle in first?" She took Cilla's leather case and shoulder bag from her. "I'll take you to your room. It's right next to Trey's on the ocean side." She started for the stairs. "I can show you around the house later while your patient is napping."

"Napping!" Trey moved to the steps. "I have no intention of napping."

"After lunch every day," Connie said in a firm voice that brooked no argument. "Dr. Jim left instructions, and you need to follow them."

Cilla struggled with a smile as she watched Trey frown at Connie's retreating back. But she didn't want to start off on the wrong foot with him. "Why don't I meet you in the exercise room as soon as I unpack?" she suggested.

"Fine." Great! Now he had *two* bossy women in the house. He'd have to set them both straight as to who was in charge around here, Trey decided. He stepped onto the first stair with his good leg, maneuvering his crutches somewhat awkwardly.

"Whoa, there," Cilla said, rushing to his side. "You shouldn't be using the stairs yet. Don't you have an elevator?" From the looks of things, the house was like a hotel, with arches leading to cavernous rooms on either side of the foyer. A quick glance had her noticing that there was no furniture in either of the two rooms she could see into. Odd.

"Elevator back by the kitchen, but it hasn't worked in years," Trey muttered, then nearly dropped a crutch.

Quickly, Cilla took both crutches from him, set them down and slipped her right arm around his waist to keep him from falling. His left knee had sustained the injury, as well as his left shoulder, so she would act as his crutch. "Let me support you on this side and you grip the railing on the other."

"You don't have to…" Before he could protest further, Trey felt her surprisingly strong hand clutch his side, then her body move close to his. As if that wasn't enough, she reached to stretch his left arm around to drape over her shoulder. A good half a foot shorter than he, she was wrapped around him in a near death grip, her windblown hair just under his nose.

He turned his head and drew in a steadying breath, only to have her scent, something fresh and lightly floral, tangle his senses. How the hell had he lost control of the situation so quickly?

"Come on, slowly now, let's move upward." Cilla urged him forward, supporting his weakened side. "Don't put your full weight on your left leg. Step up with your right, then bring the left up to the same stair, taking them one at a time."

He had to search for the humor in this. "You mean like little kids do, baby steps?" Though the house was cool, he felt overly warm and knew exactly what had caused it.

"Yes, that's right." They inched upward, slowly, carefully. How in the world had he made it down? she wondered.

Once he forgot and reached up with his left leg, but a pain sliced through his knee and he held back a moan, though just barely. Trey hated to admit she was right, that these stairs were no picnic. He was glad no one had seen him come down, one step at a time, on his butt. Connie had scolded him when he'd made it to the kitchen, but he'd spent two days confined to the upstairs rooms after ten days in the hospital, and he was antsy and restless.

Finally they reached the upstairs landing. Cilla maneuvered him to the wall of the hallway. "Just lean here a minute while I go get the crutches." She hurried down the steps.

"I have a cane in my room," he called after her.

"You aren't ready for a cane yet," Cilla told him as she returned and helped put the crutches in place. Looking around, she saw several doors leading to half a dozen rooms on both sides of the hall. Probably most were rarely used, she thought as Connie came out of a room halfway down.

"I put your things in there and opened the French doors," Connie said as she walked toward them. She'd overheard the exchange between Trey and the therapist, causing her to chuckle to herself. A firm hand was just what the doctor ordered. "It's a nice sunny room with a terrace. You can take your meals out there if you like or downstairs. I'll have lunch ready around twelve. If you need anything, just buzz me. There's an intercom in all the rooms."

"Thank you, Connie. I'm sure I'll be fine."

Connie gazed up at the man she'd helped raise from boyhood and saw he was sweating from the climb. Or was it something other than exertion that had his cheeks flushing? This might be interesting to watch. "You listen to her, you hear?"

"Yes, ma'am," Trey said with his cocky grin in place again.

"First thing," Cilla began, looking at Trey, "can you afford to have that elevator fixed?" She knew very well he could. "Because if not, I don't want you leaving the upstairs until Dr. Jim clears you."

Trey's cockiness was short-lived. "Connie, call the repairman, okay?"

"Will do," the housekeeper said, unable to hide her smile as she went downstairs.

"You look tired," Cilla said, noticing his strained expression. "Maybe we should wait until later to begin your first workout."

"No! I'm fine. How could I be tired? It's only nine in the morning and all I've done is sit around for days. Weeks." He started toward the exercise room.

Cilla had worked with many a strong, athletic type who hated being restricted in any way and wanted to rush the program. It always took some convincing that physical therapy doesn't work that way, that surgery, injured muscles, broken bones will heal but not necessarily on the patient's schedule. She could smooth the way, but she couldn't hurry their recovery.

She fell in step beside him. "Look, I know it's difficult, not being able to do whatever you want. But you should know by now that the body heals in its own time. I read your chart. You've had several surgeries and broken bones. Believe me, I'll work with you and get you up and running as quickly as possible."

That's what he wanted to hear. Maybe she'd cooperate with his plans after all. Reaching the open door to the exercise room, Trey stopped and smiled. "I know you will and I appreciate you taking me on. Jim tells me you're the best." A little graciousness, a little flattery, and she'd be eating out of his hand.

"Jim's prejudiced. He's dating my sister." Cilla stuck her head in the door to check out the equipment. A large room, one wall mirrored, Berber carpeting, assorted machines that matched the quality of the ones in her clinic. "Looks like you've got some fine equipment in here. We'll do okay." She turned and saw those green eyes studying her, his expression unreadable. "I'll just unpack and meet you back here in ten minutes."

"Great." Trey watched her walk toward the room Connie had prepared, wondering what she looked like under those roomy sweats. She seemed younger than the twenty-nine Jim had told him she was. Maybe because she didn't seem to be wearing makeup, her skin looking soft and clean, a few freckles on the bridge of her nose. Plus those fathomless eyes, blue as the Pacific.

And she smelled like heaven.

Trey hobbled into the exercise room. Jim had said Cilla was single. If things were different, he might have pursued her, making sure the few weeks they had together were memorable in every way. But he had a goal to achieve and he needed her for that and that alone. As long as she could get him on the mend and quickly, he didn't care if she looked like Godzilla.

The fact that she didn't was a bonus.

Chapter Two

The bedroom was charming, Cilla thought as she closed the door behind her. Old-fashioned but lovely with hardwood floors, a lovely Oriental rug, a four-poster bed and dresser of highly polished mahogany. She smiled as she peeked into the connecting bath and saw the claw-foot tub. Connie had unpacked for her, she was surprised to see. Wandering out through the double doors to the balcony, she breathed in the fresh salty air, pleased that her room faced the ocean side. A person could get used to this.

Although she'd often visited the homes of patients who weren't ambulatory and had the money to pay for personal calls, she'd never spent the night, certainly not for several weeks like this job demanded. But Jim had been most persuasive, his long friendship with the Templeton brothers underlying his request, and so she'd agreed. And then there was the money.

Gazing out at a small brown bird on a limb of a tall Torrey pine, indigenous to this area only, just outside her terrace, Cilla decided she just might be able to put up with her new assignment, despite Trey's impatience.

Changing into cotton shorts and T-shirt supplied by Jim to all his therapists, she wondered why Trey was in such an all-fired hurry. As often as he'd worked with a therapist, according to his file, you'd think he would know these things took time. Range of motion doesn't return to an injured joint overnight.

Tying her hair into a ponytail, she checked her appearance in the cheval glass. ''That's as good as it gets, folks,'' Cilla said aloud, then left the room.

Trey was leaning on his crutches, staring out the window as she entered his exercise room, her athletic shoes quiet on the carpeted floor. His shoulders were slumped, whether from his injury or his mood she couldn't tell. They were impressive shoulders tapering to a slim waist and muscular legs. Apparently, except for his recent injuries, he was in great shape. Men that were physically fit often resented their bodies for letting them down, even in accidents they'd brought about themselves.

''Ready when you are,'' she said, and watched him turn around.

Trey's green eyes narrowed. He'd mentally complained about her baggy sweats and now he wished she'd kept them on. She was all in white—shirt, shorts and shoes—contrasting nicely with her tanned skin. Nothing was tight on her, yet the outfit had his imagination nudging his libido. Just what he needed, a gorgeous woman with license to touch him all over. Maybe he should have stayed with the lady with pork-chop hands.

''Where do we start?'' he asked, his voice thicker than usual.

"Climb on that table, please. I need to examine the incision to see how it's healing." Cilla walked to the shelves off to the side and looked over the supplies and equipment she'd requested from Jim. Everything was there. Turning back, she saw he was sitting up, waiting.

The shelf beneath the padded table held several pillows. She picked up two and placed them at the head. "Lie down, get comfortable." Noticing he favored his sore shoulder, she helped arrange the pillows.

Carefully she unwrapped the Ace bandage from his knee, setting it aside, then the gauze. She removed a large square bandage with bloodstains. Mentally counting, she saw there were fourteen staples, the wound still red and raised. "As you probably know, Jim will remove these staples soon. There's been a little bleeding, probably since you started moving around on the crutches. I'm going to clean this up a bit." She found fresh gauze and alcohol and went to work, her touch gentle.

"How does it look, in your professional opinion?" Trey asked.

"Good. Jim does nice work."

Trey frowned. "No, I mean how is it healing and when do you think he'll release me."

Her brows rose as she turned to him. "Release you? You mean when will you be finished with physical therapy? That's always hard to say. It depends on how fast you heal and…"

"I heal real fast."

"Good. And how hard you work to…"

"I'm ready to work night and day."

Cilla finished cleaning, threw away the gauze and recapped the alcohol. "I told you earlier, these things take time. The body isn't like a car engine where you replace the parts, squirt on a little oil and it's ready to roll."

It wasn't the answer Trey wanted. "Give me your best educated guess as to when I'll be able to be on my own again."

Persistence was his middle name, apparently. "A month or two, maybe three, but don't hold me to that."

"No, that won't do." Shaking his head, Trey scooted to a sitting position, trying not to flinch at the pain in his shoulder at the sudden movement. "I can give you two, three weeks at the outside, to get me in tip-top shape."

She met his determined gaze. "And why is that?" Jim hadn't said anything about a timetable.

"Because I'm entered in the San Diego yacht races in mid-June and I have to get some practice in before the race."

Cilla was certain her face looked as dumbfounded as she felt. "You're not serious."

He grinned that disarming, boyish smile she was certain had females by the dozen falling at his feet.

"Very serious. The race is scheduled only once a year. It's my last chance to make it. I've got to be ready."

"I'm afraid you'd better not count on it." Was the man looney? A grueling race a month away and he thinks he'll be ready with a shattered knee and a badly wrenched shoulder. "You can race next year."

Damn it all, he couldn't wait until next year. There wouldn't *be* a next year for him. How could he convince her without going into something he'd rather not with her?

"All right, how about this. You get me as ready as you can, and I'll do the rest. Deal?"

That wicked smile again. Thought he had her, did he? Not so fast, chum. "We'll see. Let's take off your shirt so I can check your shoulder." With a practiced move, she tugged the football jersey over his head, revealing a broad chest sprinkled with curly blond hair, his muscles well defined. He didn't get this build from sitting behind a desk.

Cilla had to struggle to remain detached and professional with such a perfect specimen seated before her wearing only shorts. Then there was the wound.

His left shoulder was criss-crossed with three scars and dotted with still angry looking yellow, black and blue bruises. Gingerly she touched here and there and heard his involuntary intake of breath. Even if by some miracle his knee healed quickly, how could he possibly think he could work those heavy sails with this very tender shoulder in a race? Did he have a death wish or was he certifiably nuts?

She was humoring him, Trey knew. No matter. This was only day one. He'd win her over. He'd never met a female that his charm hadn't won over if he really put some effort into it.

"First, I'm going to put some heat on both of these injuries. Later we'll do ultrasound." She crossed the room to place the packs into the heater.

"What does ultrasound do?" he asked, thinking to get her talking, even though he'd had ultrasound before. The old salesman's mantra: get them to like you, get them to trust you, get them to sign on the dotted line. Only in this case, it was get her to work him hard enough to earn Jim's release in three weeks.

"It's a technique using ultrasonic waves and frequencies to aid in the healing process," Cilla explained. She placed a white cotton cloth over both wounds so the heat wouldn't be directly on the affected area.

"So it's the same as the ultrasound that doctors use to check a pregnant woman's baby?"

His question had the desired effect and she smiled.

"Similar, but not quite the same." Minutes later she placed the first heated pad on his knee.

"Ohhhh," he murmured.

"Too hot?"

"No. Feels good."

"Lie back now." When he did, she situated the second pad, wrapping it around the injured shoulder.

This one felt even better, Trey had to admit. Odd how they'd never done this in the hospital.

"We'll try fifteen minutes," Cilla said, fixing the timer. "Close your eyes and relax, let the heat work."

She saw that he actually did, which kind of surprised her. He seemed to have so much pent-up energy, like a coiled snake ready to spring. Small wonder he hated being tied down. But he was following her directions, so maybe he wouldn't be so difficult, after all.

Picking up his file, she sat down on a stool nearby and began to read Jim's notes again. He'd gone over each notation with her, explaining the injury and the prescribed treatment, but she wanted to review them.

The shock wasn't that Trey had done so many dangerous things, Cilla decided, but rather that he'd survived them all in relatively good shape, the recent injury notwithstanding. He'd broken an ankle skydiving and now had a steel plate in it. He'd broken two bones in his wrist waterskiing. He'd had his first serious knee injury snow skiing. Rock climbing, mere inches from the top, he'd fallen and broken an arm and three ribs. As soon as he'd healed, he'd gone back up and made it to the top that time, Jim had written in an aside. Can't keep a good man from his goal, she thought. Or was it a crazy man?

Playing touch football with his friends in the park, he'd been hit head-on and suffered a concussion that put him in a coma for five days. Second knee injury took place when he'd gone white-water rafting in Colorado, got tossed out on a particularly dangerous curve and landed kneefirst on a jagged rock. On that same trip, Jim had written, one of Trey's close buddies had also been hurled out, hitting his head and going under. By the time they managed to reach him, he'd drowned.

Did his friend's death deter Trey from his thrill seeking? Oh, no. He'd actually stepped up the pace. Shortly after, he'd gone deep sea diving off the Florida coast searching for sunken treasure based on a map one of his friends had found in an old book. Currently he'd been taking flying lessons, hoping to solo by the end of June, which now was out of the question. He'd also tried parachuting from a plane just for the fun of it.

All this frenetic pursuit of thrills in the last four years.

Cilla closed the file and looked over at Trey Templeton. Why? was the big question. Even now, with his eyes closed and heat supposedly making his body warm and comfortable, there was an aura of barely contained impatience about him, an eagerness to get moving. Slowly she walked over and stood looking down at him. What drives you? she wondered.

The timer went off and Trey opened his eyes. He saw her studying him, her expression puzzled and curious. "What next, coach?"

She removed the hot pads and found the professional massage cream on the shelf. "A massage. The shoulder first, I think."

Mmm. A massage by a beautiful woman. This might not be too bad, Trey decided.

Cilla dipped her fingers into the jar and applied some of the medicated cream to the area, the skin red from heat. Her touch featherlight, she gently worked around the bruises, loosening the surrounding traumatized muscles.

Back and forth she rubbed, watching his face for signs of pain, but he seemed to be handling it well. A little deeper now, easing the tense muscles, getting the blood flowing to the spot to aid in healing.

Trey never would have thought those small hands could be so strong. He'd had all kinds of massages before, but Cilla seemed to know just where the bunched muscles were and yet avoided the painful area. No question, this woman knew her job.

If only she weren't leaning so close and playing havoc with his thoughts.

Finishing the shoulder, she moved to the knee. "We've got to get this swelling down," she said, as she dipped more cream and began to massage his lower leg, working up toward the incision. She was careful, but still his skin quivered when she got too close. "Am I hurting you?"

Trey was too used to his own macho image to admit pain. "Nah, it's fine."

Cilla knew he was lying. His trembling flesh gave him away. After a bit, she shifted her attention to above the knee, working the cream into his strong thigh muscles.

Despite his best effort, Trey felt his muscles tremble and he knew his reaction had nothing to do with his injury. When pork-chop hands had massaged his leg, he'd felt nothing. Praying he wouldn't embarrass himself, he gritted his teeth and tried to make his mind a blank.

"Is there any numbness in this area?" she asked, totally oblivious to her patient's internal battle.

"Numbness? No, why?"

"That's good. Sometimes with knee surgery, the long hours on the operating table causes a trauma to the sciatic nerve which manifests itself by a numbing sensation. It quiets down after a few months, but it's better if you don't have it at all."

Her hands moved along his thigh, up and down, back and forth, feeling the muscles contract involuntarily. They'd shaved the area from just above his knee down to midcalf for surgery, and the hair was just growing back. "This probably itches like the devil, eh?" she asked, glancing at his face. His expression was tight, tense.

"Not as bad as when I broke my leg and had a cast on it." Keep talking, Trey told himself. Conversation would keep his mind off how her hands were making him feel, how her touch was coming dangerously close to arousing him. "I finally straightened a wire hanger and shoved it down into the cast. What relief."

"You could have opened up the incision," she said mildly.

"Yeah, but I didn't."

"How old were you?"

"Nine. I'd climbed that big tree alongside the house. I used to like sitting up there and daydreaming. Imagine myself as a pilot or an adventurer, king of the world. It was quiet and peaceful." He sighed, remembering. "But that day, Dad was calling me and he sounded mad. I was hurrying down when I misjudged my hold on a branch. Down I went."

Finishing, she turned to him as she put the top back on the jar. "And was your father even more angry then?"

No, it hadn't been like that. His father and stepmother, Cynthia, Gavin's mother, were going out to a party and Dad was annoyed, but not really angry. He had Connie take Trey to the hospital, with six-year-old Gavin in tow, and they'd hurried off to their party. Cynthia loved parties, and Dad did whatever it took to make her happy. Never mind that his oldest son was scared out of his wits while they set his leg and put on the cast.

Trey noticed she was staring at him, her big blue eyes serious. "No, Dad didn't get mad often."

"Mine didn't, either," Cilla said as she finished and went to clean up at the stainless steel sink in the corner. "Quite a feat, considering he and my mother raised six children, all of us only two years apart."

Trey pulled himself into an upright position. "Six? I can't even imagine it."

She rolled the ultrasound machine over, plugged it in and reached for the conductor transmission gel. "Actually, it was fun growing up in a big, noisy household. We always had someone to play with as kids. The older ones helped the younger ones with homework, baseball, chores. My brother Mike even taught me to dance." Cilla didn't realize that a certain sadness had crept into her eyes as she squirted gel onto his knee. "This will be a little cold after the heat and massage."

What had brought on that sudden sadness? Trey wondered.

Pulling over the stool, she sat down and began moving the head over the injured knee area.

He ignored the cold, more interested in her background. "Do all of you live around here?"

"All except one, my brother Mike. He lives in L.A."

"A maverick, eh? Like me."

"Not really." Mike wasn't anything like Trey. He wasn't wealthy or reckless or a playboy. She went on, telling about the rest. "Alex is a lawyer, Charles owns a construction company and Julie is a nurse—all three married, all living in or around San Diego." Cilla imagined that learning about her big family was entirely foreign to Trey's upbringing as a rich son living in this mansion on the hill. "My sister, Isabel, is single, studying for her master's degree in counseling. She's the youngest, the one who dates Jim.''

''What does your father do?'' he asked, watching her scoot the ultrasound instrument over and around, up and back. It was hard to imagine that such a simple thing would do much good, but he'd go along with it.

''Dad started out as a bricklayer, later opened the construction company Charles now operates. Mom's a seamstress. They still live in the house where we all grew up. And Mom still cooks a big dinner every Sunday, served at one o'clock. Those of us who are free just show up, along with spouses, kids and significant others. My sister, Isabel, often brings Jim. He just loves Mom's cooking.''

''But how does she know how much food to make if she doesn't know ahead of time who'll show up?''

Cilla laughed, a warm sound. ''There's never a time when there's not enough food in the Kovacs house. My mother cooks for an army, then sends leftovers home with everyone. The women help in the kitchen, and the men play horseshoes in the backyard or watch football on TV. It sounds chauvinistic but it works for us.'' She glanced at him, growing a little embarrassed. ''I know this all sounds kind of like *Little House on the Prairie* on television to someone like you. You've traveled all over the world. I must be boring you. I'm sorry. I always find the time passes more quickly and the patient is distracted from his pain if we talk.''

''No, no, you're not boring me.'' An obstinate curl had escaped from her ponytail and Trey struggled with the sudden desire to reach up and fix it. He cleared his throat. ''Your family sounds great.'' He meant it, even though he'd never known a family like she described.

''They're very special.'' Cilla knew Trey's background from Jim, knew that he'd never known his own mother, who'd died giving birth to him. She'd also been told that his father's second wife had walked out on Trey and his brother when they were both quite young, leaving their father devastated. The poor man had died shortly after. A sucker for abandoned children, her heart went out to the boy Trey had been.

The timer went off for the second time and Cilla turned off the ultrasound machine. With a soft cloth, she wiped the excess gel from his leg, then cleaned the machine before putting it away. Again she washed her hands, then gathered the gauze and Ace bandage.

"Now comes the machine workout, I'll bet," Trey said, his gaze skimming the rowing machine, the stationary bike and others.

"I'm afraid not. It's way too early for exercises that strenuous at this point. Your incision bled with the simple act of walking on crutches." She began winding the gauze around his knee. "I'm going to ice you down now, to try to bring the swelling down. Tomorrow or the next day we'll try stimulation with electrodes. It's called ramping and it stirs and arouses the muscles for range-of-motion training." Noticing his disappointment, she went on, hoping to convince him that this schedule was in his best interest. "We'll see how well your knee tolerates some simple exercises—flexing, leg raises, squats and later adding ankle weights."

Trey's mellow mood had evaporated. At this rate he'd be fiddling around here till Christmas. "I don't know if I made myself clear. I *need* to be healed and in great shape in three weeks at the most."

Cilla picked up the Ace bandage. "I don't know if I made myself clear, either. Your timetable is impossible to achieve, based on your injuries. What you want will take three *months* minimum, not weeks. Maybe more." Finished wrapping the knee with the Ace bandage, she fastened it in place and walked over to the ice machine.

"Wait a minute. Who's working for whom here?"

She waited a beat, then straightened from scooping crushed ice into a large plastic bag. "I work for Dr. Jim Gordon. I follow his orders. If you insist on changing those orders, you need to take it up with him."

Damn! Trey knew exactly what Jim would say. So much for charming his therapist into a secret pact. He'd have to go along for now, but he didn't have to like it.

Waiting by the machine, Cilla grew impatient. "Do you want to call your doctor?"

"All right, you win." His earlier amiability gone, his face reflected his annoyance.

This wasn't working, Cilla thought, deciding he looked like a pouty little boy with that unhappy scowl, as he shoved his fingers through his already unruly hair. "Maybe you'd be happier with another therapist."

No matter who Jim sent over to replace her, Trey knew they'd follow his directions to the letter. And if he caused too much of a fuss, Jim would have him back in the hospital or in a rehab center. A no-win situation. "Let's just get on with it. I'll behave. I'm not a child."

"Could have fooled me." Giving not an inch, she tied the bag of ice and placed it carefully atop his knee before fixing a smaller one for his shoulder. Looking around, she spotted the triangular leg rest she'd requested and propped it at the end of the table. "Put your legs up here. It'll take the strain off your back."

Silently he did as she requested.

Cilla set the timer, then sat down on the stool to make notes on Trey's chart. She planned to record all his protests as well as his daily treatment and physical progress. If there would be any.

When it came to healing, Terrence Templeton III was his own worst enemy.

Trey was fuming. Stretched out in a lounge chair on his bedroom veranda, he scarcely noticed the sun slowly lowering into the sea in the distance or the warm breeze mussing his hair. He felt trapped, ambushed, tricked by his doctor, his brother, his therapist and even Connie.

Every day after lunch Connie insisted he take a nap. "Doctor's orders. You need your rest," she told him, ushering him into his room and turning down the bed. "Bones heal while you sleep." Trey was certain she'd lock him in if he dared to challenge her. This was almost worse than being in the hospital. Almost.

Here it was, the third day Cilla was in residence, and he didn't feel one bit stronger than when she'd arrived. They met each morning at eight for an hour and a half, and each afternoon at two for another short session. There were heat applications, ultrasound treatments, mild stretching exercises and leg lifts, some squats, the occasional electrical stimulation, then the icing down. The machines stood idle. Hell, she wouldn't even let him put on ankle weights during leg lifts. Too soon, she'd insisted.

Alone in his room during the time he was supposed to be napping or in the evening, he would lay down his crutches and practice walking with his cane. He'd thought to get proficient, to surprise her. Except, yesterday his weak leg had begun to shake uncontrollably and he'd almost fallen. Fortunately, he'd caught himself on the arm of a chair. There'd been a knock on his door and he'd barely had time to scramble over to the bed before his doctor had walked in. Jim had come by to check on his progress. Had he fallen, no telling what Jim would have done. Probably hauled him back to the hospital.

So he was being a good boy, but it was killing him. He heard a sound and turned to gaze out toward the beach where a man was riding a horse at a good clip on the packed sand. What he wouldn't give to be out there, running free, wind whipping through his hair, urging the stallion on. Would he ever be free like that again? he asked himself, swiftly moving into self-pity.

The phone next to his bed rang. Trey answered on the second ring. Recognizing the caller, he grinned. "Hey, Max. How're things?"

For ten minutes he talked with one of his close friends, Max Varner, who liked to live wild and spontaneously like Trey. The two of them, along with Chet Norris, Mel Fisher and Russell Fox, pals that went back to their college days, had had so many good times together. Only Mel had gotten married, and that had lasted less than a year. Like his buddies, Mel didn't like to be pinned down, to stay in one place too long, to do something until it became boring. Variety peppered with a certain amount of risk—that adrenaline rush—was the ticket. That's when you felt alive.

"Don't worry, Max. You can count me in. I *will* be ready for the sailboat race," Trey told his friend, his voice firm.

"I sure hope so, buddy," Max answered, sounding a shade skeptical, "'cause otherwise I'm going to be short a crewman. The knee's coming along okay, then?"

"Hell, yes." Trey lifted his bandaged leg high as he could and felt the quivering begin. Frowning, he lowered his leg. "Another couple weeks and I'll be there for the practice runs."

"Great. See you then, Trey."

Slowly Trey hung up the phone. He couldn't let Max or the rest of his friends down, now, could he? He'd simply have to get more vigorous exercise done on the q.t. after Cilla went to bed. Connie had taken to serving their dinner, alone or together, on the veranda, since Trey wasn't to use the stairs and the elevator wasn't repaired yet. Tonight, after dinner, he'd listen when she went to her room next to his until all was quiet. Then he'd sneak across the hall and work out.

More than one way to skin a cat, he thought, finally smiling. He heard the tapping on his door and called to Connie to come in. Dinner had arrived.

They'd finished eating, so Trey topped off her wine and refilled his own glass. He was in a better mood, certain that his plan for tonight would move things along more rapidly. Sipping the robust cabernet, he leaned back in his chair and noticed that Cilla had been gazing out to sea for some time, lost in her own world.

She'd changed into a black silk blouse and beige slacks, sandals on her feet. He saw that her toenails were painted a vivid pink which seemed almost too frivolous for her no-nonsense demeanor. Her hair looked freshly shampooed, shiny and brushed, just skimming her shoulders. She wore pale pink lip gloss and no other makeup that he could see.

She didn't need any.

She was a natural beauty just as she was, Trey thought. If they'd met under other circumstances, if he were strong and hardy again, he'd definitely make a move on her. Cilla Kovacs was the stuff men's dreams were made of.

Except right now, she was a nightmare standing in his way.

Maybe if he turned up the charm a notch.

''Penny for your thoughts,'' he said, smiling across the table.

Reluctantly Cilla dragged her attention from the lovely scene before her. No way was she going to tell him that she'd been thinking how wonderful it would be to have a place on the ocean where she could run on the beach every morning and dive into the waves whenever she felt like it. It wouldn't have to be a big place. Certainly nothing like this cold mausoleum.

"You're very fortunate to have grown up here with that beautiful view," she hedged.

He glanced out toward the water. "Yeah, I guess. But I hate this house."

Cilla sent him a questioning look. "Then why do you live here?"

Trey shrugged his good shoulder. "When my father died, as his older son, I inherited the mansion on the hill, as I call it. He'd inherited it from his father, and so on. Until I turned twenty-one, it was maintained by a trust he'd set up. The house is hopelessly outdated, ancient, with none of the character or charm some old homes have."

Interested, Cilla wrinkled her brow. "Then why don't you sell it and move? Or change it to suit your idea of home?"

Again that little shrug. "I'm not here much, usually on the go. I did get rid of most of the antiquated furniture that had been here probably since the turn of the last century. I had the kitchen remodeled to suit Connie, and her suite, as well, which is downstairs. I bought new furniture for my room and kept one or two guest rooms. All the rest are empty."

What he said simply didn't make sense to Cilla. "So you're just going to rattle around in this huge, nearly empty house that you hate?"

"For a while." She couldn't know that he didn't have

all that much time left, and he had no intention of telling her, of inviting her pity. He certainly had no intention of spending his remaining six months remodeling this old place. If he had his whole life in front of him, years and years, he might, but...

But he didn't have years and years. He had six short months, give or take. And he'd better get cracking on his plan to moonlight some exercises or he'd be stuck here for all those months. That truly would be a fate worse than death.

"A while," Cilla repeated. "Then you do have plans to move or sell or whatever after a while?"

"Yeah, whatever." He held up his half-empty wineglass, noticing hers was still full. "This isn't bad, is it?"

He wanted to change the subject. Well, why not? After all, it was his house. She picked up her wine, sipped. "It's nice."

Trey put on a mock frown. "Nice? Nice is how your maiden aunt looks. Wine deserves a more thoughtful description." He swirled the red liquid in his glass, squinting as he reexamined it. "Like full-bodied, flavorful, wonderful bouquet. Tickles the tonsils." He had her smiling, which was a start.

"I'm not an expert on wines. I like the red wine my father makes. It's kind of strong so you can't drink too much. But, oh, it's so smooth and mellow. Warms you down to your toes."

"Ah, now there's someone I'd like to meet. He could teach me about winemaking. That's something I haven't tried."

Cilla hid a smile as she pictured them—the bricklayer and the playboy. Dad would wear his trademark overalls and Trey would be in Armani. "Maybe one day you will meet him."

Setting down the wine she really didn't want, she stifled a yawn. "I think I'll turn in. Must be the ocean air. Makes me sleepy." She rose and saw him reach for his crutches. "No, don't get up. Really, I'm right next door. Enjoy the rest of the evening. I'll see you tomorrow morning at eight sharp."

"I'll be there, raring to go."

She just knew he would be. "Good night." Cilla walked through his sitting room where an arch off to the left led to his bedroom. Leroy Neiman paintings on the wall—football, basketball, tennis. An oversize leather chair with ottoman facing a big-screen television. On the opposite side was a large pool table and a full-size juke-box. And by the door was a red-and-white barber's pole.

Stepping into the hallway and closing the door behind her, Cilla wondered if Trey would ever grow up.

On the veranda Trey smiled as he heard her bedroom door next to his sitting room close. He checked his watch. Only eight-thirty. He'd give her half an hour to settle in. He knew she'd showered before coming to dinner, the faint scent of bath powder clinging to her, so she'd probably just undress and get into bed. Maybe watch a little television or read for a while.

Using his crutches, he walked to where he'd left his cane. Switching to it, he practiced strolling back and forth. Slowly, carefully. Yes, he was getting better at it. In thirty minutes he'd leave his room, listen at her door to make sure all was quiet, then mosey on across to the exercise room.

It's hard to keep a good man down, Trey thought, whis-tling.

At precisely nine Trey left his room, quietly closing his door. Balancing with his cane, he went to Cilla's door and cocked his ear to listen. No television or radio sounds. All was quiet. Using great care not to fall and give himself away, he moved to the exercise room, went inside and snapped on the light.

He'd made it.

He'd never been one to take orders well. Even as a child, he'd balked at direct commands from his father, his stepmother and even Connie. He'd had difficulty in school with authority figures. So it just stood to reason that he wasn't going to knuckle under to a small slip of a girl telling him what to do in his own home. Girl? He remembered the fragrance of her freshly bathed skin, the way the silk blouse had clung to her very feminine form. All right, make that woman.

With no small difficulty he got himself onto the mat on the floor, annoyed that he was breathing hard as if he'd just run around the track field. He'd just do a few sit-ups, some quad stretches. Move things along a tad faster. What could it hurt?

He lay back, propping his hands behind his head, his legs straight. He pulled himself up to a sitting position and...and felt a swift, sharp pain travel from his hip to his left knee. Or vice versa. He couldn't tell which.

No big deal, Trey decided, catching his breath. No pain, no gain. He did it again and it didn't hurt so much the second time. He smiled grimly, felt his face flush as he did it again. After ten, he was sweating profusely and his knee was throbbing. He lay there for a few minutes, catching his breath.

He couldn't stop this soon. With no small effort, he dragged himself over to the rowing machine. He'd take it easy, not use the leg bends but just exercise the shoulder, get his strength back. After several minutes of painful maneuvering, he managed to get himself into the seat and grab hold of the oars. He'd always been good at this. He pulled back once, felt himself slide forward on the runners beneath the seat. He also felt a fiery pain in his shoulder.

Breathing hard, Trey knew that the first few would hurt. But he had to keep going. Again, he pulled back on the oars, his face a grimace as a pain shot through his knee as well. Just a few more, he told himself. He'd show Cilla that... Whoa!

What was that noise? He stopped in midmotion. Sounded like a door closing and a squeaking board in the hallway outside the exercise room and...

One sharp knock and the door swung open. Cilla stood silhouetted in the doorway.

Busted! Damn.

Chapter Three

Trey noticed she was still wearing the silk blouse and slacks even though he'd been picturing her snuggled down in bed fast asleep by now. The way she walked in and calmly closed the door, slipping her hands into her pockets and leaning against the counter unnerved him. Instead of annoyance or anger, he thought he detected disappointment on her face.

"*What* are you doing?" Cilla asked, her voice calm and cool.

Dropping the oars, Trey let the rowing machine slide him back. "How'd you know? I was being so quiet." He had trouble meeting her eyes, feeling like a kid again, caught doing the forbidden.

"I had a feeling. You seemed distracted at dinner, almost anxious to have me leave. I thought perhaps you had a plan." She studied him a long moment before she spoke again. "Perhaps it's not in you to follow Jim's schedule,

Trey. You're going to wind up hurting yourself more. I'm sorry, but I won't be a party to that." She sighed with regret. "I'll leave in the morning." Turning, she put her hand on the doorknob.

"Wait!" Trey saw her pause. "I can explain."

Slowly Cilla swung back, finding his eyes. "I'm listening." Though she couldn't imagine what explanation he could have worth risking further harm to his already ravaged body.

Painstakingly Trey got himself upright, noticing she wasn't making a move to help him. He grabbed his cane and hobbled over to the massage table, hoisting himself on it. His ribs ached, his shoulder throbbed and his knee radiated pain. He gritted his teeth, trying not to let her see the extent of his discomfort. "You don't understand," he said, his voice low and husky.

"Make me understand."

Drawing in a shaky breath, he searched for the right words. "It's kind of a long story. My great-grandfather, Jonathan Townsend, came out west in a wagon, literally. He made good as a young man and bought acres of prime land dirt cheap, married and had a son. However, he died at thirty-seven from an infection he got chopping wood."

Trey eased his legs onto the table, trying to ignore the pain. "His only son, my grandfather, Terrence Templeton, was a carpenter who loved to build. He started up in northern California, putting up homes and churches and schools and libraries and city offices. He was so popular they named the city he built after him."

"You mean Templeton up in Northern California was named after your grandfather?" Cilla asked, more than a little surprised.

"That's the one. Later, he moved south and built this house for his family."

"I still don't see what all this has to do with you trying to rush your recovery."

He held up a hand. "Hold on. I'm getting to that. One day, two weeks after his thirty-seventh birthday, my grandfather was up high on the girders of a building because he was a hands-on owner, and he slipped and fell to his death." Trey looked at her now, saw she was listening intently, but he couldn't tell from her expression what she was thinking.

"Now we come to my father, Terrence Templeton II, and my uncle, Stephen Templeton. Uncle Steve, a mild-mannered professor of English who'd never married, died of a massive coronary at thirty-seven. My father was a workaholic, like my brother, Gavin. He tripled the family wealth and now we have real estate holdings, hotels, apartment buildings, you name it. The man was a near genius when it came to business, but he flunked Father-hood 101."

Absently rubbing his sore shoulder, Trey saw the quick sympathy in her eyes. But pity wasn't what he wanted. "He married a pretty but frail young woman named Carolyn, who died giving birth to me. So Dad hired Connie who was married to a day laborer, Luis. She took care of me and the house while Luis was in charge of the grounds. Dad went on a business trip and came back with his new bride when I was only two. Cynthia was blond and brown-eyed, a real beauty, and he was mad about her. She loved partying, shopping, traveling. She let Connie do all the child rearing because by then Luis had died and they'd had no children. Gavin came along the next year, but Stepmommy-Dearest wasn't any more interested in raising her own son than someone else's. So Connie raised us both."

Cilla still didn't know where all this family history was

leading, but she could see his unsupervised workout had taken its toll on Trey, his forehead damp from his exertion, his leg trembling. She could no longer stay uninvolved despite her annoyance. Moving to the table, she began unwrapping his knee, hoping the damage wasn't too bad.

Trey went on. "One day when I was thirteen and Gavin ten, while Dad was on another business trip, Cynthia moved out with as many of her things as she could stuff into the convertible Dad had bought her, and we never saw her again."

Cilla's hands stopped moving. "That must have been really hard for all of you."

Trey shrugged, then winced. "Gavin and I didn't miss her much because she'd hardly been around anyway. But Dad did. He tried everything to find her, with no luck. However, he also couldn't stop loving her. He neglected the business, himself and us, just sat in his den staring at her picture. One morning about six months later, he just didn't wake up. The doctor told us he'd died of a broken heart."

Cilla was skeptical about that last part. "I'm not sure it's possible to die from a broken heart."

"I'm not either, but that's what we were told. One more thing. The day my father died was his thirty-seventh birthday."

Finally she saw where he'd been headed with all this. "How old are you, Trey?"

"I'll be thirty-seven in six months. Now, do you get it? The magic number, the black number, the family curse. All the Templeton males die during their thirty-eighth year."

Rolling up the Ace bandage, she looked at him. "You're an educated, intelligent man, Trey. You don't honestly believe in curses, do you? Do you think some witch way back when put a curse on your family for imagined wrongs? Really!''

He leaned forward as she began removing the gauze, saw that it was stained with blood, but he had a more important point to make. ''How else do you explain all my male relatives dying, all in different ways, all at the same age?''

She had no reasonable answer for that. ''How does your brother feel about this so-called curse?''

''He doesn't believe in it. But he's only thirty-four. When I die this coming year, maybe he'll change his mind.'' His voice held no self-pity, rather a determination that baffled her.

Cilla tossed the stained bandages into the trash can. ''Let me get this straight. Because the relatives you mentioned all died at thirty-seven, you're certain you will, also. And you want to try every foolish and reckless thing you haven't yet experienced because you're convinced you won't have a chance later. Because of the curse. Is that about it?''

Put that way, she made it sound a little silly, but he wasn't laughing. ''Yeah, that's right. I can't seem to convince anyone, but you can't ignore facts.'' He winced as she cleaned off the blood along his incision. ''Until a couple of years ago, I worked with Gavin in the company.''

''But wait. Connie obviously stayed on after your father died and raised both you and Gavin, right?''

''Yes. My father had it all outlined in his will. He'd also appointed a vice president of Templeton Enterprises to act as CEO until we came of age and finished college. The bulk of the assets were maintained by a trust, including this house, handled by a trustee Dad had appointed.''

It was a lot to digest. "Are you saying your father made all those arrangements because he knew he was going to die?"

Again, that small shrug. "Call it what you want, but I think after Cynthia left, Dad didn't want to go on living without her."

"And you took ownership of this house?"

He nodded. "As the oldest son, it came to me. Other than this house, Gavin and I share everything else equally. I was never as gung-ho about business as my brother. He lives for and dreams about business all the time. When I finally sat down and figured out that I didn't have long to live, I told him I was leaving and he could run the company any damn way he liked."

Cilla began rewrapping his knee. "What did he say to that?" Jim had told her very little about Gavin Templeton, although he had mentioned that the man was serious, intense and focused.

"He tried to talk me out of it, but he couldn't. So I said goodbye to desk work and started doing things I'd always wanted to do. Hang gliding. Climbing mountains. Racing cars. Learning to fly a plane." As she finished, he caught her gaze. "Everyone says 'life is too short,' but when you *know* it is, it's like a wake-up call. You'd better take the time to smell the flowers, to try to see the world and all it has to offer, to live life to the fullest. Because you're dead a long, long time."

Stepping back, Cilla put her hands in the pockets of her slacks, wondering what to say to his lengthy story. "I believe that life is too short for most of us. But I still don't believe in predestination. Or in curses."

"You don't have my history or you would."

"I don't think even that is a license to be reckless."

Trey sighed tiredly. "The opposite of reckless is cowardice. Like my father, who just gave up, lay down and died rather than be man enough to face life and care for his two sons who desperately needed him.'' Thinking he'd already revealed way too much, Trey withdrew almost visibly.

Cilla wondered if he really believed all that curse nonsense or if it was just a sympathy ploy to get her to do what he wanted. He seemed sincere, but was that a practiced expression? She hated being so suspicious, but charming people could put one over on an unsuspecting person. She'd try to check out his story with Jim and maybe Connie.

''Be that as it may, I was hired by your doctor to rehabilitate your knee and shoulder, to get you walking as soon as possible, considering your injuries. He gave me a schedule to follow, one that's safe and sound. I'm not going to rush you through it so you can go out there and do some crazy thing. You saw how just a few minutes on the machines opened up your incision. Too many of those and you'll not heal properly.''

''I'll try to follow Jim's schedule,'' he said, wishing he didn't feel so defeated, ''but I need to work out more than a couple hours a day. Please, Cilla. Don't leave. Help me.'' Easing his legs over the table, he reached for his cane and stood up.

She wished he didn't look so appealing. ''All right, we'll do more. But slowly and on my terms. And the next time I catch you doing something stupid like this, I really will leave.''

Trey was stuck and he knew it. His body wasn't cooperating any more than Cilla or Jim were. He'd have to go along with the program, at least until he felt stronger. ''I understand.''

''Good.'' Taking his arm, she led him out of the exercise room and walked him to his bedroom door.

''Maybe if you came in and tucked me in, I'd stay in bed,'' he said with a sly smile.

''If you can pump along on that rowing machine, I'm sure you can get yourself into bed.'' She let go of him as he opened the door. ''And stay in it.'' She turned and went into her own room.

With a sigh of regret, Trey stumbled in. Making his way to his bed, he wasn't sure which hurt more, his shoulder or his knee. Time for a pain pill, he decided, even though he'd promised himself he'd tough it out without medication.

Not tonight. He lay down, waiting for the pill to kick in. Maybe he'd dream of Cilla, her soft hands, that heavenly cologne she wore. He closed his eyes.

It was late afternoon of the next day, and Trey had to admit she'd given him a good workout. He would be on his back on the massage table and she'd lift his injured leg up high, holding it up over her shoulder, then gradually stretching, stretching those impaired muscles. He found himself breaking out in a sweat as she pulled higher, longer, then slowly let it back down.

Then there were the squats, where he'd hold on to the table edge and bend as if to sit down, but hold it there for the count of ten while his muscles strained. Twenty of those at a time, then twenty more had his leg quivery as Jell-O. For his shoulder, she had him pull wide elastic bands gripped in his hands, starting at his midriff, then slowly stretching his arms wide. He couldn't believe how two sets of twenty would have his arms trembling.

But, Trey decided, they were making progress, and that was the important thing.

Cilla checked her watch and decided there was time to give her patient a treat. "Can you roll over on your stomach?" she asked, ready to assist him.

"Sure, why?"

"I noticed your back seems to be hurting a bit so I thought you'd enjoy a full body massage, get those tight muscles loosened up."

Little did she realize that his muscles were tense because her clever hands had been moving freely all over his body, causing a good deal of havoc in ways she either didn't notice or chose to ignore. Still, it did sound good. "That would be great." He shifted, stuffing a pillow under his head.

Cilla warmed her hands under running water, dried them thoroughly and reached for the professional massage cream. Rolling some between her hands, she began high on his back close to the uninjured shoulder. Patiently she worked the muscles, her hands sliding on his slick skin, digging deep here and there where she felt a bunching. She smiled as she saw him close his eyes. Few people could resist a massage.

Even when she worked his sore shoulder, he didn't mind, for her touch was gentle yet firm. Warm afternoon sun poured in through the slanted blinds, making him drowsy. He was almost dozing when he felt her turn under the waistband of his shorts so she could go lower without getting lotion on the material. Just that slight touch and his body reacted.

He needed to wrap his mind around a conversation instead of how she was sending shivers to his system. "What made you choose physical therapy as an occupation?" he asked, grasping at the first subject he could think of.

Cilla pressed with the heels of her hands as she carved

a path up the broad muscles of his back. His skin was smooth and taut with not an ounce of fat. "I enjoy helping people and I know firsthand how important therapy is. Not just to aid in the healing process, but to keep muscles from atrophying when the patient is no longer in control." She hesitated a moment, wondering if Trey could relate, then decided to tell him. "My brother, Michael, the one in L.A., has a rare muscle disease that causes spasms and loss of control. When he's not in remission, he often has to resort to a wheelchair, because, even though his brain sends messages to his muscles, they don't always respond. Physical therapy helps him get through those periods."

"Why is he in L.A. when you could help him right here?"

"His specialist has staff privileges at a hospital up there. Michael, his wife and two boys live near the hospital so when he has relapses, they can rush him right over."

Her hands at his waist were playing havoc with Trey's nerves. He struggled to find a less depressing topic. "So tell me, who's the man in your life? I'm surprised you're not married, as attractive as you are." He angled his head, trying to glimpse her face.

Cilla decided there was a compliment in there somewhere, but she'd be wise to ignore it. "Just never had time, I guess. There was school and work and my family." She reached for the jar of cream. "Why don't you turn over?" she suggested.

"Oh, come on. No man in your life, ever?" Trey maneuvered his body over, propping the pillows beneath his head.

"Not anyone serious." She poured cream into her hands, wanting to shift the focus back to him. "What about you? I don't see a lady of the house, unless you've got her stashed away in one of those many rooms up here? Or is there a bell tower?''

Trey laughed. ''No, the only woman who lives here is Connie.'' In the next moment his laughter faded as her hands began massaging along his rib cage, then softly sliding onto his chest.

Cilla's fingers glided through the silky blond chest hair, and she swore she could feel his heart pick up its beat. She felt her own pulse quicken, a reaction she seldom had with any patient. She kept her eyes cast downward. ''I like Connie,'' she said, to divert herself from her wayward thoughts as much as to make conversation. ''She's no-nonsense yet she's got a soft heart.'' Cilla had wandered the house several afternoons while Trey was supposed to be napping, and had wound up in the kitchen chatting with Connie.

''Yeah, she's a good old gal, except for this one tiny little bad habit.''

''What's that?''

''She steals. A kleptomaniac.''

Cilla stopped in midstroke, her brows raising. ''That sweet woman steals?''

''You bet. A leaf here, a snippet there. Her favorites are African violets. Didn't you see them all over the kitchen?'' His lips twitched as she went back to massaging. At last, they were on safe ground.

''I did. Big, healthy plants. I thought you said she took only a leaf or two?''

''Right. She puts the leaf in water, roots form, she transfers them to her little pots, and before you know it, she's got plants everywhere. I expect a few stores are on to her. When the doorbell rings, I never know if it's the cops coming to get her.''

Finished, Cilla recapped the jar. "I think you're making all this up. Connie has an honest face."

"Sure. That's why she gets away with it." He sat up and gave in to an irresistible impulse, reaching to tuck a loose strand of hair behind her ear.

Cilla felt his fingers stray to stroke along her cheek, lingering much longer than necessary. In his green eyes she saw a growing interest, one she reluctantly shared. This wouldn't do. Medical professionals should not get involved with their patients. Besides, despite her reaction to his charm, Terrence Templeton III was definitely not the kind of man she needed in her life.

Breaking the look, she took a step back and went to wash her hands.

Slowly, Trey swung his legs over the side of the table, struggling with his own reaction to Cilla Kovacs. She certainly was nothing like the women he'd known. She was dedicated, hardworking, honest. There was also a vulnerability about her that told him she wasn't the sort for brief romances. And those were the only kind he could have.

But he was curious about her, so he returned to their previous subject, thinking if he revealed a bit, she'd open up more. "The reasons I haven't anyone special in my life are twofold. First, I don't think it's fair to get serious with someone, knowing I won't be around that much longer. Second, I haven't found anyone special enough."

There was that silly curse idea again, Cilla thought as she dried her hands. "Maybe you should take that chance. Maybe you'd have a daughter and not a son. And just maybe the curse would be broken."

"No, it wouldn't."

Crossing her arms over her chest, she regarded him. "You know, it's really sad, the way you think. You've left out some pretty important things. Like, what about love? If I knew—knew for an absolute fact that I had only six months left—I'd want to be with people I love, with that special someone, if possible. Not racing around the world looking for new thrills. Everyone needs to be loved. How can you so easily dismiss love from your life?''

A frown of exasperation marred his almost-perfect features. ''I have lots of friends and they care about me.'' Suddenly, the words sounded hollow, and Trey wasn't sure he believed them. He scooted off the table and reached for his crutches. ''Maybe if you were facing what I am, you'd feel different. If I did love someone special, I'd just wind up hurting her when I...when it ended.''

It was Cilla's turn to shrug. ''A person can get run over by a bus or die in their sleep—without a family curse. Happens all the time. Besides, shouldn't you let the woman decide if she wants to take a chance on loving you?''

He didn't like where this was going. ''If there was a woman, yeah, maybe. But it's a moot point since there isn't one.'' He hobbled over to the intercom. ''Want some coffee or a cold drink?''

Perhaps he needed to be alone for a while. ''I'll go down and get it. What do you want?''

''Iced tea with lemon and two sugars. Please.''

''Try not to do anything foolish while I'm gone.'' Cilla left the exercise room, went downstairs and found Connie at the sink cleaning greens for a salad.

''Good morning.'' Connie's smile was warm. ''How is it going?''

''Coming along, I guess. Mind if I take up some iced tea?''

''Sure, sure.'' Connie dried her hands and hurried to the refrigerator. ''You should have buzzed me. I would bring it up.''

"That's all right. I can use the break." While Connie got down two glasses, Cilla was drawn to the broad windowsill by the breakfast alcove where half a dozen African violets in various pots thrived. "Looks like you have a green thumb," she commented.

Connie laughed as she fixed the tray. "My one big sin. I steal leaves and root them into those plants."

Cilla waited for her to explain.

Connie made a self-deprecating sound. "Old habits, they die hard. When I was a little girl in Mexico, we were very poor. My mother raised six of us while our father worked the California fields and sent us what money he could. My mother loved flowers, but we could scarcely afford food. So she'd go to the market and snip a leaf here and there. She would nurse them along and soon we had flowers both in the house and outside. My mother said the plants at the store wouldn't miss a leaf or two. She always told me you can't be too sad when you see such beautiful flowers all around."

Cilla smiled at the touching story. "Your mother was right."

"Sit down for a minute, please," Connie said, pulling out a chair for her at the round table. "Tell me, how is Trey really doing?"

She wouldn't tattle on him and mention the night he'd tried to work out alone, yet Cilla had a feeling this little woman with the wise eyes knew her employer far better than he thought. "He wants to hurry the therapy more than is good for him. He finds it hard to take direction." Which was putting it mildly.

"This I know," Connie said, taking the chair next to Cilla. "He's an impatient one, pigheaded even. I raised him. I should know. But he's got a good heart."

Cilla saw the affection in her dark eyes. "I think you're

right. I'm just trying to make sure he doesn't injure himself further.''

"Yes, yes, that is good. I know he misses his visits to the Boys & Girls Club, but it can't be helped. He sent them a check, but it's not the same."

Interested, Cilla leaned forward. ''The Boys & Girls Club?''

"He didn't tell you, eh? It's in San Diego, a poor section. Trey read about it and went down there. The building they use was falling apart and the kids had almost no equipment. Trey had the building fixed up with a basketball court, added a cafeteria and bought balls and hoops, a bunch of games. He goes twice a week when he's in town to teach the kids and to just talk to them. Like a big brother.'' She studied Cilla's face for a long moment. ''See, he has a good heart.''

"That's very generous of him." That was something she hadn't suspected about Trey. But then, perhaps his generosity had roots in his lonely childhood, growing up without a mother and a mostly absent father.

"There's more, you know," Connie went on. "I hate it when everyone thinks Trey is just a selfish run-around. Oh, he likes the ladies, but he has a soft spot for kids. There was an old school in the barrio section of San Diego, shut down, no money. Trey had it fixed up real nice, found some teachers and now it's only for homeless children. They wanted to name the school after him, but he wouldn't let them. Everything he does, he does quietly. His brother, Gavin, he gives to lots of charities. Writes a check and that's that. Not Trey. He's arranged for those kids to have a dance, a prom, the ones graduating. He got the boys suits, the girls dresses and even haircuts.'' She beamed with pride. ''I know two ladies whose children go to that school. They cry when they see Trey.''

"I had no idea," Cilla commented. She'd been wrong to think Trey couldn't relate to the common folk. Loneliness knew no financial boundaries.

Connie worried the edge of her apron as she looked up at Cilla. "I tell you all this because I don't want you to give up on him because he is difficult. I know he doesn't like to listen and…"

"Don't worry, please." Cilla reached over and squeezed the older woman's hands. "I don't give up easily. Besides, he's cooperating better after…after we had a talk."

Nodding, Connie looked relieved. "I'm glad. Thank you." She turned to the tray she'd prepared. "I'll take this up for you."

"I can handle it." Cilla took the tray from her just as the front doorbell echoed through the house. Following after Connie, she headed for the front stairs, but her curiosity had her pausing as the door swung open.

"Connie, my love, how *are* you?" the young woman gushed as she sauntered inside as if she owned the place, carrying a huge stuffed bear. Tossing back her long, blond hair, she removed her sunglasses and flashed Connie a megawatt smile. "It's been just *too* long."

The housekeeper's face revealed nothing. "Hello, Ms. Monroe."

"And where is our boy? I thought I'd come by and cheer him up." Glancing toward the stairs, she spotted Cilla holding the tray. "Oh, you've hired on extra help. Good. You shouldn't work so hard." Dismissing Cilla as obviously household help, she moved toward the stairs. "Is Trey in his room? I have something for him."

"What would that be?" Connie asked stiffly.

She held up the yellow stuffed toy. "Why, Pooh Bear, of course." She started up.

"Wait, please, Ms. Monroe." Connie rushed over. "This lady is Trey's physical therapist. He's been badly hurt and shouldn't have visitors just yet. You can come back another day."

"Oh, piffle on that, Connie." Her long-lashed gaze took Cilla's measure more thoroughly. "I'm Jolie Monroe, an old, *dear* friend of Trey's."

"Cilla Kovacs," she said, her voice cool.

"Mmm. He's upstairs, right?"

Cilla nodded as Connie's frown deepened, her dislike of this "old, dear friend," becoming obvious.

"Maybe next week would be better," Connie suggested.

But Jolie Monroe was already climbing the stairs, giving them both a careless wave. Her skintight yellow jumpsuit threatened to split a seam or two, but she wiggled on.

Connie knew when she was outmaneuvered. "He's in the exercise room, across the hall," she called after Jolie.

"Maybe I should get another glass," Cilla said as she watched the blonde turn the corner. Then again, maybe *she* would be the fifth wheel on the wagon.

"No!" Connie stated emphatically. "That woman, she's trouble. Married twice, divorced twice. Always hanging around the men. She's going to talk Trey into something not good for him."

Cilla was tired of this little game of protecting Trey at all costs. "Connie, he's a big boy who makes his own decisions, right or wrong. She can't talk him into something he doesn't want to do." With that, she set off up the stairs, thinking she'd place the tea things on the counter and leave the two old and dear friends alone.

The door to the exercise room was ajar so Cilla nudged it open wider and went in. Jolie was sitting on the massage table alongside Trey at his good side, both her arms encircling him. There was a bright-red lipstick smear on his right cheek.

"Just set it over there, dear," she purred. "I'll take it from here."

Looking embarrassed, Trey disentangled her arms from his torso. "Jolie, it was nice of you to drop by, but I have to work out. It's important that I get back on my feet quickly."

Cilla set down the tray and tossed ice cubes into the two glasses. She'd fix Trey's because she'd said she would, and her own, but damned if she'd wait on that silly woman. She was a therapist, not a waitress.

"Oh, sweetie, surely a little old hour with Jolie won't hurt you." She licked her lips suggestively. "It might even do you a whole lot of good."

She was actually blinking and batting her eyes at him, Cilla noticed, just like someone sent from Central Casting to star in a B movie. But Trey didn't seem to know his lines, squirming slightly away from her, then grimacing at a sudden pain. Fascinated, Cilla sipped her tea and continued to watch.

Jolie slid closer, hot on his trail. Trey glanced at Cilla and saw the amusement in her eyes. Just then Jolie leaned closer, and her pink tongue licked his right shoulder.

"Mmm, you taste so...so manly," she said, her voice husky.

Trey had had enough. His hands gripped her wrists and he yanked just enough to scoot her off the table. She stood there, shock registering on her face, followed by a flash of anger.

"Just what in hell are you doing?" she demanded.

"I'm *trying* to tell you, to show you, that I can't do this now. Cilla and I have work to do." He let go of Jolie and waved a hand to include the exercise machines. "See all this equipment? I need to get going on them so I can function without those,'' he said as he pointed to his crutches.

Cilla could tell that pouting came naturally to Jolie as she rearranged her face and appealed to him one more time. ''All right, sweetie, you work those little old muscles. Then I'll swing by for you about eight in my new Jag and we'll hit the hot spots. A night on the town is just what the doctor ordered.''

Trey noticed Cilla's lips twitch and felt a slow burn. He'd never been a big fan of Jolie's, though she'd gone on one or two fishing trips with the gang. However, this phony concern of hers and that fake Southern accent were too much for him to handle just now. ''Look, Jolie, I can't go out. Not tonight, not for a long while. Now, please, you have to leave. I'll call you if I need you.''

Amazed at her self-control in an embarrassing situation, Cilla watched the spoiled young woman quickly compose herself, then flash him a smile. ''Don't bother, sugar. Not until you improve your disposition a whole hell of a lot.'' Still, she leaned to him and planted a juicy red kiss on his surprised face before undulating toward the door. ''Take good care of Pooh.'' She slipped out and just barely avoided slamming the door.

Cilla thought Trey definitely could use something cool. She handed him the iced tea, fixed the way he liked it.

Trey reached for the tissue box and wiped his face, his expression irritated, before taking the tea and downing half the contents at once. He glanced toward the silly bear Jolie had brought him slumped in the corner. ''Get rid of that thing for me, will you?''

''I could give it to one of my nieces,'' she suggested.

''Fine. Just get it out of my sight.''

Cilla couldn't resist a little teasing. "I think it's kind of cute. Shows that she cares for you."

"Ha! I don't think so. Jolie's between husbands, looking for someone to bankroll her again." He sipped his tea, telling himself to relax. "Besides, we've always been just friends."

"Uh-huh." Cilla set down her glass and went to get a damp cloth, returning to his side. "More lipstick on your cheek. Just friends, eh?" Not that it was any of her business, but Jolie Monroe was a card-carrying phony-baloney and, even though she'd only known Trey a week, she would hate to see that woman get her clutches on him. It took a truly strong man to resist a sexy barracuda like Jolie.

Cilla had been pleasantly surprised that he'd gotten rid of her so quickly.

"We *are* just friends, and barely that," Trey insisted as he finished cleaning his face. "After that performance, she's way down on my list."

"'Methinks thou dost protest too much,'" Cilla answered, turning her back so he wouldn't see her smile.

Actually, she was pretty certain that Trey had Jolie's number. Not that she cared. Although she had felt some sort of anxious twinge when she'd walked in and found Jolie draped all over him. Not that what he did made a bit of difference to her.

Did it?

It was evening, and Trey was out on his terrace on the chaise lounge flexing his leg muscles. He absolutely was getting stronger. He could feel it. Ten days of gradually increasing workouts was paying off. He'd like to do even more, but he knew it would be just his luck Cilla would catch him again. He had no doubt she'd leave for good with one more incident.

The soft breeze on his skin felt good. All he ever wore were T-shirts and shorts these days. In the distance he could hear the ocean waves rolling in then rushing out. There was something soothing to that sound.

But another sound intruded on his thoughts.

Frowning, he sat upright and cocked his head this way and that, listening. He'd heard another sound, music coming from nearby. A piano. There it was again. Show tunes. The love song from *The Phantom of the Opera*. Reaching for his cane, he moved to the railing. The music was coming through the open French doors of the library just under his bedroom. Since he was certain Connie didn't play, the pianist must be Cilla.

Curious, Trey walked with the aid of his cane to the far end of the hallway to the elevator that had finally been repaired. In minutes he was crossing the marble foyer, heading toward the library, the sound louder now. The library door was slightly ajar, and he pushed it open, then strolled inside.

The piano was a white baby grand situated at the far end by the French doors. His father had bought it for Cynthia, but Trey couldn't remember her playing too often. She just liked the idea of having a piano in the house. He was certain if she could have shoved it into the trunk of her convertible, she'd have taken it with her when she drove off.

He was also certain that no one had ever played that piano the way it was being played tonight. Not loud or showy, but soft and dreamy. Her back to him, Cilla's capable fingers caressed the keys as he recognized a Stephen Sondheim medley. There were no music sheets and she wasn't looking down at her hands, but rather she was gazing out into the night through the open doors. She wasn't a professional, just someone playing for her own pleasure. A melancholy song and, though he couldn't see her face, he could easily picture the sad look that lingered all too often in her blue eyes.

What put it there? he wondered.

Trey debated about going in, perhaps joining in. He could pick out a few tunes with two fingers, mainly "Chopsticks." He'd just about decided he would surprise her when he saw her rise and slowly walk to the open doorway of the balcony. She wore a floor-length robe in some light-blue fabric, and her hair hung softly to her shoulders.

He was about to step in when he heard a tremulous sigh escape from her. Something was bothering Cilla, but it was none of his business. He didn't want to intrude on a private moment.

As she walked out onto the bricked terrace, he reversed his steps and headed for the elevator. A part of him—a large part—wanted to go to her, to turn her into his arms so he could chase the sadness from her. But the other part—the smart part—advised him to let sleeping dogs lie.

He didn't know Cilla Kovacs well enough to encroach on her privacy. Yet the truth was, he wished he did.

Chapter Four

Dr. Jim Gordon smiled his approval. ''The knee's coming along just great.'' He spoke to Cilla, who was standing next to the table where Trey was stretched out. ''Now that I've removed the staples, let's just put a light Teflon bandage on for daytime and leave it unwrapped at night.'' He stepped back. ''You're doing a fine job, Cilla, as always.''

''Thanks.'' She wouldn't complain about her patient in front of his doctor, but all three of them knew getting Trey to listen had been uphill all the way.

''Hey, don't I get any credit around here?'' Trey interjected.

''Sure you do. You get credit for following instructions, for once in your life.'' An old friend as well as Trey's doctor, Jim told it like it was.

''My reputation precedes me,'' Trey mock complained as he sat up. ''What next, Doc?''

"I'd say the stationary bike, and if you tolerate that well, the rowing machine. How sore is your shoulder?"

Trey slowly raised both shoulders in an exaggerated shrug. "Much better."

"Okay, then." Jim glanced at his watch. "I've got time for a quick swim, if that's all right with you," he said to Trey.

"Sure, no problem. As you know there's a changing room with lockers and a shower next to the garage, and a couple extra pairs of swim trunks if you forgot yours." Trey eased his legs over the side. "Maybe I'll go down with you and..."

"No, not yet," Jim insisted. "Those steps down to the sand are way too steep." He turned to Cilla. "How about you? Can you use a little break?"

Cilla saw the disappointment on her patient's face and hesitated. It wasn't that she needed a break just now, but maybe Jim wanted to talk to her alone about Trey. "I'd like that. Meet you at the top of the stairs in ten minutes."

"Terrific." Jim was aware of Trey's frustration, knew he always liked to be in the thick of things. "Maybe next time, buddy. Why don't you take a rest?"

"Yeah, sure." Using his cane, Trey walked out, feeling like a kid who'd been banished to his room. Angry with himself that Cilla going swimming with Jim mattered to him at all, he dropped into the chaise on his veranda.

He'd barely had time to work up a good pity party when he heard voices, followed by a warm peal of feminine laughter. Scooting closer to the ledge, he realized he'd never heard Cilla laugh out loud. The two figures came into view, leaving the terrace as they headed for the stairs, towels over their shoulders.

Cilla was wearing some sort of a cover-up so he couldn't tell what her suit was like. Remembering that he had his binoculars in the next room, the ones he often took on trips, Trey hurriedly grabbed his cane. He had to search around on the closet shelves but finally found them and went back outside.

He removed the lens covers and adjusted the focus. There they were, dropping their towels on the sand and gazing out at a fairly calm sea. The binoculars were powerful; he'd bought them in Germany some years ago. Jim and Cilla seemed like they were close enough to touch. Trey saw that they were chatting, but he couldn't tell what was said. Suddenly Jim threw back his head and laughed.

Trey struggled with an uncharacteristic wave of jealousy. Jim was a serious guy. What had she said to make him laugh like that? Or was the good doctor suddenly seeing Cilla in a new light, even though he'd been dating her sister? Trey ground his teeth, wishing he could race down there, take her hand and be the one to lead her into the water.

He watched Jim run ahead and saw Cilla remove her cover-up. She was wearing a one-piece black bathing suit, not deliberately sexy yet he could see every curve. His mouth dry, he saw her run into the waves, walk out a ways, then dive under, surfacing moments later alongside Jim. Tossing her wet hair back, she trod water as they talked. Were they discussing him, doctor to therapist? Or were they speaking of more personal, more intimate matters?

Annoyed with his train of thought and the fact that he'd worked himself up unnecessarily, he lowered the binoculars. He shouldn't be watching like some lovesick jerk, which he wasn't. It was more that he was jealous not to be able to join them yet.

Trey knew he didn't adjust to change well. If that was selfish, it was also honest. He wasn't good at compromise, either, and he knew it was one of the main ingredients in a serious relationship.

Not that he was interested in a long-term relationship. He didn't have enough time left for that, nor would it be fair to the woman to get seriously entangled with a man whose time was limited. However, while his body healed, he certainly had the time for a little playful lust with someone he'd come to genuinely like.

That was all there would be, could be, of course. He'd been up-front with Cilla, so she knew as soon as he got the go-ahead from Jim he'd be on his way. The yacht races off the coast were coming up soon, and after that he'd been invited to do some kayaking up in Alaska before the weather changed. So much to see and do, so little time.

"How can you so easily dismiss love from your life?" Cilla had asked him. Maybe she'd known love from that big family of hers, but he hadn't seen many examples. And those he'd seen—like his father so nuts about Cynthia that he just gave up and died without her—didn't impress him. Besides, this conjecturing could all be moot. After all, what made him think Cilla wanted anything to do with him? He'd stroked her cheek and seen her reaction, but she'd quickly backed away.

Still, curiosity had him raising the glasses again. They were both sitting on their towels on the sand, chatting like old friends. Which they were. And he was stuck up here.

Trey had suspected that life wasn't fair. Now he knew it.

He was on the stationary bike at last. Cilla secured his feet on the pedals and set the timer.

"Not too much resistance at this stage." Hand on his back, she watched his legs go around and noticed the grimace on his face. "Try it backward at first. It's less of a strain."

He did and found she was right. Trey gave her his cocky grin as he settled himself more comfortably in the seat.

Cilla sat down on a stool nearby, thinking of her conversation with Jim yesterday. She'd asked him some questions about Trey, and they weren't about his health. After all, Jim had known both Templeton men since entering college. He was Gavin's age, so Trey had been three years ahead of them. They'd both been pretty much in awe of him.

"Trey excelled in just about everything," Jim had said as they'd sat on the beach. "Football, basketball, tennis. He hardly ever studied, yet he got great grades. And girls? He had them following him around like lovestruck puppies."

"But no one special?"

"Nope. He played the field, in college and after. I don't think I've ever seen him with the same woman more than a couple of times." Jim looked at her, his eyes questioning. "Are you interested in Trey, Cilla?"

She frowned. "No, of course not. He's a patient. I just...just wanted to know more about him. So I'd know how to approach his case, that's all."

Jim continued searching her face. "Well, I can see how you'd be attracted. Trey's handsome, generous to a fault, fun to be with and a hell of a nice guy."

"Did I say I was attracted?"

Jim's smile was knowing. "You didn't have to. Now that I think about it, you'd be good for him. He needs a settling influence, someone with both feet firmly planted on the ground."

"Is that how you see me?"

"Don't be insulted, but yeah. You're solid, honest, steady."

Which added up to boring. Let's not forget boring. Just the way she'd dreamed of being thought of, Cilla thought. Not that she was a femme fatale or wanted to be. Perhaps she was more serious and focused than most women her age, certainly more than Isabel, her sister, whom Jim was dating. No one ever thought of Isabel as boring.

Cilla had changed the subject then, but last night as she'd lain in bed, she'd gone over her conversation with Jim, as she had just now. Was she attracted to Trey? Probably a little. After all, she was human and he was, as her roommate, Jan, would say, quite a hunk. Or was it a babe? More than likely, both.

Then she remembered how Jim had described her, making her sound about as appealing as someone's maiden aunt. Was that how Trey saw her?

The door to the exercise room swung open and Connie stuck her head in. "Cilla, there's a phone call for you. She said it was important. You can take it in the hallway, just out here."

Instantly anxious, Cilla slipped off the stool. "Did you get a name?"

"Marcy Kovacs in Los Angeles, I think."

Oh, no! Michael's wife. Cilla hurried to the door, calling over her shoulder to Trey. "Stop when the bell rings and don't do any more." She followed Connie to the phone on the small hall table, her heart pounding.

Hanging up minutes later, Cilla slumped into the wing chair alongside the table. The news wasn't good, even though Marcy, as always, had tried to be optimistic. Mike had relapsed, the muscles in his legs unable to hold his weight. There was a new treatment the doctors were going to try. Marcy insisted that there was no need for Cilla to drive up there and that she'd call later to update her. Cilla had offered to go up and watch the boys, but Marcy said her mother had them.

Closing her eyes, Cilla prayed that this new treatment would put Mike back in remission. The last bout had lasted nearly four months, weakening his already ravaged body. Choking back tears, she remembered how thin he'd been, almost frail. But Mike was a fighter and he'd rallied. He would again. He just had to.

Pulling in a long, calming breath, she walked to the exercise room. And heard before she saw that Trey was pumping away, much faster than she'd allowed, his face red with exertion. She slammed the door shut and marched over to him, ignoring his quick hang-dog, guilty look as he ground to a halt.

"Do you know who that was on the phone?" she began, her voice dangerously low yet trembling with temper. Not waiting for a reply, she forged ahead. "My brother's wife. Mike had a relapse, and he's back in the hospital for Lord-only-knows how long. He has to go through some probably painful new procedure, then fight to get his muscles to work right, even though he knows this will happen again and again, because there's no cure for his illness."

"Look, Cilla, I'm sorry. I…"

Pacing to the other side of him, she was too busy building a head of steam to stop now. "Meanwhile, you're in here pushing yourself to the breaking point yet again, possibly causing irreparable harm to bones just beginning to heal." She stepped closer, leaned down until she was inches from his face. "Do you know what Mike would give to have your healthy body, which would be just fine if you followed a simple set of directions? You brought all this on yourself, but he didn't and he doesn't deserve…''

A sob caught in her throat and she knew she was close to breaking down. ''I can't do this.'' She turned and rushed to the door.

''Cilla, wait!'' Trey scrambled off the bike, but his cane fell from where he'd propped it. Swearing under his breath, he glanced up and saw that she was gone.

In her room, Cilla let the tears fall. Life wasn't fair, she silently screamed. Mike was such a sweet guy who just wanted to live a normal life with his wife and two boys. But the insidious disease was always hovering, waiting to rob him of his strength, his family, his work. It simply wasn't fair.

Wiping her face, she realized she'd behaved badly. Very unprofessionally. It was just that after hearing such terrible news, when she'd walked in and seen Trey going off on his own again, she'd simply lost it.

Maybe she shouldn't be here. Cilla knew she was a good therapist, but apparently she wasn't emotionally qualified to deal with a headstrong patient like Trey. Jim would be disappointed, but he'd find someone else. She would consider this a personal failure, yet better to leave now and cut her losses.

Shaken but certain what she had to do, Cilla yanked her suitcase from the closet just as two knocks sounded at the door. She might as well get this over with and tell him she was leaving.

''Come in.'' She wiped the tears away.

Using his cane, Trey walked in slowly, his green eyes troubled as he noticed her suitcase. ''I'm so sorry about your brother.''

She fumbled with her tissue. ''Thank you.''

He stepped closer, needing to apologize. ''I should have

listened to you, I know. I promise—no, I *swear* I won't
do anything against your orders again. Not ever.''

Gazing up at him, she thought he seemed so sincere.
Like the last time. ''Trey, I think you need someone else.
Maybe a male therapist. I can't seem to—''

''No!'' With one step, he closed the gap between them,
dropped his cane and placed his hands at her waist. ''You're
the one I need.'' He reached to wipe away her tears with
his thumb, feeling guilty. Here he was, rushing his schedule
so he could race a sailboat, while her brother was fighting
just to survive. The comparison wasn't lost on Trey. ''Please
don't cry and don't leave. I'll do what you say, honest.''

For the second time in one morning, Cilla did something very unprofessional. She leaned into him, her arms
going around him, and laid her head against his heart. His
hands moved to encircle and hold her closer. She needed
to be held, just for a little while, and he was so solid and
strong. It had been a very long time since she'd felt such
a need, if she ever had.

But she couldn't indulge herself too long, so finally she
tried to pull back, but he held her all the closer.

''Don't move. Not yet. Let me hold you.''

Cilla was too worn out to fight that. Later, she couldn't
say how long they stood there, holding each other up,
offering and receiving the comfort that only comes from
knowing another human being cares, if only a little.

Finally, she drew back, picked up his cane and handed
it to him. ''I...thank you. I behaved badly and...''

''No, *I* behaved badly. And it won't happen again
or...or you can beat me with my cane.''

She sniffed, then smiled. ''Yes, that might work. I'll
add it to my 'to do' list.''

''Put your suitcase away, please.''

With a trembling sigh, she did as he asked.

* * *

Trey stood at the top of the steep steps leading down to the beach. The subdued lighting on the terrace behind him lent a surreal glow to the palm trees dotting the perimeter. Colored lanterns lit the stairs, and a nearly full moon overhead was surrounded by a bevy of winking stars. It was a lovely night, yet he was feeling uncharacteristically melancholy.

Cilla had worked him only an hour that afternoon after the phone call, then had given him a short list of flexes and stretches to do while she left to run a couple of errands. Probably went to talk to her parents about Michael, because when she returned she passed on dinner and stayed in her room. Trey hadn't seen her again until he'd strolled outside and noticed her down on the beach sitting on a large piece of driftwood.

Her back was to him so he couldn't tell if she was crying again or just brooding. She wasn't dressed for swimming, probably she'd just gone down to sit and think, to let the endless waves soothe her. He should leave her alone, Trey thought. She obviously needed some private time.

Cilla watched the water rush closer with each pulsing beat, the froth whirling around some of the moss-covered rocks, then the rush back, pulled by the ageless rhythm. She'd always loved the sea, finding serenity in knowing that the ocean waters had been here for thousands of years and would likely be for thousands more. Continuity. Permanence. Uniformity.

Unlike so much in life, always changing, unreliable, often difficult to understand. For instance, why was a good person like her brother stricken with a disease that would doubtless end his life long before his time? She'd been pondering that question for years, yet had no answer. Perhaps it wasn't something mere mortals would understand.

Stretching out her legs, Cilla settled more comfortably on the rough piece of driftwood. The clouds had deserted the moon in the midnight blue sky so that its silvery glow drenched the smooth sand with light. How beautiful it was here, so peaceful. It was impossible for her to imagine wanting to leave this tranquil spot to run around the globe seeking thrills. What made a man look for more and more stimulation from dangerous escapades? Was it the fact that Trey had never had close family ties that would make him want to remain home? Was it ego to see how high he could climb or how deeply he could dive?

Or was he running scared and this was his way of coping with what he thought was his imminent death?

Even though Cilla thought believing in curses was silly, apparently it was very real to Trey. Or was that just an excuse to indulge himself in all manner of fun pursuits while his brother worked on behalf of both of them?

A silvery fish leaped high in the air, then dove back into the water, showing off. Was Trey showing off with his antics? She'd read that children raised without parental love were always seeking approval and were needy for love, yet afraid to trust the emotion. Cilla had talked about that with Jim and he'd more or less agreed with her analysis, knowing both brothers firsthand.

"Take Trey," Jim had told her, "he's a soft touch for anyone in trouble. He's financed one of his friend's drug rehab program not once or twice, but three times. He never gives up on a friend. And not just by giving money. He visits the guy, talks to him by the hour, trying to help him lick his addiction by sheer force of his personality.

But, on the other hand, he's unable or unwilling to have more than a fleeting relationship with a woman.''

"Because he believes he's going to die soon?'' she'd asked.

"Maybe,'' Jim had answered thoughtfully. "Or maybe he feels unworthy of love because he never had it from either mother or father. He likes women, has fun with them, but only fleetingly.''

"How about his brother? Is he the same?''

Jim had shaken his head. "They're nothing alike. Gavin is serious, business-oriented, almost compulsive. Knowing what his mother did to his father, he's afraid history will repeat itself, so as soon as a woman starts hearing wedding bells, she's out of his life. Yet I've never known a man who needed love more. Trey has lots of friends, both men and women, but Gavin's a loner by choice.''

"He doesn't trust anyone, not even male friends?''

"Not many. I've known him for sixteen years, roomed with him in college, and while I believe he likes me, he's not a confiding sort of friend. But if I needed something, he'd go to the wall for me. Trey would, too.''

"So they're both loyal. Choosy but loyal.''

Jim had smiled at that, but he'd agreed, Cilla remembered. She also remembered a psych course she'd taken in college and been told that everyone is influenced more than they realize by their background—their parents, siblings, birth order, financial circumstances, health, etcetera. She believed it then, and she believed it still.

Rising, Cilla stretched her arms above her head, wondering why she was spending so much time trying to dig into Trey's psyche, to understand him. He was a patient, just a patient, who'd be out of her life in a few more weeks, something he wanted more than she. No getting around it, she found him very appealing. The way he joked and kidded around during the workouts most days even though she knew at times he was hurting. The affectionate, irreverent way he was with Connie, apparently the only woman who'd ever had any real influence on him.

And the way he'd held her after she'd learned of Michael's hospitalization. His touch had been kind and supportive, not in the least sensual—though her thoughts had floated in that direction afterward. Fortunately, she'd pulled herself together and hoped he hadn't noticed.

Dusting off the seat of her shorts, Cilla decided it was time to climb back up and...

"Oh, no!" she whispered as she caught sight of Trey inching his way down the small steps using his cane, one hand on the rickety railing. "What are you doing?" she yelled at him as she rushed up to meet him.

His grin was cocky. "Coming down to enjoy the view more closely."

Cilla slipped an arm around his waist to brace him. "Why didn't you call me from the top?"

Taking a baby step down, he shrugged. "It's nine. I think you're off the clock."

"I'm never off the clock." Carefully she helped him descend until they were on the sandy bottom. "Your cane won't work in this. Let me help you over to the log."

"Yes, ma'am." He let her guide him and saw she was in a pretty good mood. He'd stood up at the top watching her, finally deciding she might like some company after all. He could certainly use some.

"I hope I'm not intruding on your personal time," Trey said, lowering himself to the log.

Cilla gestured toward the water as she sat alongside him. "Hey, it's a public ocean."

For several minutes they were quiet, watching the sea waves gallop to shore.

"Mesmerizing, isn't it?" Trey asked.

"Mmm-hmm. I decided a long time ago that one day I'd live on the ocean. Preferably Big Sur or Carmel, maybe Monterey. All I need is a million bucks or so." She laughed. "If you're going to dream, dream big, I say."

Trey's eyes narrowed as he gazed up at the stars. "That's beautiful country up that way. Once upon a time I'd planned to get rid of this white elephant and build something more to my taste up along there. But then...well, we can't have everything."

"No, we certainly can't." Although, if he'd get over this silly curse business and stopped physically abusing his body, he could easily have his dream. Cilla didn't see much point in going into all that. He wasn't one to change his mind easily.

But she could try. Angling her body so she could look at him, she decided to do just that. "You're absolutely and positively convinced that this curse thing is going to be the end of you?"

He didn't turn to look at her, but a muscle in his jaw clenched. "Yeah, I am."

"Okay, let's suppose, just for a moment, that you stop all your risky escapades, that you lead a normal life, avoiding anything dangerous. And let's suppose that your thirty-seventh birthday comes and goes, and nothing happens. Not the whole year long, and suddenly you're thirty-eight." When he started to interrupt, she put up her hand.

"Wait. Hear me out. Now, let's suppose again another scenario. Suppose you're well into your thirty-eighth year but you've injured yourself two maybe three times after these current wounds heal. You're fast coming up on your thirty-eighth birthday and you're sure you haven't got much time to live, so you try some truly daredevil stunt just for the thrill of it. And you die. That's not the curse. That's your doing.

"While I believe there's a master plan for most of us and we live as long as we're supposed to, I don't believe we can tempt fate by throwing ourselves in front of a train to test that theory. Sometimes our death comes about by our own reckless hand."

His expression contemplative, Trey turned toward her, stretching out his legs. "You think I have some sort of death wish?"

"Do you?"

"No. Absolutely not." Feeling frustrated since no one seemed to take him seriously, Trey ran a hand through his thick hair. "I don't want to die. I'd like nothing better than to live a long life, to work again with Gavin, to be carefree about things and not have this hanging over my head. But…"

"But you're only *guessing*. You noticed that several of your male relatives died in their thirty-eighth year—and some of them died in accidents—and you surmised you would also. You have no concrete proof, no diagnostic forecast. Your medical records show you're in excellent health, if not for the injuries you brought on yourself. And they will heal. Why not take a chance on life instead of a doomsday that in all probability will never happen?"

Unconvinced, he nevertheless felt he ought to put up a good defense. In reality, he'd never had anyone, not his doctor or his brother, try to persuade him so eloquently. "Okay, let's say I disregard the facts as I know them. Say I tear down this monstrosity of a house and begin to re-build a new one. Or sell it and move. Maybe I meet some-one and marry them. Then, a year from now, when the

Grim Reaper comes calling, I'll leave a new widow all alone where we relocated or alone to finish a monumental job of reconstruction. Know anyone who'd want to take on a six- to twelve-month marriage?''

Apparently he didn't realize he was quite a catch, handsome and very wealthy. ''Put an ad in the paper and you'd have a list as long as your arm. But you said you had set aside the idea of the curse. No curse, no death scene. You and the new Mrs. Templeton would live happily ever after in your dream home.''

Slowly, sadly, Trey shook his head. ''If only it was that easy.''

Cilla touched his arm, anxious to convince him. ''It *is* that easy. All you have to do is believe my version instead of yours. Come on, Trey. You're a risk taker. Take the biggest risk of all, a leap of faith that your life will be long and happy.''

She was so passionate in her argument that he almost believed her. Almost. ''What if you're wrong? I don't want to check out of this vale of tears while sitting at a desk computing last year's earnings. I want to go out having fun, maybe just having climbed Everest or winning a bicycle race in Spain or completing the Iditarod. Something new and exciting.''

''What could be more exciting than holding your own child for the first time?''

His head jerked toward her. ''What?''

''You heard me. You have time to marry and father a child. A legacy, something real and permanent, not some silly trophy for winning a race. Maybe Jolie Monroe. She seemed eager enough.'' That was really a stretch, Cilla thought, but there had to be one woman out there that he cared about.

''Jolie? You've got to be kidding! I'd have to be crazy

to want to be her *third* husband. I'd die early with her, from boredom.''

Cilla couldn't help smiling. ''All right, not her. But you must know all sorts of women. Pick one and go to work on her.''

Trey grew weary of the subject, which was going nowhere. Here he was in the moonlight on a deserted beach with a beautiful woman and all she wanted to talk about was how to fix his psyche. ''Tell me, are you a matchmaker on the side? Do you charge extra for analyzing your patients?''

Chagrined, Cilla looked away. ''You're absolutely right. I apologize for overstepping my boundaries. Again, very unprofessional.''

''Hey, it's all right.'' He managed to move closer to her on the skinny log. ''I know how you medical types are. Can't turn it off. Always serious, always working.''

There was that word again: *serious*. Implying *way too serious*. Did the whole world consider her serious? Cilla wondered. Preoccupied with her thoughts, she didn't realize how close Trey was until his good arm slipped around her shoulders and drew her toward him.

Cilla looked into his eyes. ''What are you doing?''

He lowered his head and touched his lips to hers, softly, gently, tasting, exploring. Very nonthreatening. Almost chaste.

Drawing back, Trey watched her eyes open, saw a vulnerability he hadn't noticed before. ''I'm testing to see if you're human, not a therapy automaton programmed by Jim.''

That got to her. As her brothers often told her, she could never resist a challenge. Cilla's hands bunched in his shirt as she yanked him to her and crushed her mouth to his, feeling the heat of anger mingled with a rising passion.

For years she hadn't dared let herself need or act on a desire for intimacy. There'd been school and her residency and her work and Michael's illness and her dad's emphysema. Obligations, duties, responsibilities had kept her from reaching. She'd hidden the wanting under a professional mask.

But not now, not tonight. Trey's challenge had released in her a craving to be held tightly, to be kissed thoroughly, to prove that, first and foremost, she was a female and not anyone's automaton. When he took over the kiss, sending the tip of his tongue in to dance with hers, she couldn't control a sigh of pleasure. Somewhat awkwardly, with both of them seated, he wrapped his arms around her and she felt the hot beat of his heart thumping against her own.

Who would have guessed? Trey asked himself as, edgy with need, he drew her closer still. Little Priscilla Kovacs, always so cool looking, so calm and efficient, with the exception of today when she'd let down her defenses and cried. She set off shivers along his spine and ignited aches that had him throbbing. As her hands moved up to thrust in his hair, he saw stars behind his closed eyelids more brilliant than in the night sky.

Inwardly he cursed his infirmity, for he would like nothing better than to pick her up, carry her to his room and into his big bed. He would show her a night she'd long remember and in doing so, make a few memories of his own.

A bird calling to its mate brought Cilla back to the real world with a snap. She pulled away from him, breathing hard.

"Is that human enough for you?" she asked, her voice husky. She'd made her point but at what cost?

Rising, hoping her legs would hold her, she moved toward the stairs. "Walking up is easier than down. See you in the morning." With that, she scampered up the steps leaving Trey staring after her.

Chapter Five

Seated on his terrace on Sunday morning, three weeks after he'd come home from the hospital, Trey hung up the phone and wanted to hit something really hard. He'd had to call his buddy, Max Varner, to tell him that he wouldn't be joining the guys next weekend for practice runs for the San Diego yacht races. Furthermore, he wouldn't be able to make the race at all.

Jim had stopped in again yesterday, but Trey knew what he was going to say before he spoke. The shoulder was healing well, but the strain of working the heavy sails would put his recovery back to square one. And the knee, while stronger, wouldn't hold up to scrambling all over the deck of a sailboat. Besides, the slightest bump could open up the incision.

With a sinking heart, Trey had listened as Jim told him he'd be risking permanent damage to the knee. Should that happen, he'd be facing big-time restructuring, possibly a steel plate and a durable leg brace, limiting future activities. Trey got the message.

But he didn't like it.

Earlier he'd called around and finally located Will Mathers, an old friend who agreed to replace him on Max's boat so the team wouldn't be short a man. Both Will and Max had been dutifully sympathetic, telling Trey there'd be other races.

Not for him, Trey was certain.

So he planned to spend the day brooding, angry that his body had let him down at a crucial time, struggling with his envy of the guys who'd be out there sailing with the wind and the sun, the laughs and camaraderie that he'd miss.

Connie had roasted a chicken and made potato salad, put the bowls in the fridge for whenever Trey and Cilla wanted to eat, then left to visit her sister's family in Chula Vista. Cilla had suggested working out, but he'd declined her offer, preferring to sit on his veranda and contemplate the sorry state of his life.

She was annoyed, but then, she simply didn't understand. No one did. Eyes shaded by his sunglasses, Trey watched a gull dip into the sea and come up with a fish in its mouth, then fly off. Things were pretty bad when he started envying seagulls.

Cilla had tried to be sympathetic or, at the very least, understanding. But the longer Trey's face became, the shorter her fuse. He hadn't moved out of his room since Jim left yesterday. Obviously, he didn't handle delays well. She knew how much he'd wanted to race that boat. Too bad. Life was full of disappointments. Grown-ups learned to handle them.

By eleven she'd had it with his juvenile sulking.

She made a quick phone call, then knocked on his door and walked in without waiting for a reply. "Put your shoes on. We're going for a ride." Spotting his Adidas, she carried them out onto the veranda and plunked them down next to the lounge chair he was sprawled on.

He continued staring out to sea. "I'm not going anywhere."

Hands on her hips, she regarded him. He hadn't bothered to shave and he wore a San Diego Chargers shirt with white denim shorts. Broody, sexy male. Smiling to herself, she thought he'd fit right in.

"Yes, you are. Mental attitude is half the battle in healing. You're going to backslide if you sit here much longer looking glum. Now, put those shoes on or I'll put them on for you."

Trey hadn't had anyone give him orders like that since he'd been a kid and Connie had gotten after him. Women who issued orders rarely gave up. Sighing heavily, he dragged a hand over his face. "I'm not cleaned up to go anywhere."

"You look fine." More than fine, Cilla thought. There was something about a blond man with stubble that was sexy as hell. He'd had a day's growth of beard the evening she'd kissed him as hungrily as a desert walker might gulp water. The memory of that kiss brought color to her cheeks even now, so she deliberately shifted her thoughts. "Come on. We haven't got all day."

Frowning, he sat up, put one foot on the floor and reached for a shoe. "Where exactly are we rushing to go?"

He wasn't thrilled, but he was moving. Score one for our side, Cilla thought. "You'll see."

Noticing how he struggled with the shoe because his injured leg didn't want to bend readily, she stooped to help him. She was aware of suspicious green eyes watching her as she laced up first one, then the other.

Despite his morose mood, Trey was curious. "Connie's gone, so you're going to kidnap me, is that it? Take me to some faraway retreat where you'll make me your love slave."

Finished, Cilla rose. "You should be so lucky." She handed him his cane and waited while he got up. "To the elevator."

Trey had no idea what game she was playing, but anything was better than hanging around this big, empty house feeling sorry for himself.

Cilla pulled her white Jeep Wrangler into a tight spot between a huge gray SUV and a bright-green Volkswagen right in front of a large two-story house with a wrap-around porch. There wasn't another parking spot to be had on the entire crowded block. "I have good parking karma, or so my dad says," she bragged with a smile as she turned off the engine. "Wherever we go, I seem to find the one and only place."

Trey was only half listening as he stared at the black shutters that contrasted with the neat, gray paint job that looked newly finished. He counted six windows on the top floor and three large ones on the lower level. There was a porch swing hanging from double chains and pots of healthy geraniums sitting along the wide railing. The lawn was freshly mowed, and three circular flower beds with white brick borders were overflowing with plants in a riot of colors. A bird feeder dangled from a branch of a tall tree alongside the brick walk.

The houses up and down the block were similar, middle-class comfortable, Trey decided. Suburbia at its summer best.

"Who lives here?" he finally asked, turning to see her watching him with amusement. On the way over they'd talked about the weather, the Padres home game tonight, all manner of things. But when he'd asked again where she was taking him, she'd smiled enigmatically and told him to be patient.

"I used to. Now it's just my folks and my sister, Isabel." Stepping down, she slammed her door and walked around to hand Trey his cane. When he just sat there looking hesitant, she had a momentary pang that she'd made a bad decision. "Something wrong?"

Trey heard shouting and laughter coming from the fenced backyard barely visible from where he sat. He remembered Cilla telling him that her mother made Sunday dinner for her available family members every week, served promptly at one. It was almost noon.

Feeling uncharacteristically out of place, he looked at her. "I don't belong here, Cilla. This is your family's Sunday dinner."

"Did I forget to mention that any of us are free to bring a guest or two without warning? More than three and we have to call. In case you're worried, I called Mom and told her I was bringing you." Cilla smiled as she reached for his hand. "She said she's going to send some of her chicken soup home with you to help you get better." She tugged on his fingers. "Come on. You'll be fine, I promise."

Reluctantly Trey stepped down. "I don't know about this. You should have told me. I would have shaved. We could have stopped and gotten flowers or a bottle of wine or—"

"Look at all the flowers Mom has, and more in back. And I told you, Dad makes his own wine. Wait till you taste it." She took his arm.

They'd barely stepped onto the sidewalk when a soft-ball came sailing over from the direction of the backyard. In a move as graceful as it was spontaneous, Trey reached out and caught it with his right hand.

"Good catch!" A tall, dark-haired man came through the gate toward them. He had a lean face with inquisitive eyes that probably missed nothing. The resemblance to Cilla was noticeable. And he hadn't shaved, either.

"Alex, this is Trey Templeton," Cilla said. "Trey, my brother, Alex."

"The lawyer, right?" Trey held out his hand. He knew he usually had no difficulty meeting people. Then why was it that the thought of Cilla's family intimidated him? he wondered.

"Guilty as charged." Alex shook hands as he slipped an arm around his sister. "Hello, brat," he said to Cilla, planting a kiss on her head.

"No respect. I get no respect around here," Cilla mock complained as she gave him a quick hug. "Everyone here already?"

"Everyone except Michael and his gang." His look was assessing, but he smiled at Trey. "Come on back and I'll introduce you around."

Trey shot a please-don't-leave-me look at Cilla as Alex shepherded him into the midst of the boisterous Kovacs family.

There was a makeshift softball game going on, some boys were playing marbles and Jimmy Buffett serenaded from a boom box propped on the porch. Beer cans were cooling in an ice-filled tub and soft drinks were piled in another. Everyone was dressed summer casual, yelling at one another, comfortable with each other.

Trey had never seen anything like it in his life. Not up close, anyhow. Movies didn't count.

He was dragged over and introduced to Alex's wife, Jenna, and their nine-year-old son, Ernie, who happened to be wearing the same Padres shirt as Trey, which had the boy giving him a shy smile. Then there was the oldest sister, Julie, the nurse, married to Sam, a cardiologist and their very active five-year-old twin girls, Debbie and Dorian, both climbing a huge maple tree near the back fence. Another brother, Charley, who ran the family construction business since their father retired, and his wife, Laurie, who was expecting number three next month. Their two boys, C.J. and Tommy, each wearing too-large mitts, were out waiting for Alex's next pitch.

"I'd ask you to join us," Alex said, then looked down at the still-red scar on Trey's knee, taking in the cane, "but maybe next time."

Trey nodded and Alex turned back to the boys. Cilla hovered nearby, hugging and talking with each one as Trey prayed he'd remember their names. Especially since the siblings all resembled one another with their auburn hair and deep-blue eyes.

"Feeling overwhelmed?" Cilla asked Trey as the impromptu ballgame resumed.

To say the least, Trey thought, but he didn't want to tell her that he felt like a fish out of water. "They seem like a great bunch."

"Yes, they are. I wish Mike could be here, too. You'd like him." A worried frown creased her brow.

"What's the latest on his condition?" Had he been so self-involved that he hadn't even asked her about her brother lately? Trey was uncomfortable with the answer.

"He's holding his own is all the doctors will tell us. I went to see him the other day while I was running my errands. He looks so pale, and he's too thin." She watched her nephew leap up and catch a high fly ball, remembering when all of them were younger, playing ball in this same backyard, and Mike was healthy and whole. "Way to go, Tommy," she called out.

"You have to believe he'll get better," Trey found himself saying. He'd never known anyone, much less someone he cared about, who had a potentially terminal illness. Cilla had encouraged him so often that the least he could do would be to return the favor. "Remember what you said, that mental attitude is half the battle. He's a fighter, right?"

Cilla blinked back a rush of tears, surprised to hear her own words bounced back at her. "Yes, he is," she whispered. When he squeezed her arm, she managed a smile.

Shaking off the somber mood, Cilla took Trey's hand. "Let's go inside. There're more people for you to meet."

Bracing himself for more of the same, Trey followed.

Inside, the tantalizing aromas in the kitchen had his mouth watering as he sniffed at pots bubbling away on the big stove, their lids dancing as steam rose. The oven bell buzzed and Isabel, Cilla's younger sister and a redhead, bent to remove a batch of rolls before shoving in another pan, then turning to welcome Cilla's friend.

"I've heard a lot about you," she told him, her eyes twinkling. "From Jim. He thinks you're…exceptional."

Trey laughed. "I'll just bet he does. I give him a lot of grief."

Cilla glanced around. "Where is Jim?"

Isabel sighed. "At the hospital, where else? Some fool was waterskiing too fast, fell off and broke his leg. I'm surprised he didn't break his hard head."

Trey cleared his throat, wondering what all Jim had told Isabel about him.

"He'll try to make it later," Isabel said. "Anyhow,

welcome to the Kovacs madhouse,'' she told Trey with a genuine smile.

''Thanks.''

''Mama! Wait!'' Cilla hurried to take a large tray from her mother as she came up from the basement. ''This is too heavy for you to carry.'' She set the tray laden with jars of pickles, peppers, olives and covered dishes on the counter.

''Cilla!'' Comfortably in her sixties, Anna Kovacs wore a big apron wrapped around her slightly overweight frame. Her dark hair, barely streaked with gray, was in a bun, and she had on rimless glasses. With a loving smile she gave her daughter a hug. ''We don't see enough of you these days.''

''I know, Mama.'' She turned to Trey, drew him closer and introduced him.

Anna hugged Trey as if he were one of her own. Taken aback, never having had much experience with touchy-feely, he found himself almost at a loss for words. ''It's good of you to let me come,'' he finally managed.

''My children's friends are always welcome.'' She glanced over her shoulder. ''Take him to Papa, Cilla. He's in the smoking room.''

''Is there anything we can do to help?'' Trey asked, though he was about as helpless as a newborn in the kitchen. Good manners drummed into him by Connie made him offer, anyway.

''No, no, you go with Cilla. Isabel helps me.'' With a fork, she stabbed fat, juicy pickles and put them on a plate.

Trey followed Cilla down a narrow hallway toward a closed door at the end. ''What's a smoking room?'' he asked.

Cilla laughed. ''That's what we always called it because it's the only room Mama used to let Papa smoke in.'' She leaned close, as if to reveal a confidence. ''It's also where he makes his wine.''

''Ah, I see. Sort of like a den. Off-limits to others.''

''Mmm-hmm.''

''Used to? He doesn't smoke anymore?''

''No, he's got emphysema. Not really bad, but there's an oxygen tank on the premises, just in case. Now he just sticks his old pipe in his mouth unlit and chews on the stem.'' She gave three solid knocks on the door, then waited.

''Cilla!'' exclaimed a deep voice. ''Come in.''

''We all have our own knocks so Papa knows who wants him,'' she explained, her lips twitching. ''It's the birth order.''

''Clever,'' Trey said as Cilla shoved open the door. There was a lingering fragrance of cherry tobacco in the room and around the man who was seated in a comfortably worn lounger, his pipe in one hand and a small glass of dark-red wine in the other.

As Cilla rushed over to hug her father, Trey had a chance to look him over. He'd been expecting a big man from the sound of that voice, but Mihal Kovacs was no taller than his daughter. His head was bald except for a fringe of reddish-brown hair tinged with gray. But the thing that made him stand out was a dark handlebar mustache, both ends waxed and curled to perfection.

''Papa, I want you to meet Trey Templeton, the man I'm currently working with. Trey, this is my father.'' There was no mistaking the pride in her voice.

Trey reached to shake the older man's hand. ''Glad to meet you, sir.''

Mihal made a dismissing gesture. ''No one calls me sir. Papa or Mihal is just fine. Sit down, both of you.'' He gestured toward a small two-seater couch as his light-blue eyes flickered over Trey, ending up at his injured knee. "I see you got knees like me." Setting down his glass, he yanked up his gray trouser legs, revealing scars around both knees. "That's what thirty years in construction can get you."

Trey just nodded, hoping Mihal wouldn't ask how he got hurt. He felt uncomfortable in front of this hardworking man who'd sustained his injuries on the job, while his had come about through his own frivolous action. He glanced at Cilla, wondering if she'd had a hidden agenda in bringing him here. But she had her back to them, taking down two glasses from a small cupboard.

"I told Trey about your wine, Papa."

"Sure, sure. Pour yourselves some." He downed the last of his and held out his glass. "And me, too."

Cilla hefted the half-full gallon jug and played hostess, all the while eyeing her father. "How many glasses does this make? You don't want Mama to get after you, right?"

Again that dismissive wave. "She's not *my* Mama, she's yours." He clinked his glass to Trey's. "Women, always after you for something, right?"

Trey grinned, liking Cilla's father. "I agree." He took a sip, his eyes smiling into Cilla's. He felt the wine shoot heat all the way down to his toes, warming his blood. He swallowed and blinked as his eyes watered. "Good stuff," he commented.

Mihal nodded and winked. "You betcha. I make the best." He fingered his pipe longingly as he studied Trey. "So, you know my Cilla long?"

Here it comes, Cilla thought, rushing to head him off at the pass. "A few weeks only, Papa. Dr. Jim sent me to do therapy on Trey's knee."

Oddly annoyed that she answered for him, Trey spoke

up. "She's great, your daughter. I'd still be on crutches if it weren't for Cilla." Which wasn't exactly true, but he thought her father would like to know she did good work.

"Yeah, sure, I know." His gaze narrowed as he looked from one to the other. "What kind of work do you do, young man?"

Oh, Lord, the inquisition, Cilla thought. But before either of them could reply, there was one loud knock at the door and her mother stuck her head in. "Dinner, folks. Come to the table."

Saved by the knock, Trey thought, rising. For the first time since he'd quit working with his brother, he felt embarrassed about his lifestyle.

The afternoon hummed along like a surreal play he was attending without benefit of a program, Trey decided. The huge mahogany dining room table, covered by a delicately embroidered cloth, somehow managed to seat everyone including all the children. Everyone, that is, except Anna Kovacs whose chair sat empty while she strolled around, pouring lemonade or milk, refilling dishes, cutting a child's meat. No one but Trey seemed to think it was unusual that she didn't join them but preferred serving the food she'd cooked all morning.

And what food it was. Trey had actually toured Hungary and several surrounding countries some years ago, but he hadn't tasted such delicious abundance. First there was soup with chunks of chicken and slender noodles in a rich broth. That was followed by cabbage rolls stuffed with pork and rice, chicken paprikas with tiny dumplings that melted in the mouth, potato pancakes with warm homemade applesauce, veal meatballs in mushroom gravy and cucumbers in sour cream. The hot rolls with unsalted butter were as light as air; he had three of them.

There was little formality as dishes were passed and called for, folks reaching, children chattering while adults talked and laughed with a warm familiarity Trey found himself envying. He'd been to the homes of friends, lots of them, but he'd never seen anything like the good-natured ribbing, the obvious affection, the underlying love that swirled around the Kovacs table. What must it have been like growing up in a household such as this? The respect they all showed for Papa Kovacs, listening attentively whenever he spoke, and the fondness he could see in Mama's caring touch as she moved about. He wondered if these people knew just how lucky they were.

"I can't believe you eat this way all the time," he murmured to Cilla. "Do you think your mother would move in with me?"

Grabbing a fat pickle as the dish went by, Cilla laughed. "What about Connie?"

"She needs a break." Wiping his mouth on the white linen napkin, he sat back, wondering if his expanding girth could handle another stuffed cabbage, then decided not to be greedy.

"Here, one last one," Mama Kovacs commented, sliding the final cabbage roll onto his plate as she and Isabel began to clear. "I saw you watching it." She squeezed his shoulder as he thanked her.

Next came a rich, strong coffee laced with cream and tiny sugar pellets along with strudel—apple, cherry or cheese—the dough as soft and flaky as any he'd eaten. There was also a walnut torte with butter icing that Trey sincerely regretted not having the room to try. And small glasses of blackberry brandy for the adults, ginger ale for the children. He was impressed how the children were included in everything.

"More coffee?" Mama asked, pausing behind him with the pot.

"I couldn't eat or drink another thing, Mama. Thank you. It was all wonderful." She beamed her pleasure as she went on.

When had he started calling his hostess "Mama?" Trey wondered with a jolt, hoping no one else had noticed. He'd never in his life called anyone Mother or Mom or Mama. Cynthia had instructed Gavin and him to call her by her first name. But everyone called this warm, generous woman mama, and he'd just followed suit.

Trey stole a glance at Cilla and saw she was smiling at him, a smile he'd not seen on her before. He was getting in way over his head here, he decided, uncertain how to stop the runaway train.

Chauvinism was alive and well in the Kovacs household as all the women put away leftovers and did cleanup while the men and children went out back for a rousing game of horseshoes. Bracing his bad leg with his cane, Trey managed to score a few points. When Cilla came out on the porch and frowned at him, he just shrugged and grinned, safe in the midst of the guys. But he did quit after one game and moseyed over to where Ernie was fooling around with a bag of marbles.

"Looks like we have more than a Padres shirt in common," Trey commented as he eased himself down in the grass alongside the boy. Ernie was small for nine and wore glasses. Trey had noticed he hadn't caught a single throw in the ball game nor did they ask him to play horseshoes.

Ernie looked up, only slightly curious. "You like marbles?"

"Sure do." Trey studied the ones the boy had on the ground. "Wow, look at this one. I used to have one like this. We called these magic eyes because of their deep blue centers.'' He held the marble up to the light. ''I'll bet this is one of your best.''

''Yeah, but I've got one better.'' Ernie's hand dug around in his bag and came out with a big gold shooter.

''Whoa! You're right. That's a yellow jacket, a real beauty.''

''Want to play a game?'' Ernie asked casually, squinting up at Trey as if it didn't really matter to him one way or the other.

''I'd like that.'' They started lining up their marbles, the boy looking pleased.

Cilla drove her Jeep through the twilight of a warm summer evening, her thoughts scattered. After cleanup, she'd come out and found her shy little nephew playing marbles on the ground with Trey, the boy grinning as he shot another one out of the circle. She'd leaned against the porch pillar and watched them, wondering how this man who seemingly knew nothing about children had honed in on the one kid who didn't quite fit in. The game ended and Ernie whooped with delight as he realized he'd won. Naturally, he wanted to play another, but Trey had shaken his head and, with no small effort, gotten to his feet. Noticing how unsteady Trey was, sweet little Ernie had grabbed ahold of him and they strolled around the yard until Trey could walk on his own again.

Now she slid a glance over as Trey sat in the passenger seat staring straight ahead, his expression unreadable. She couldn't help wondering if he knew how natural he was with children, this man who'd opted not to have any of his own. She should have guessed when Connie told her about his involvement in the Boys & Girls Club. He'd certainly charmed Mama and Papa, accepting a quart of chicken soup, some sugar cookies and a jug of wine to take home amidst sincere invitations to return soon. He'd seemed genuinely moved.

"My family can be a little overpowering in large numbers," she said, breaking the silence.

"No, they're not at all. They're great. I wish…"

When he didn't go on, she did. "What do you wish?"

He sighed, shook his head. "Nothing."

"Hey, I took you out to cheer you up, not to drag you down."

"I know. I'm fine, really. Just a little tired." Not physically, Trey thought, but mentally. Tired of wishing his past had been different. Like maybe if *his* mother had lived, things would have been better. Self-defeating to think like that. Couldn't think too much about the future, either. Okay, the present then. Squaring his shoulders, he turned to look at Cilla.

The occasional streetlamp shone in on her skin, dappled from the passing trees. She wore a long, oversize bright-green T-shirt over white shorts. She looked so natural, so lovely that he again wondered why there were no men beating down her door.

"You ought to have boyfriends galore or even a husband by now and a couple of kids. How come you don't?"

"I think we've already had this discussion," Cilla said as she stopped at a light. An elderly couple, likely in their eighties, stepped off the curb arm in arm, each supporting the other as they slowly walked to the other side. They glanced neither left nor right, but when they reached the far sidewalk, they looked into each other's eyes and smiled, then strolled on.

"Look at those two," Cilla commented, her gaze still

on them. "I'll bet they've been together longer than Mama and Papa, yet they're still in love."

He kept staring at her profile. "I'll bet that's because, in his eyes, she's still as lovely as she once was. As you are now."

Faintly surprised at his romantic tone, she turned to him. "My, aren't you poetic tonight?"

"What I was going to say earlier is that I wish you could forget about my shoulder, my knee, the therapist-patient thing and just look at me as a man."

The light changed and the driver behind them gave a quick toot on his horn. Dragging her gaze from his, Cilla stepped on the gas, driving on autopilot. Nervous about where this conversation was headed, she considered carefully before answering. "I do think of you as a man. You're so...so male, how could I not?"

"Good, because I think of you as a woman. A very attractive woman."

What did he expect her to say to that? Though she really didn't want to, she'd have to put a halt to this. She'd never, in six years as a therapist, gotten involved with a patient. Of course, she'd never been drawn to one before quite like she was with Trey. Still, she was certain Jim wouldn't approve.

Turning the Jeep into the lane leading to the Townsend mansion, Cilla felt her stomach clench. "Look, Trey, I hear what you're saying, and I find you attractive, too. But we have to put our personal feelings aside while I'm your therapist because—"

"Did you take some sort of oath? Thou shalt not have feelings of a personal nature for thy patient?" He was smiling as she stopped in the circular drive, but his voice was edgy.

"No, of course not." She removed the keys and turned

toward him. "But there are unwritten rules all professional people have to follow. *Should* follow."

Unhooking his seat belt, Trey angled his body so he was facing her. "So then, you're saying if it weren't for these unwritten rules, you'd go to bed with me?"

Well, that was certainly a leap. "No. I could, yes, but...wait! What I mean is, if we were just two people who'd met under other circumstances and were attracted to each other, we'd be free to pursue that thought. But as it is..."

"You can't." Trey reached over, tucked a lock of her hair behind her ear, noting its softness.

"Exactly." Cilla marveled that a mere touch of his hands could cause her breath to hitch, her heart to pick up its rhythm.

"That's a shame because Ernie tells me you're a real cool babe." He subtly shifted his fingers to her nape, stroked there.

"Ernie said that? I don't believe you. Little, shy Ernie?"

"Believe it. He called you a *hottie*."

"Oh, no!"

"'Still water' and all that." He felt her lean into his touch, knew she wasn't aware she had.

"He's only nine," Cilla insisted as a shiver slid up her spine.

"A very advanced nine. He also said your hair was as silky as a moonbeam with a fragrance that keeps him awake nights." At her shocked look, he gave her a crooked smile. "Okay, so that last part was mine." His fingers tangled in her hair just before he plunged both hands in and drew her face to his. Just before his mouth took hers.

Free-falling, Cilla thought. The suddenness, the fierceness, the wildness made her feel as if she were free-falling, diving through the sky without a chute. Passion exploded just that quickly, just that deeply, and she moved closer to the flame. Wanting this, needing this.

Trey plunged and plundered, needing to know if that first kiss and his reaction to it had been a fluke. But no, her fiery response, her fluid mouth, her tempting taste had him drowning in sudden need, in a bright flush of passion. His hands at her back kneaded the flesh beneath her thin shirt before moving to the front and settling on her breasts.

That move had Cilla pulling back from him, her eyes hazy with desire but determined to put a halt to things. Slowly, reluctantly, she removed his hands. Trying to slow her wildly beating heart, she drew in a long, shaky breath. ''Trey, we can't do this.''

''Why not?'' He nuzzled her cheek, hoping to convince her.

''For all the reasons I mentioned and more.'' Like the fact that he'd already told her he had no interest in the long term, in marriage and a family. Like the silly curse he believed in and would die trying to outrun.

Trey had always believed *no* was *no* when a woman said it, but he had a hard time accepting this refusal. ''Cilla, we're both free, both attracted, both with obvious needs. What's the harm?''

Easing back fully onto her side of the car, she reached for the door handle. His last statement made it easier to step back. ''I don't do one-night stands.'' With that she got out and went inside.

It was late, nearly midnight, but Cilla couldn't sleep. Slipping out of bed, she put on her short robe and stepped out barefoot onto her bedroom veranda. The moon was finally full, high in the sky, bathing the back lawn, the beach and the restless sea in its silvery light. Not a golden, harvest moon but a lovers' moon. Only there were no lovers here to enjoy it.

She'd gone to her room after walking away from Trey and been there ever since. Thinking, worrying, wishing. Her first instinct had been to start packing, to leave tonight, slipping a note under his door with a brief explanation. Nothing personal, just that she'd had to go and she'd see that Jim sent over a replacement therapist.

But after a long, contemplative shower, she'd decided to stop always choosing the easiest path, to stop running from her problems. She'd almost left twice before, threatened to, because Trey wasn't cooperating. But wasn't it her job to persuade the patient to do the best thing where his rehabilitation was concerned? When had she become such a coward, ready to run the moment things became difficult?

Standing at the railing, Cilla heard the wind shifting through nearby palms, felt a breeze drift through her hair. She would stay and face things, but it wasn't going to be easy. When she'd admitted her attraction to Trey, she wasn't just agreeing with him to be nice. She'd been attracted since day one, even when he'd been obstinate and pouty. She'd come to see the giving side of him, the caring, compassionate side. And now that he knew how she felt, she didn't know how long she could keep resisting him with the memory of his kisses dancing in her restive dreams, awake or asleep.

Professionalism aside, giving in to her desire now would likely cause more heartache later when he finished healing and left on another dangerous endeavor, as he surely would. She'd tried convincing him the curse was only in his imagination, but the fear was too ingrained in him.

It was the eternal male-female conflict. He wanted a good time for as long as it would last while she was falling in love with him and was thinking forever thoughts. But how could you consider a future with a man convinced he had no future?

Cilla heard a sound behind her and turned. Trey stood by the double doors wearing the same white shorts with an unbuttoned blue shirt, one hand on his cane, his green eyes a dark jade. She'd been so lost in her thoughts that she hadn't heard him come in.

"I don't think of you as a one-night stand, Cilla," he said. "I never have." He saw that her eyes were luminous in the moonlight, and then her lower lip trembled. He dropped his cane and closed the distance between them in two long strides, taking her in his arms.

Cilla closed her eyes and breathed in his special scent as her own arms encircled him, wanting to be closer and closer still. She might not have forever, but she would have this. Her lips sought his, and the taste of him exploded on her tongue, seeping into her pores, her very heart. When he shifted and took her deeper, it was as if she had no will, no choice but to follow.

Trey was losing himself in her rich, dark taste, the scent she wore that he could recognize across the room, the touch of her hands burrowing beneath his shirt, spreading heat. Each time they came together, there was this all-consuming passion that quickly rose to the surface, keeping him off balance. He'd hoped she wouldn't send him away when he'd walked in, but he hadn't dared believe she'd welcome him like this.

When he pulled back from her and searched her eyes, he saw that she was as baffled as he that together they could set off such fireworks. "I want to make love with you," he told her, his voice husky. "But only if you want it as much as I do.'' He had to be certain. This was too important to mess up.

"I want that, too," she answered, her voice certain.

He bent his head and kissed her with infinite care this time, wanting to show her that he could be gentle. Arms entwined, they slowly made their way over to the bed she'd only recently vacated, the top sheet askew from her thrashing about. He didn't notice, didn't care as he lowered her to the mattress and followed her down.

"What about your knee?" she asked.

"What knee?" he murmured.

Now that he finally had her with him, Trey felt no need to rush. His lips roamed over her face, her silken throat, raining kisses and little love bites. Low, meaningless whispers gave way to moist kisses that had his heart pounding like a trip-hammer. With trembling hands he gently removed her robe and gown with anticipation, not unlike unwrapping a gift, leaving her skin shimmering in the moonlight.

Cilla had trouble lying still as he learned her every secret while his hands sent thrills and chills through her system with their random searching. He kissed her everywhere, always returning to take her mouth in a soul-shattering kiss. She felt a shudder race through him and knew the time for slow loving was over.

A throaty moan escaped from her parted lips as his mouth settled on one breast, then the other, drawing on her until she wanted to beg but had no breath left. Finally he moved over her and joined with her as she arched to meet him.

In the dark of night, all that could be heard above the pounding waves was their harsh breathing. Slick skin slid against sleek skin as green eyes locked with blue. He wanted to watch her while she climbed, when she reached the summit. He hoped he could hold off answering his own needs, which had been building for weeks.

She was so lovely, he thought as he tried to stay in control. She looked at him with a curious mixture of vulnerability and trust. Straining with him, finally he felt her release and saw her stunned surprise. With no small measure of satisfaction, he let himself follow.

Some time later Trey rolled from her, taking her with him, careful to avoid putting his weight on his injured leg, which was throbbing now. But a little pain had been worth it. Cilla lay with her cheek against his heart, her pulse slowing, her hand toying with the hair on his chest. It had been a very long time since he'd felt so good, so content, Trey thought, wondering if she felt the same.

"Are you all right?" he finally asked.

"Mmm."

He'd take that as a yes. Holding her close, he caressed her hair absently, wondering where to go from here. There was no going back in their relationship. How could he possibly ignore her small but strong therapist hands working on his body without wanting her, now that he'd known her passionate touch? Already he felt a stirring that told him he was ready for more.

"Cilla, what made you change your mind?" He had to know.

She thought about the question and all of its ramifications before answering. "I'm not sure, except I think the world is a scary place and no one gets out alive. But even scarier is getting out without ever knowing love." Easing her head back so she could look into his eyes, she knew she had his attention. "Do you know what I mean?"

Trey studied her serious face for a long moment before pulling her closer. "Yeah, I think I do." What he didn't know was what he was going to do about it.

Chapter Six

Cilla went in the back door and on through the kitchen, stopping to snag a bottle of water from the fridge.

"How was your walk?" Connie asked, glancing up from the sink where she was cleaning vegetables.

"Great. It's a beautiful day. I think I saw a dolphin. Do they ever come in this close?" Tilting her head back, she drank thirstily.

"I guess." Connie studied her more closely. "You seem awfully happy this morning." Her knowing look said it all. "I don't think it's the dolphin making you so happy, eh?"

Cilla couldn't resist bending to hug the little woman. "I just love the whole world today, Connie." Stealing a carrot stick, she headed for the elevator.

"Trey has a visitor," Connie said.

Stopping, Cilla turned back. "Is Jolie back?" She'd seemed like a woman who didn't easily accept a refusal.

"No, one of Trey's playmates, I call them. Men who still act like boys." Disapproval was evident in her tone. "This one, Russell Fox, has more money than brains. Such a waste, if you ask me."

Cilla felt the first flutter of nerves. "Is he here about that sailboat race? Because Trey's already decided not to go on that."

"I don't think so." Connie rinsed the vegetables in the colander, then reached for a hand towel. "He's bad news, I know."

Thoughtfully Cilla chewed on a bite of carrot. "You're thinking he wants Trey to go off on some new adventure with him?"

Connie nodded as she dried her hands. "Usually that's what he wants."

She had to be philosophical about this, Cilla decided. "Trey's smart. He turned down the race because he knew he could have permanent injuries. He knows how to say no."

"You better hope so," Connie commented as Cilla stepped into the elevator.

Riding up, Cilla frowned. She had to trust him, to believe he'd finally realized that if he harmed himself further, even the six months to a year he believed he had left would be painful. He surely wouldn't do that to himself. Or to her.

The past week had been one of the happiest of her life. They'd gotten some serious workouts in, but mostly they'd spent the days exploring these shiny new feelings. They walked on the beach, swam in the warm ocean, with Cilla ever watchful of his injuries, and they'd carried a picnic basket lunch down to the sand to eat on a blanket they'd spread in a small cove, then napped in each other's arms.

And, oh, the nights! He'd shown her the heights and depths of physical pleasure while she'd shown him that the addition of love made all the difference. She was madly in love with him, though she'd never told him. Certainly he'd never said those three little words. But there were times when she'd catch him studying her, his emerald eyes serious and contemplative, as if trying to look into her very soul. When that happened, she would face him, let him see her heart there, his for the taking.

They didn't talk of the future or even the past, living in the here and now. Cilla dared not think about what lay ahead, though Trey hadn't mentioned the curse in a while. Her ardent hope, her fervent prayer was that the love he'd found with her would make the difference, that he'd put aside his fears about a curse, and work toward building a future with her.

Arriving on the second floor, Cilla pushed open the elevator door. Although she had such high hopes, she'd never been one to believe that things fell into your lap simply because you wanted them to. She was well aware of how strong a person Trey was and that his beliefs were just as strong. She would take one day at a time, grateful for the hours she had with him, and worry about the future later.

Walking down the hallway, she heard two male voices coming through the open door of Trey's sitting room. No, she would not stand there and deliberately eavesdrop. Cilla went into her own room and stepped out on her terrace. The voices were even clearer here. She knew she probably should go shower, but she couldn't seem to move.

''You've got to admit, it's a sweet deal,'' said the man Cilla decided had to be Russell Fox, Trey's friend. ''Two weeks in Alaska up close with the glaciers. I read where a big one is moving. We'd fly into Juneau, where I've got a guy lined up to take us kayaking in the Gulf of Alaska. Then on to Fairbanks and go farther north by dogsled with a guide. Perfectly safe. Finally, we'd fly home from Anchorage.'' There was a pause. "Hell, I'll foot the bill if Gavin's got you on a tight leash."

"You know that's not it," Trey answered, sounding torn. "Look at this knee," he went on. "I've been told if I injure it again, I'll be facing major reconstruction, maybe a permanent brace."

"Hey, think positive, here. Why would you injure it? I went kayaking a couple years back. Didn't have so much as a scratch. And dogsledding, all you do is sit there and let the huskies do the work. Paul's going and Ken. What do you say?"

Cilla could hear Trey sigh the way he so often did when he wanted to do something but knew he shouldn't. "I don't know. How soon do I have to let you know?"

Oh, no! Cilla thought. He was actually considering it.

"Let's see. Today's Wednesday. We're leaving Friday. I've made arrangements but I've got to know if I should put your name in. Paul's friend, Sal, wants to go, but I said I want you."

"Yeah, okay. I'll call you."

"Look at that face," Russell exclaimed. "You *want* to go. I can see it."

"Sure I want to go. It's just this knee…"

"Hey, we've all had a few broken bones. Remember that time in the Canadian Rockies when I broke my leg in three places and had to finish the trip in a hip-to-toe cast?"

Trey chuckled. "Yeah, I remember."

"This is the opportunity of a lifetime, Trey. This guide's been on TV and written a book. Says he'll take us up into the wilderness where only a few guys have ever gone. It'll be better than that trip we took down the Amazon two years ago.''

"It sounds great, Russ,'' Trey answered, excitement in his voice. "I've always wanted to go up that way.''

"This is your chance, buddy.'' Russell's chair made a scraping sound on the wood floor.

Cilla had heard enough. Quietly she closed the double doors and let out a ragged breath.

So here we go, she thought. Missing out on racing the sailboat, he now wanted to go kayaking.

From what she'd heard, Trey and Russ and the other men mentioned had been friends for years. They'd traveled the world over together, shared all sorts of experiences, probably some good and some bad. It would take a lot for a guy to choose a woman over that kind of bond. Even loving him, how could she compete?

Toeing off her running shoes, Cilla stretched out on the bed and stared up at the ceiling. By now she suspected that Trey was aware she had fallen in love with him. But she also knew that he was afraid to love, thinking he'd be gone in a short time and it wouldn't be fair to the woman. Personally, she didn't believe in silly curses and was more than willing to risk loving him.

But there was something else here. As she'd told Connie, Trey was a grown man who could say no if he wanted to. Was he going off on these jaunts because he'd become addicted to danger and was using the idea of a curse to justify his actions? If so, she certainly didn't want to become further involved with a man who could so easily be persuaded to drop everything and try another dangerous pursuit. If his feelings for her were as strong as hers for him, he wouldn't even have considered Russell's invitation.

She would have to see what he decided to do, because at this point the ball was in his court. He could choose fun and adventure and possible permanent injury or he could choose a woman who loved him, one who offered him a family, children. She'd seen his face at her parents' home, the naked longing he tried to hide. Together they could make up for his somewhat bleak childhood and give to their children all the love he'd never known.

But it was up to Trey. She wouldn't ask him not to go, wouldn't make a fool of herself and beg him to stay with her, for his sake as well as her own.

Rising to go in to shower, Cilla prayed she'd be able handle his decision without breaking down.

The workout on Wednesday afternoon didn't go well. Trey was distracted and remote, his mind obviously elsewhere. He hardly spoke at all and didn't meet her eyes when he did. Cilla knew he was wrestling with his decision, but she couldn't help him.

After the second time he dropped the five-pound weights he was using to strengthen his arm and shoulder, he swore and grabbed a towel. "Let's call it a day, okay?" he told Cilla. "I don't feel like doing any more today."

"Fine." She began cleaning the mat.

Trey grabbed his water bottle and drank deeply. He hadn't been using his cane since after lunch, though there was still pain. He'd half expected Cilla to chastise him for rushing things again, but she'd been oddly quiet. Of course, he'd hardly been a chatterbox. He had a lot on his mind, a great deal to think about.

Russ had built a good case for going to Alaska with the guys. Trey wanted to go, yet he didn't. Not because of his knee. Because of Cilla.

He'd known for a long time now that he cared about her. Far more than he was comfortable with. He hadn't intended to fall in love—if, in fact, that's what this was. He'd thought to have a little fun while he healed, then get on with his agenda. This Alaskan invitation had come too soon. If he could have had one more month with her, maybe by then he would have gotten her out of his system. Maybe.

A while ago, when she was massaging his leg, the thought that he soon wouldn't ever feel those small, capable hands work on him again had depressed him. More upsetting was the thought that she wouldn't be coming willingly into his bed if he told her he was leaving before Jim released him. That bothered him more than ever.

The past week, making love with Cilla, joking around and laughing with her, just *being* with her, had been like an awakening. He'd never in his life felt so cared for, so alive, so happy. Was that love? He'd seen examples in her parents' house when Mama had stroked Papa's cheek as she passed his chair at dinner. And when her big, gruff construction worker brother, Charley, had sat alongside his wife, his large hand resting on her pregnant belly. Yeah, he'd seen a lot in a short time, things he hadn't ever seen growing up or among his buddies, most unmarried.

Now that he thought about it, most of the guys he hung around with were like him: from wealthy, broken homes, sort of rudderless, unable or unwilling to sustain a lasting relationship. Trey knew the curse was his reason for living on the edge, but what about his buddies? Why hadn't they, most in their midthirties, settled down, found meaningful work, started a family? Alongside men like Cilla's father and Charley and Alex the lawyer and even Jim the doctor, he and his friends led a frivolous life. Until recently that hadn't bothered him. It was beginning to.

Bending to pick up the weight he'd dropped, he felt a pain slice through his thigh from his knee. Damn, why wasn't this healed by now! Trey didn't want all this deep thinking, these tough decisions. He wanted to be carefree again, out there living life to the fullest like before. Why, suddenly, did that statement sound childish and immature?

Turning, he saw that Cilla was folding clean towels at the counter. She was in yellow shorts and a navy top today, her familiar fragrance perfuming the air. She was so lovely, easily the most responsive woman he'd ever known. He'd never had trouble walking away from women when things cooled. But with Cilla, it hurt to think of his life without her.

Moving close to her, he waited until she looked up. His eyes bored into hers as if the answer to his problems could be found in their deep-blue depths. She didn't move, didn't smile, just stood quietly watching him. He leaned down and touched his lips to hers, brushing lightly. But the spark ignited and he turned up the flame, drinking from her. The kiss lasted only a short time but was powerful enough to shake him to his soul. Stepping back, Trey realized he was trembling. No woman had ever made him tremble before.

Without a word he left the room, closing the door behind him.

Was that a goodbye kiss? Cilla wondered, her hands shaky. It certainly felt like it. Lowering her head, she let the tears fall.

Trey spent Thursday in his room. Cilla had knocked, asking if he wanted to work out, but he'd told her he didn't feel like it. Connie had taken in a lunch tray and later a dinner tray, but he'd hardly touched either.

That evening Cilla walked out onto her terrace and saw that Trey was on his next door, seated in his lounge chair, looking morose. She decided she had to make the first move.

"Trey, could we talk, please?" she asked.

He took his time answering. "We don't have anything to talk about." With that he rose somewhat unsteadily and went inside.

Cilla knew that Alaska had won and she'd lost.

Friday morning Cilla stepped out of her room, and the first thing she saw were three suitcases standing outside Trey's door. She walked closer just as he came out wearing a dress shirt and slacks, a sports coat slung over his arm. He was clean shaven, but there were dark circles beneath his eyes.

"I've had an offer I can't refuse," he began.

"Yes, I know."

"I want you to know I appreciate everything you've done for me." He watched her face drain of color and felt like the heel he was. "I tried to warn you..."

"Yes, you did. It seems I don't follow instructions well."

"Hey, that's my line." From somewhere he found a small smile and gave it to her. "Take care of yourself, Cilla." He kissed her forehead, knowing if he touched more, he'd never leave.

"You, too."

He handed her a folded check and stepped around her, heading for the elevator. Four months till his birthday. He had a lot of living to do before then. This was the best way. He'd get over Cilla and she'd forget him. Far better than marrying her and dying shortly after.

Trey moved into the elevator and pushed the button.

Blinking back tears, Cilla went back into her room to pack.

The weather in June in San Diego was unpredictable. Where visitors expected warm sunshine, they often faced days filled with a chilly rain. It was just such a day that Cilla welcomed her new patient to Dr. Jim's physical therapy facility two blocks from the hospital.

It was ten days since she'd returned from her stay at the Templeton mansion.

It hadn't been easy, explaining things to Jim, who wisely didn't comment much, though she could see he read between the lines and guessed some of it. Then there'd been her family, with Mama calling to invite "that nice young man with the big appetite" back for another Sunday dinner. Mama was even better at reading between the lines than Jim, and her sympathetic understanding was almost Cilla's undoing.

Work was her salvation, and she threw herself into it, putting in ten- and twelve-hour days at the clinic, doing everything but sweeping up. Her job occupied her days and even evenings, but the nights were the worst. Though she'd be physically tired, her mind wouldn't close down, thoughts whirling around, making her restless. And when she finally did fall into a restive sleep, dreams of Trey walking with her on the beach or sharing a picnic lunch on the sand or floating on the foamy waves would have her awakening with tears on her cheeks.

His wonderfully handsome face seemed forever locked in her mind's eye. She relived the hours she'd spent in his arms in his big bed, wondering why she was torturing herself like this.

It had to stop.

And it would, today. She had a new young patient who would require lots of attention and patience.

Eleven-year-old Timmy Lockhart had been in an auto accident and had his arm broken in two places, his elbow all but crushed. After reconstructive surgery, he'd been in a cast from his shoulder to his wrist for months. Finally, cast off, he had to slowly learn to use his arm again.

Which is where Cilla came in.

After all the surgeries, the days in the hospital, the awkward cast, Timmy was understandably hesitant. After helping him onto the table, Cilla noticed how protectively he guarded his arm.

"Timmy, my name is Cilla," she began as the boy's mother watched from a chair nearby. The center wasn't too crowded today, only three other tables occupied with patients in various stages of their therapy and two assistant therapists working with them. "I'm going to help your arm to be as good as new. Okay?"

He nodded but he didn't look convinced. "Is it going to hurt?"

"Perhaps, a little. Those bones and muscles have been locked inside your cast for a long time now and they're stiff. We need to work them so they move freely, like your other arm." Cilla saw that he seemed to relax a bit. "Do you play ball?"

"I used to, before this. Catcher. I miss it."

"Tell you what, Tim. If you do exactly as I say, you'll be playing ball again real soon. Deal?"

This time the nod came more readily. "Okay."

She heard the door at the front open, smelled the rain as someone came in, but Cilla ignored it as she handed her patient a rubber ball. "I want you to squeeze this ball, not hard, just nice and easy. And keep squeezing it. The muscles in your hands connect to other muscles that stretch all the way up your arm so we start this way. I'm going to go read your chart while you do that, okay?" She saw him nod. Smiling at his mother, Cilla turned.

And her heart jumped into her throat.

Standing by the front desk alongside the grinning receptionist was Terrence Templeton III wearing a damp navy shirt and khakis, his blond hair wet and gleaming, his smile a little uncertain. In his hands he held what had to be at least two dozen long-stemmed yellow roses.

Since Cilla seemed rooted to the spot, Gloria, the receptionist, felt she had to say something. "You have a visitor, Cilla. A former patient, I believe."

Her eyes locked to his, Cilla finally found her voice. "Yes, thank you." She walked closer, but stopped again, her thudding heart bouncing around in her chest, her thoughts in a scramble. He looked so damn handsome. Why was he here? Did he think they could just take up where they'd left off after he was through playing boy explorer? Or, dare she hope, was he back for good?

"Hi, Cilla," Trey began. "Mama told me your favorite flower was the yellow rose." He held out the bouquet.

"Mama? You talked to my mother?" She took the flowers, burying her nose in the sweet scent.

Trey nodded. "Just came from there. Had a couple questions for her and Papa."

"Questions?" Cilla knew she was sounding a little ditzy but her mind couldn't seem to wrap around a coherent thought.

Aware of her confusion, he edged her over to the side of the room, since therapists and patients alike had stopped working to stare at them. "Yes, questions. I don't know much about Hungarian weddings, and I..."

"Weddings?" Now she was behaving like a parrot. Enough. "Trey, what on earth are you talking about?"

Setting aside the flowers for now, he had her cornered beside an empty massage table. "I suppose I should start at the beginning." Feeling a momentary panic, he slid a nervous hand through his damp hair. "Alaska was a bust, you see."

So that was it. He hadn't enjoyed himself so he'd come back wanting to play house again. "So Alaska wasn't as great as you'd been led to believe, eh?" Not even for six dozen roses would she go back to the way things had been.

Trey gathered his thoughts and went on. "Oh, Alaska was beautiful, everything I'd dreamed of. The glaciers were magnificent, the scenery unbelievable and kayaking is probably a lot of fun. If you do it with the right person." He zeroed in on her, placing his hands on her cheeks, framing her face. "The thing is, I wanted to kayak with you. I wanted you there to see those powerful glaciers. Everywhere I looked I saw your face. I kept turning around because I thought I heard your voice." He shook his head in amazement. "Nothing was any fun without you there, Cilla."

"Really?"

"Yeah, really. I don't know when it happened or how it happened, but I don't want to be without you. I love you. Will you marry me and take a chance with me? I'm still not sure about the curse, but I don't want to hop-skip around the world trying to outrun that when I could be with you. Please, Cilla, marry me."

Her lips smiled as did her eyes. "I'm not afraid of some silly old curse. Yes, I'll marry you."

"It has to be soon, though. Papa's over at the rectory, posting the bans starting next Sunday."

Surprised pleasure lit up her face. "You told my parents before you asked me? Pretty sure of yourself, Mr. Templeton."

"Only because I love you, Mrs. Templeton-to-be, and I knew I wouldn't take no for an answer. So, we're on?"

"You bet." When he bent his head to kiss her, she was ready, throwing her arms around him and holding him close.

All the people in the center burst into cheers and applause.

Blushing, Cilla smiled hugely.

Hugging his bride-to-be, Trey laughed out loud. "Something I didn't think of. My brother, Gavin's, face when he hears I'm getting married. He's never going to believe it!"

* * * * *

Millie and the Millionaire

Chapter One

Gavin Templeton had never considered begging anyone for anything in his entire life—but this morning he was uncomfortably close to doing just that. In his office on the top floor of Templeton Towers, he sat at his desk across from Hannah Atkins, his executive secretary, who'd just announced that she had to take an indefinite leave of absence.

Hannah was far more than his secretary. She was his right hand, his girl Friday, the only woman who knew him just about as well as he knew himself. What was almost more important, she knew the ins and outs of the day-to-day operations of the firm, keeping track of minutia with voluminous notes and her phenomenal memory.

As the CEO of Templeton Enterprises, Gavin was involved in multiple deals almost daily, flying off on the company jet to meet with corporate players often at a moment's notice, entertaining businesspeople in town to sign contracts, negotiating the delicate details of multi-million-dollar takeovers. Hannah smoothed the way in all his dealings.

So attuned was Hannah after years of working with him, that she often anticipated his next move, his every need, and quietly took care of it all. An attractive, well-dressed, slender woman with a trim figure and sharp blue eyes, Hannah had been widowed twenty-five years ago when her daughter, Emma, was two. His father had hired her on, shortly after, and she'd worked her way up. Her company knowledge was legend and her loyalty to Gavin absolute.

How could he let her go, even for a short time?

"Hannah, you can't leave just now," Gavin repeated the words he'd just said moments ago. "This is a very crucial time. The Blair merger is days away from completion. We have to go over the contracts, check them out with Legal, set up the meetings. And then there's the Hudson buyout that needs special handling." Gavin shook his head. "Absolutely not. We can't spare you."

Hannah busied herself placing several stacks of files on the solid oak desk that was clear of clutter except for a phone with a number of lines plus intercom and a yellow pad and pen. "Gavin, you know I wouldn't leave if it wasn't of the utmost importance. But as I've told you numerous times, family comes first with me. My daughter needs me and I have to go."

Using family as an excuse was foreign to Gavin's thinking. His father had died when he was ten and his mother had taken off the year before. He had only his older half brother, Terrence Templeton III, known as Trey, but the two men led very different, independent lives. At one time he and Trey had been co-CEO's, but for the last four years, Trey had opted to chase another dream. Even though his brother had recently married, Gavin held out little hope that Trey would return. In Gavin's book, work came first and always would, in direct opposition to his brother.

He tried his most persuasive tone as he leaned forward. "Hannah, how else can I put it except to say I need you here with me to solidify these two very important mergers worth millions. Why can't your daughter come here?"

Obviously trying for patience, Hannah sighed. "I told you. She's in the intensive care unit of a hospital in Albuquerque. The twins came earlier than expected and there were complications. Emma's husband is on submarine maneuvers Lord only knows where, not due home for weeks. I have to go. But I'm not going to leave you in the lurch. I've made arrangements for a temporary replacement, a woman who is the epitome of efficiency."

Gavin scowled. "You've been with Templeton Enterprises longer than I have. No one knows these complicated dealings as you do. No one can take your place."

Hannah checked her watch, then sat down opposite her boss. "While that's very flattering, it's also hogwash. An experienced executive secretary can slide in here, and you won't even know I'm gone." Noting his expression didn't change, she went on. "Let me tell you about Millie. She started Crandall Secretarial Service about five years ago, sort of a Kelly Girl outfit, only highly specialized. She employs nine people—seven women and two men—she's personally trained and she herself takes on only the occasional assignment. But I persuaded her that you needed her special touch."

Gavin hated change, unless he brought it about. Still, he knew when he was up against a brick wall. "You'll have time to bring her up to speed on things pending, to tell her how we do things around here?''

''Yes, of course. That's why I gathered those files. If you'll go over them with me, then I'll update Millie this afternoon before my plane leaves at six.''

''Millie. An old-fashioned name. How old is this woman?''

''Thirty, I believe. I've been friends with her mother for years. Millie was named after her grandmother, Mildred.''

He had no choice but to accept. ''So you've already approached her and she's willing, knowing this isn't an eight-to-five job, that I'll need her to go with me to all meetings, take notes, be available early and able to stay late when needed? And she's familiar with contracts, legalities and...''

''Yes, yes.'' Hannah nodded. ''Yes, she knows all that. She'll arrange her schedule to accommodate yours. Her mother watches her son when Millie's working.''

''Son? Oh, no!'' Gavin felt that the main reason he and Hannah got along so well was that neither of them had someone at home who'd be upset if dinner was late or if they had to take a sudden trip out of state. ''How old is this kid and where's his father?''

''I believe Joey's ten or eleven. As to the father, Millie divorced him when the boy was very young, two or three. She has sole custody and I don't know the man's whereabouts.''

Gavin rose, started pacing. ''What if the kid has a crisis in the middle of merger talks which, as you well know, can go on for days? Or what if the husband shows up and causes problems?''

Hannah frowned, growing impatient. ''Listen, I can't guarantee no problems will come up. But Millie is the sole support of her son, her mother and herself. She needs to succeed. She'll make herself available.''

Unconvinced, Gavin stopped in front of her. "What if I hire round-the-clock nurses for your daughter and double your salary? Will you stay then?''

Looking disappointed in him, Hannah stood. "This isn't about money, Gavin. By the way, I've offered quite a bundle to Millie to cover for me on such short notice.''

"Exactly how much?'' When she named a figure, he didn't flinch. "I just hope to hell she's worth it.''

She walked to the side of his desk and picked up the top folder. "She is. You'll see. Now, let's go over these so I can get moving.''

Reluctantly, Gavin sat down.

"So that's everything,'' Hannah said, closing the last folder and leaning back on the couch in Millie Crandall's office. "I've marked down the phone number where I'll be staying and my cell number in case you get stuck. But I really don't think you will. I've heard nothing but good things about you and your company.''

"From Mom, you mean? She's a bit prejudiced, but, thanks.'' Millie stared at the six file folders on the low table in front of the couch, wondering if she'd bitten off more than she could comfortably chew.

"Do you have any questions?'' Hannah asked, glancing at her watch.

"It's not really the work that intimidates me. You've explained it thoroughly and I think I can handle it.'' She angled her body toward Hannah and crossed her slim legs. "It's the man himself. I've read a little about Gavin Templeton and frankly, he seems on the stuffy side and a bit arrogant.''

Hannah laughed. "Not really. I started working for him

when he was fresh out of college—young, nervous, hesitant. He's matured, of course. He's not so much arrogant as confident. After all, he's been running a billion-dollar corporation for twelve years now and doing an outstanding job, according to the board of directors. He's a formidable negotiator which is one reason he's so successful. He took his father's company and tripled its assets.''

Her deep-blue eyes still showed concern. ''But what's he like as a person? If I'm to be available practically twenty-four/seven, I'd like to know.''

''Well, he's tall, handsome, impeccably dressed. He has an apartment right in the Templeton Towers where he does some entertaining, and you might be called upon to assist him in that, as well. He's very focused, but he has a good sense of humor when he lets his guard down. He runs religiously for an hour every morning or works out in the company gym when it rains.''

''No wife? I've seen his picture in the papers occasionally, always with a different woman.''

''No wife and no steady girlfriend.'' Hannah decided to confide something that might help Millie understand Gavin. ''His mother walked out on the family when he was a child, and rumor has it that his father died of a broken heart shortly after. Which, I think, is why Gavin steers clear of serious relationships. Yet, you know, I've never met a man who needed to be loved more.'' She gave Millie a contemplative look, then stood. ''I've got a plane to catch. I want you to know I appreciate this so much, Millie.''

''No problem, and don't worry. Gavin and I will be fine.'' As Hannah left, Millie strolled over to the window in her office overlooking a small flower garden she herself had planted to improve the view. The warm June sunshine sprinkled down on the white hibiscus and the small flowering plum tree as well as the mixed portulaca and jaunty marigolds. The three large red poinsettias along the stucco wall were her favorites. The colorful scene always soothed her.

And it would appear she might need soothing during the coming days. Or weeks, Hannah had said, for even after her daughter was released, she'd likely be unable to care for her twins alone for a while.

Millie ran a hand through her short, black hair as she headed for her desk to pack her briefcase. In went the six files, her electric memo pad, cell phone, notebook and several yellow pads. Hannah had said it would be best if she'd go meet Gavin Templeton ASAP. After a quick phone call to her mother to say she didn't know when she'd be home so she and Joey were to go ahead with dinner, Millie left her office. She'd already briefed her girls and the part-time receptionist.

Hurrying outside, she saw that the downtown San Diego traffic was already congested and it was only four o'clock. She walked briskly to the parking structure that housed her car, her stomach experiencing a few butterfly flutters. Was she nervous, excited or worried? Millie asked herself.

Probably all three, she decided as she got into her six-year-old white Mustang. If this job worked out and she'd be able to pay off some bills, she just might be able to invest in a new car.

Gavin was pacing, as he always did when he was nervous. Which wasn't all that often. Except when his girl Friday left him with scarcely eight hours notice. And her dubious replacement was due any minute.

Turning, he walked the other way toward the windows. This high up, it was impossible to see much besides

clouds and the occasional plane passing by. If he looked
down, the cars on the street would look like toys, the
people like so many ants. He always enjoyed this view,
seeing it in the hushed silence of his executive office. But
today, he hardly noticed as he strolled on, his strides
growing agitated.

The Blair merger was his top priority, a very complicated deal he'd been working on for four months. Earlier
in the week, he and Hannah had been closeted with their
CPAs and half the legal department, ironing out details.
There were more to go over. And in two days the high-
muckety-mucks from Blair would be in Templeton's conference room to discuss the last proposal and hopefully
finalize everything.

A lot was riding on this merger, the second in a three-
way acquisition, including the pending Hudson buyout,
that would mean Templeton Enterprises would have control of the huge airplane replacement parts market in the
western United States. Gavin had been working on ac-
quiring the three companies for over a year, and now the
first was already signed, sealed and delivered, the other
two very close.

In the past during tense discussions, he'd always had
Hannah at his side, verifying information, handing him
necessary data, cross-referencing, checking questionable
figures on her cell phone. How in hell was he going to
complete this huge deal with a new assistant and only two
days to finalize all the contracts and paperwork?

Gavin continued pacing.

Millie stepped off the elevator after the somewhat diz-
zying ascent up twenty-six floors of the Templeton Towers, the heels of her black pumps sinking in plush gray
carpeting. The walls were a soft burgundy with comple-

menting paintings artfully placed and a discreet black sign that read Templeton Enterprises, Inc. A large receptionist's desk faced the private elevator. Seated there was a mid-twenties blond woman who smiled a welcome.

"You must be Millie Crandall." As Millie nodded, she stood. "I'm Tara. Mr. Templeton is expecting you. This way, please."

A lot of wasted space, Millie thought as she followed the receptionist out of the large mostly empty waiting area and down a wide hallway. Wallpaper in a gentle geometric design of burgundy and gray kept the decor in theme. Finally they reached double doors at the far end.

Tara knocked twice, then swung open one door and entered, ushering Millie inside. "Ms. Millie Crandall, sir." With that, she discreetly withdrew, closing the door behind her.

He was standing facing her at the far wall of windows, somehow shaded so the heat of the sun didn't penetrate. Millie was used to quick perusals in her line of work, judgments that more often than not were uncannily accurate after years of experience.

Gavin Templeton was tall, an inch or two over six feet, his blond hair neatly trimmed, his face tanned, his brown eyes assessing. He wore a snow-white shirt with a subdued paisley tie that matched his suspenders, and a dark-blue suit, the jacket of which was draped over the back of his leather desk chair. He wasn't smiling and there was an impatience about him, a contained energy about to burst yet kept ruthlessly in check.

The private office was larger than her entire nine-hundred-square-foot building, Millie noticed. His oak desk was large and uncluttered and there was a casual conversation grouping near the door with a couch, two wing chairs and a table. A bar was along one wall as well as a big-screen television, and there were two doors leading she knew not where. A rest room or his living quarters, perhaps? On the paneled walls, she recognized a Monet and a Renoir, and had a feeling they weren't copies.

This was money with a capital *M,* but done in good taste.

Gavin walked closer, stretched out his hand. "Gavin Templeton."

"Millie Crandall," she answered, touching her hand to his, finding warmth and a mild jolt that surprised her. Hannah had been right, Millie thought. He was handsome, but she rather thought he knew it.

Gavin invited her to be seated on the couch, thinking a less formal setting might relax her. "Can I get you a drink? Or coffee?"

"Coffee, black, would be great."

Gavin poured from the ever-ready pot, studying her as she gazed about the office. Not tall, maybe five-seven. Slender yet womanly. She was wearing a tailored black suit with a white blouse, his favorite color combination, and he fleetingly wondered if Hannah had mentioned his preferences to her. He thought her black curly hairstyle suited her. Her face was oval with high cheekbones, her inquisitive eyes a dark blue. She was distractingly attractive. He much preferred working closely with a woman old enough to be his mother, like Hannah.

It would only be for a short time, he assured himself as he carried her coffee over to the table and sat down in the chair opposite her. "I take it Hannah briefed you on everything?"

"I think so. If you'd like to go over the papers..." She opened her briefcase which she'd set on the couch beside her.

"Okay, yes." Unable to sit still, uncharacteristically

jittery, Gavin got up to pace. "Read me Hannah's notes on the first file and your thoughts on how we should approach that account."

Millie hadn't had very long to study them, just the short time with Hannah, but before she'd opened her secretarial service, Millie had been executive assistant to the vice president of a bank and was quite familiar with mergers and their many ramifications. One by one she went through the files aloud while he paced. Twice, he interjected a comment or two, then resumed walking.

A little undone by his nervous strolling, Millie kept going, wondering why he was so twitchy. Finally, she'd had it, talking to his retreating back.

"Mr. Templeton, do you always pace like this during a conference?"

She'd caught him off guard. "Uh, no, not always. And please, call me Gavin."

"Okay, Gavin. Please stop pacing. Personnel transitions are difficult, I know, but I really am good at what I do. Tell me how you want something handled and I'll do it."

Removing his hands from his trouser pockets, Gavin stared at her a long moment, then walked over and sat down. "I know you've got some experience in this area. Do you see any obstacles we haven't covered?"

"Not in the short time I've had to study the contracts. I'd like to go over them more thoroughly at home tonight, then discuss them again tomorrow, if that's all right with you."

Tomorrow. Well, he'd have to put up with the delay. After all, what had he expected, that she'd have absorbed all the complicated data in a couple of hours? "Fine." He got up and opened one of the doors along the side wall. "This is Hannah's office. Yours now. She cleared off her personal stuff so it's ready for you. If you need anything, let Tara know. Or me.''

Stuffing everything in her briefcase, Millie stood. ''All right then. I'll see you tomorrow at?''

He frowned, thinking. ''Is seven too early?''

''No, seven's fine.'' She'd miss her hour's chat with Joey before school, but it couldn't be helped. She had to start off on the right foot with Gavin Templeton. She'd make it up to her son later.

He walked her to the door, handed her a card. ''My private line here, my apartment and my cell number. If you have questions, any questions, please don't hesitate to call.'' He had his apprehensions, but he had no choice but to trust this woman. A lot was riding on how well she was able to assist him. He had half a thought to offer to shake hands again to see if that tingle he'd felt had just been nerves. But he decided not to.

With a tight smile he opened the door. ''I'll see you in the morning.''

Millie returned the smile and left, reminded of something she'd learned when she'd worked for the banker: the rich really are different.

Gavin frowned at the sheaf of papers spread out before him on the conference table where he and Millie had been going over facts and figures for several hours. He'd had juice, coffee and assorted Danish delivered, but coffee was the only thing disappearing.

''I can't believe this slipped by both of us. Hannah and I have gone over these numbers repeatedly.'' He sat back, looking at Millie, seated next to him. How could this young woman, new to his firm, have found this potentially damaging discrepancy the first day on the job? Nevertheless, he was glad she had.

It would seem corporate types tried all kinds of shenanigans when big bucks were at stake and their attorneys were adept at concealing them in deliberately misleading language. "What in hell were they trying to pull?" he muttered, voicing his thoughts.

Millie's brows went up. "A fast one?" she suggested as she refilled their coffee cups.

"How did you even find this?"

She took a hot sip before answering. "I'd gone over everything twice last night, but something was bothering me and I couldn't put my finger on it. So I went to bed, thinking I'd get up early and take a fresh look at the papers again." Stopping to take another drink, she fished around in the pile of papers, searching for one in particular.

Gavin had a quick flash, a mental image of Millie in a short gown, lying in bed, that lovely black hair on a white pillow case, moonlight coming in through an open window and...

He cleared his throat and straightened in his chair, annoyed with his train of thought. Whatever was he thinking, fantasizing about a woman he'd just met? He must be working too hard.

"But I couldn't get to sleep," she went on, "so I got up and went back to it. Along about three, I found what I felt was suspicious wording." She leaned closer, pointing to a section she'd highlighted. "This second clause gives Blair Industries the right to reclaim everything in six months if Templeton Enterprises hasn't acquired Hudson, Inc. *and* hasn't shown a minimum ten percent profit within that period of time. I read it over and over and, although it's couched in confusing language and intertwined with another perfectly acceptable clause, I believe I'm right. Please, read it again. I could be wrong...."

Gavin took the paper she offered and rose to pace. It wasn't that he needed to walk, but rather that the fragrance she wore was playing havoc with his concentration. Something light, alluring, enticing his senses and his mind to wander in a direction it had no business going.

Gavin read the highlighted clause again and arrived at the same conclusion. "I'll be damned. And I thought George Blair was a thoroughly stand-up guy." He reached for the phone. "I need to get Legal in on this. And find out why they didn't catch it. And I'm wondering why neither Hannah or I caught it after weeks of fine-tuning."

"In fairness to Hannah, she told me she hadn't gotten to really studying the Blair or Hudson papers as thoroughly as she should have because of concern for her daughter. She had a lot on her mind."

Gavin thought she was probably right about Hannah. But what was *his* excuse? Although he felt that a good executive knew how and when to delegate, still the buck stopped at his desk. Perhaps he'd been leaning a little too heavily on trusting others. Hannah was very good, but he'd known she'd been distracted from the moment she'd received the call from the hospital.

By the time Millie finished her coffee, one of the legal eagles had picked up the paperwork, looking chagrined and worried, and taken it back to his department. Gavin swung toward her, a genuine smile on his face.

"You just may have saved this company a whole bunch of money. Thanks. I owe you."

"Just doing my job." The job she knew he'd been sure she couldn't do as well as Hannah. The find had been a fluke, but one she'd taken advantage of, glad that Gavin appeared to trust her now.

"Okay," he said, revved up and ready for more, "let's

go over the Hudson buyout with a fine-tooth comb. And I hope to hell they're not as devious.''

Two days later the Blair merger went off without a hitch, after the offending clause had been revised. George Blair swore he knew nothing about that, but Gavin didn't believe him and decided to keep an eye on the man in the future. Eventually he would ease him out of the company he'd acquired, even though George had started the business from the ground up. Sentiment had no place in business, Gavin felt, so he would retire George without a moment's hesitation. Nobody got the chance to buffalo him twice.

The Hudson buyout, which had been in the works for some time, was next on the agenda. Millie and Gavin felt that the paperwork was all legit, but Henry Hudson was still balking, mumbling about another offer.

''That son of a gun is angling for more money,'' Gavin commented after hanging up from yet another call to Henry. ''I doubt there's another offer.''

''I doubt it, too,'' Millie said. ''I checked into Hudson Inc.'s background. They're over-inventoried and cash poor. Some of their stock is obsolete. It's not worth a penny more than you're offering, if that.''

Seated behind his desk with Millie opposite him in one of the wing chairs, he raised a surprised brow. ''How did you find all that out?''

She shrugged. ''I used to be assistant to one of the vice presidents at a bank with branches all over, including Detroit, where Hudson's headquarters are. There're a few people at the bank who still owe me favors.''

''I'm impressed.'' And Gavin didn't impress easily. Who was this wunderkind who'd dropped in his lap? If only his naturally skeptical mind could stop questioning the ease with which she'd come through for him. Twice.

"I'm not trying to impress you, just trying to fill in for Hannah. I talked to her last night. Her daughter's still in intensive care, but the infection is beginning to respond to the medication. They almost lost her, you know."

No, he didn't know. He'd had Tara send flowers, but beyond that, he'd had no contact with Hannah. Gavin tried to keep things between himself and his staff strictly business. The only one allowed the familiarity of using his first name was Hannah and now Millie. Entanglements led to problems. His father had met his mother, so the story went, on the job, and that had certainly turned out badly.

Instead of commenting, he rose to go look out the window. Over the years Gavin had come to the conclusion that his mother had been a gold digger who'd probably researched Templeton Enterprises and set her cap for the lonely, widowed CEO. After getting her to marry him, she'd bided her time until she could leave with all the assets she could finagle out of his lovesick father. At least his dad had been smart enough to get her to sign a prenup, but she'd still managed to get plenty. Was it any wonder that Gavin kept his staff at arm's length and generally didn't trust women?

Millie's gaze followed him, watching as he rolled his broad shoulders, trying to ease tension. What an uptight man he was, she couldn't help thinking. In the short time she'd been working alongside him hour after hour, he'd received no personal calls, not even his brother, no friends dropping by to ask him out to lunch. People drifted in and out of his life merely to do business and after that was settled, she doubted if he could pick them out of a lineup, so fleeting was his interest.

She knew he'd been basically abandoned at an early

age, raised by a housekeeper. Hadn't there been anyone who'd loved the boy he'd once been? She thought of her Joey, and a smile automatically formed. Joey with his tousled blond hair and curious blue eyes, his winning smile, his infectious laugh. She loved him with all her heart and told him so daily. She loved him enough for two since his deadbeat father only showed up erratically and caused trouble even on those sporadic visits.

Joel Crandall was a selfish, self-centered loser always chasing a dream that never came true. He'd been so all-American handsome when they'd met which had appealed to her at eighteen, blinding her to his flaws. It hadn't taken her long to wake up, thank goodness, but by then they'd been married and she'd been pregnant.

Odd how she'd been drawn to tall, handsome blond men like Joel since her teens. But since Joel had walked out on his family, unable to handle fidelity and fatherhood, she'd been wary of such men. Joel had been a hard lesson for her. If she were to be utterly truthful, she'd have to admit that Gavin Templeton held that basic attraction for her. But she'd be a fool to give in to the same temptation twice.

And Millie Crandall was no longer a starry-eyed eighteen-year-old who believed in love at first sight.

Gavin was still standing at the window, and she wondered what he was thinking. It was late afternoon and they'd been working since seven. Joey's Little League team had a game tonight and, though she'd told him she didn't know if she could make it, maybe she could. "Is there anything else you need me for right now? Because if not, I'll just go in my office and clear up a few things before I head home."

"Sure, go ahead. I'll see you tomorrow." Gavin still didn't turn around.

He was certainly a hard man to read. Millie gathered up her things and made her way to the office she was using temporarily.

Seated on the bleachers alongside her mother, Millie cheered with the other parents and relatives as Joey's team scored again. Of course, they were still behind by three, but no one seemed to mind. It was a compatible group, most just hoping their kids were enjoying the game, win or lose. She'd checked them out before signing up her son to make sure there were no parents so hell-bent on winning that they spoiled the game for everyone.

Of course Joey, ever hopeful, had given his father a schedule of all their games, but, true to form, Joel hadn't shown up even once. Millie didn't miss him since inevitably they'd have words over something, but she felt bad for Joey who kept scanning the stands looking for the father who never had time for him.

"He's a no-show again," Lois Donovan commented.

"He's got better things to do than watch his son play ball, I guess," Millie told her mother. "I just wish Joey wouldn't be hurt time and time again."

"Don't worry, honey. One day Joey will catch on that his father's not worth a moment's concern. It's sad that he has to learn that harsh lesson at such a young age." Lois sighed heavily. "Still, I'm worried he'll grow up judging all men by his father's rotten example."

Another boy got a base hit and everyone stood and cheered. Millie saw that Joey was up next and waved to him as she caught his eye.

Sitting back down, Lois went on with her usual crusade. "What that boy needs is a good male role model." She looked pointedly at her daughter. "I know you had a bad time with Joel, honey. But it's been nine years since the divorce, and I can count on the fingers of one hand the number of dates you've had.''

Why was it that they got on this subject so often lately? Millie wondered. ''Mom, don't start, please. I don't need a man to make my life complete. And Joey's doing just fine.'' She watched her son swing awkwardly at the ball and miss by a mile.

''Balderdash, Millie, as my mother used to say. You both need a good man, if you ask me.'' She saw her grandson bunt the ball out-of-bounds and frowned. ''One that could teach Joey baseball would be a start.''

''I'll start interviewing ball players tomorrow,'' Millie said, deciding that the only way to live with her mother's constant harping about men was with a sense of humor.

''Now, that's *not* what I meant and you know it.''

Joey hit a fly ball next, which the pitcher caught easily. Millie watched her son walk off the field dejectedly, even though his teammates patted him on the back to console him.

She knew Joey wasn't the only kid in Little League who wasn't a natural-born athlete, but for his sake, she wished he was a bit more coordinated. Still, she had no intention of recruiting a man to help her son play ball better.

''Did you tell Joey we'd go for pizza afterward?'' Lois asked, apparently deciding to change the subject since she was getting nowhere.

''Yes, I did.'' The ringing of her cell phone had Millie reaching toward her canvass bag. She frowned as she recognized the number of the caller just before answering.

''Millie, it's Gavin. I've just made arrangements for my pilot to fuel up the jet. Henry Hudson has upped the ante, wanting us to also take his factory in the bargain, for more money, of course. And he swears there's another offer. I have to check this out in person. I need you to meet me at the airport, hangar 21. Pack for a couple days stay, just in case. How soon can you be there?''

Millie drew in a long, steadying breath as she absorbed all that and checked her watch. Six-thirty. Game not over, so she'd have to arrange a ride home for her mother and Joey, preferably with a parent who also had promised pizza. She'd have to drive home, shower, pack, get to the field. ''By nine?''

There was a short burst of static, then Gavin's voice came back on. ''All right, if that's the best you can do. With the three-hour time difference, we'll be arriving in the middle of the night. The company owns the Westchester so we'll be staying there. We can go over strategy on the flight over. Bring everything you've got on Hudson, Inc.''

''Okay.''

''See you shortly. Dress casual.'' And he disconnected.

Millie took a stunned moment to assimilate what had just happened. Then she turned to her mother to explain, and hoped she'd understand. She hated leaving them on such short notice, but she'd told them up-front before she took the job with Templeton Enterprises that this sort of thing could happen. She'd also mentioned that the amount of money she would make from this job would make life a good deal easier for them all.

Lois, a practical woman, understood, though she wasn't happy. But as Millie walked to the chain-link fence where Joey's team was hanging out and spotted her sweet-faced son laughing with one of his friends, her heart felt heavy, knowing she was about to erase that smile. One day, she vowed, her company would be out of the red and she'd give herself a shorter workday and spend more time with her son.

But not today, she thought as she motioned Joey to join her.

Chapter Two

At five to nine Millie stepped out of the cab she'd hired to take her to the fence at hangar 21 at Lindbergh Airport. A short distance away sat the silver plane with black lettering declaring it to be the Templeton Enterprises jet. She paid the taxi driver, grabbed her briefcase and leather bag and walked to the gate where a uniformed agent checked her ID and waved her toward the plane.

It was a beautiful night, cloudless, the stars filling the sky, a warm breeze drifting through her hair, still damp from her hasty shower. She wore a black silk blouse, bone linen slacks and leather flats. Gavin had said casual so she'd give him casual.

A gray limo was parked by the steps leading to the plane, one she recognized as part of the Templeton fleet. Gavin had phoned again, suggesting he send a car for her, but Millie had declined since she wasn't sure how long it would take to get ready. As she got closer, she noticed

Gavin impatiently pacing toward the front of the plane and wondered if Hannah had ever kept him waiting.

He spotted her and retraced his steps. He was wearing a loose black shirt over pale gray slacks, perhaps to match his plane. Heaven forbid there should be a color clash. Reaching the stairs, he looked up.

"She's here, Emil. We're ready when you are."

"I hope I didn't keep you waiting too long," Millie said, mostly because she felt she ought to say something.

"No, you didn't." He took the bags from her and indicated she should go aboard.

Climbing the stairs, Millie felt that Gavin was anxious to get going and a bit annoyed she couldn't have shown up earlier, but his monumental control over his emotions wouldn't let him show any sign of agitation. What must it be like to hold yourself in check like that all the time? And why did he?

The copilot welcomed her warmly. Entering the main cabin, she was instantly impressed. She'd never been aboard a corporate jet before, hadn't realized they were plush as well as utilitarian. Thick gray carpeting, single chairs and double chairs upholstered in deep navy, paneled walls. A conference table, a television bracketed to the wall, a small galley with a door on each side leading to other rooms.

"This is very nice," she said as Gavin set her briefcase down on the large round table and slipped her suitcase into a bin next to his by the galley.

"I like it. Gets me where I'm going. Commercial flights these days are one delay after another." He moved to one of the large chairs and touched the intercom button. "Are we all set, Emil?"

"Yes, sir," came the reply.

"Good. Let's go." He motioned her to the chair beside him. "Better buckle up."

A woman in a navy uniform with gray piping, her blond hair in a French twist, came out of the cockpit with an empty tray in her hand. "Can I get you anything before takeoff?" she asked, smiling.

The man knew how to surround himself with lovely women, Millie thought, as she asked for a cup of black coffee. She'd need to stay awake if he wanted to strategize on the trip. Personally she'd just as soon sit back and stare out at the stars.

Gavin asked for a soft drink, and when the flight attendant returned to serve them, he smiled at her somewhat absently. "Thanks, Gina."

"You're welcome, Mr. Templeton," she murmured before taking a seat in the back and strapping in.

Millie had also thanked her, but she couldn't help noticing how the woman's face had lit up when Gavin had called her by name. She supposed it was bound to happen when a man was handsome, wealthy and available. He must have to beat them off with a stick. Yet he seemed oddly oblivious.

"As soon as we reach cruising altitude, we'll get to work," Gavin told her.

He hadn't thanked her for rearranging her schedule to accommodate him, but he knew she'd agreed to be on call twenty-four/seven. Millie sighed, resigned to the fact that she *had* signed on for that. Quit your bitchin', she told herself, and enjoy the view as the interior lights went off and the plane began taxiing down the runway.

Wasn't this just the life? Millie thought, gazing out the window as the city lights blinked and winked. Wouldn't Joey love to see this? Hopefully, one day soon, she'd take him on a trip, his first on a plane.

She glanced over at Gavin and saw that his eyes were closed. He probably had done this so often the thrill was gone. Too bad, she decided, leaning closer to the window, because it was an awesome sight as the powerful jet zoomed upward.

Millie swallowed a yawn as she checked her watch. They'd been at it for more than three hours, brainstorming, hashing out details. It was past midnight and she was bone tired. Pushing aside her third cup of coffee, she stood, stretching her arms overhead to relieve the kinks. Surely he wasn't going to keep at this all night.

Gavin stopped writing in midsentence, glancing up. The silky blouse clung to every curve as Millie twisted this way and that. It wasn't a calculated sexy move, but the effect was the same. He swallowed around a dry throat and tossed down his pen.

"What do you say we quit for tonight?" he suggested.

"I'm all for that." Millie sat back down and began stacking the papers, suddenly aware that her hands were trembling.

Gavin noticed, too. "Are you all right?"

"Just too much caffeine, I think. And I didn't have time to eat. I was going to take my son out for pizza after his Little League game, but...oh, well, there'll be other games."

For the first time in a long while, Gavin focused on someone else's needs, a person instead of Templeton Enterprises. He never had to make concessions with Hannah because she lived alone with no one to worry about but herself. But this woman had a child.

"I dragged you away from his game. I'm sorry." He remembered a long-ago day when he and Trey had played on different Little League teams. Their father hadn't made it to a single game, only the housekeeper, Connie, ever showed up. Trey had quit halfway through the season, his disappointment in his father ruining the game for him. But Gavin had stuck it out, vowing not to let his father spoil his love of baseball. He hadn't thought of that in years.

Gavin sounded sincere, Millie thought, his expression melancholy. "Joey knows I'll make it up to him."

"Some things you can never make up to kids." Annoyed that he'd revealed too much, he rang for the flight attendant. "What have you got back there to eat, Gina? This young lady's hungry."

The smiling Gina rattled off a none-too-shabby list of gourmet items.

"What sounds good to you?" Gavin asked Millie. "I should have thought about something to eat sooner."

"You order, but I'm not going to eat unless you join me."

"Okay, then. Tomato bisque, crab salad and hot tea for two. Please, Gina. And some of those little imported crackers."

Gavin noticed that Millie's hands were still shaky and there was a vulnerability about her that he hadn't seen before. Maybe he hadn't looked closely enough. He felt like a heel as he took her hands in his large warm fingers. "You have to stop me when I get carried away and lose track of time. Sometimes I forget to eat. That's my choice, but it isn't fair to you." She had such soft skin and she was wearing that same enticing scent.

"Don't worry about it. I sometimes do the same thing." Why was he touching her like this, almost absently, probably unaware that he was starting a slow, smoldering fire, one she hadn't felt in some time? She tried to tug her hands back, but he held on, watching as he rubbed warmth into her chilled fingers.

"Tell me about your son," Gavin found himself saying. For reasons he couldn't fathom and didn't want to explore right now, he wanted to know more about Millie Crandall and thought a good place to begin was with her child.

Millie was surprised at this sudden interest, mostly because Hannah had told her Gavin rarely asked personal questions. However, she was always glad to talk about Joey.

"He's a great kid—smart, funny, loving. He likes school and gets good grades. He's not much of an athlete, but he tries."

Smart, funny, loving. Would anyone have described him like that as a child? Gavin wondered. Smart, maybe, but the other two were doubtful. "What's his name?"

"Joey, and he's eleven."

"Named after his father?" Gavin noticed a slight frown appear as she pulled her hands free of his.

"Sort of. His father's name is Joel."

"You have custody, I assume. Does Joel take him for weekends or vacations or…"

"Rarely, a while back. Not at all anymore." Millie's frown deepened and her voice cooled. "I have sole custody, but Joel was entitled to take him every other weekend. However, he was always much too busy to visit his son, although he's good at making promises. Big, empty ones, like he'll take Joey to Disneyland or he'll show up for the father-son banquet. Then he'd back out at the last minute and not even call."

"I see. What does he do for a living that he's so busy?"

She almost laughed out loud. "Joel's an entrepreneur, always starting some kind of new business that's going to make him rich, that takes up all his precious time. When one goes bust, he tries to get funding for another of his wacky ideas."

Now he heard the bitterness, the underlying anger. ''I suppose he figures that if he supports the boy, he's doing his part.'' Like his own father had.

''Supports the boy?'' she asked, her brows raising. ''Hardly. At first I thought he'd pay the monthly child support the court ordered simply to stay within the law and maybe because it was the right thing to do. I was employed by the bank then, working my way up, and we could really have used the money. I kept waiting for the check that never came, fool that I was. Finally, when he was about six months behind, I hired a lawyer and took Joel to court. They ordered him to pay with interest, but he skipped town for a while. I got really tired of it so I offered him a deal he couldn't refuse. I had him relinquish his parental rights in exchange for forgiving his past and future child support payments.''

''And he took it, gave up his child?'' Why was he surprised? Gavin thought. Many parents gave up their children, either by neglect or by walking away.

''Oh, he took it, all right. So now I don't have to wait for his bouncy checks and I don't have to watch my son stand at the front door waiting for his dad to pick him up. It's sad because Joey still hopes his father will show up at his ball games, but Joel can't be bothered even though Joey mailed him a schedule. That's all right. Mom and I are there, and to hell with Joel Crandall. I work, I support us and I don't need his damn money. I...oh, God!...I'm sorry.''

Feeling tears closing in, Millie got up and headed for one of the doors off the galley, past a wide-eyed Gina, hoping to find a rest room.

Gavin stood, staring after her, then sat back down with a heavy sigh. He never should have started this, shouldn't have questioned her. Why had he abandoned his stay-detached policy? Why did he want to know more about this woman?

Because she'd appeared so in control, so self-assured and yet, tonight she seemed so different—defenseless, in need of a friendly ear. And he, who almost never offered, had volunteered, much to his regret. Now he had an upset woman on his hands.

Gina served the bisque as Millie came back, looking composed once again though her eyes were red. Gavin stood alongside her chair.

"I owe you an apology," she said softly.

"No, I owe you one. I shouldn't have probed." He waited until she looked up. "I'm sorry."

Odd how suddenly those two little words relaxed her by making him appear more human. She'd been quite intimidated until now. "I didn't get much sleep last night and…"

"And I've been working you too many hours and not even making time to eat." He reached over and took her hand, noticing it was once more chilly. "I'll watch that in the future, I promise."

"I'm not fragile, really."

He gave her a mock frown. "You, fragile? What you did, remove your ex from Joey's life at the expense of child support, took a lot of guts. No, you're not fragile, and now Joel knows that, too."

He really was much nicer than she'd been led to believe. "Thank you." Still, years of keeping her guard up were deeply ingrained in her.

Wanting to put her unfortunate and unprofessional moment behind her, Millie tasted the soup. "Mmm, this is delicious."

Gavin followed suit and the rest of the meal passed with easy conversation as they chatted about Detroit. Millie had never been there, so he familiarized her with the city's layout, hotels and restaurants.

"Once it was a beautiful place, but all the good stores deserted the downtown area for the suburbs and it's pretty much going to pot these days. Templeton Enterprises owns an apartment building on the outskirts, the Westchester, where we keep a suite of rooms for the occasional business trip. That's where we'll be staying."

Millie, feeling much better after her meal, leaned back and sipped her tea. "So where will we meet with Mr. Hudson?"

"At the Westchester, but we'll have to visit the factory first to check it out so we can discuss it intelligently. I doubt that we'd be interested but I want to see why he's suddenly so anxious to tie it into the whole package."

"Good, because my banker source says the factory's nearly fifty years old, located in a run-down section, only one ragtag shift working."

Gavin nodded. "I rather thought so." He glanced at his watch, saw that it was past midnight. He checked with Emil and learned they'd be touching down in half an hour. "No time to catch a nap, but you can get a good night's sleep in the suite. I've arranged for the limo to pick us up for the factory tour at nine *after* breakfast. I'm not having you skip meals again."

"I'm not much of a breakfast person."

"Sure you are. Most important meal of the day. Our meeting with Henry is at one o'clock in our suite. I've ordered lunch so we can study him before we begin negotiating."

"How shrewd of you."

He shrugged. "I've got a lot of experience sizing up people, as I'm sure you do."

"It helps." She smothered a yawn.

Gavin got up from the table as Gina walked over to clear. "Come on, let's sit down. Maybe we can catch a few winks before landing."

Gratefully Millie settled in the large leather seat and raised the footrest. Between missing out on a good deal of sleep and her crying jag, she felt wiped out. Searching around, she tried to find the seat belt, but found it was stuck.

"Here, let me." Gavin leaned over her, freeing the strap and even fastening it for her. As the lock clicked in place, he looked up and realized his face was mere inches from hers. His heartbeat picked up as he met her eyes, dark blue and suddenly aware.

"Thank you," she said, her voice husky.

"What is that fragrance you wear?" he asked. "I've been trying to place it."

She smiled but her lower lip trembled. "I have a friend, Jerry, who works for a cosmetic company. He's always experimenting, and this is one of his special blends."

He found himself mesmerized, unwilling to pull back, his gaze settling on her full lips. What would it feel like to kiss her, to pull her into his arms and...

What on earth was happening here? "What's it called?" he asked, because he had to say something.

Jerry called that particular fragrance Temptation, but she wasn't about to say that out loud. "I forget."

Finally Gavin straightened, sat down in his chair and belted himself in. He leaned his head back and closed his eyes.

He was getting in way over his head, something he'd vowed years ago he'd never do. He'd been tempted before, but not like this. Where was the cool detachment, the almost haughty business demeanor that never let him down?

Where was Hannah when he needed her?

* * *

By the time they reached the Westchester, it was nearly two in the morning and Millie was dead on her feet. The corporate suite was lovely, done in pale green and peach, though she wouldn't have cared if it had been decorated in bright orange and psychedelic blue. All she wanted was eight hours of oblivion.

She had to settle for five and hope a hot shower, followed by a blast of cold water, would make up the difference. Rubbing herself dry, a mental picture of Gavin leaning over her seat in the jet popped into her mind. He'd been close enough that she could see the tiny lines at the corners of his brown eyes as he'd shifted his gaze to her mouth. And that business about her cologne? What had that been about?

Whatever it was, she wasn't having any, Millie decided emphatically. She hadn't taken this job for romance or a quick fling. Applying moisturizer, she had to admit to herself that the man attracted her. But she had no intention of acting on that attraction. She'd been down that rocky road before, and it was full of potholes.

Today she would make every effort to keep their relationship strictly business.

Minutes later, dressed in a navy suit with a striped blouse, she walked out into the conference room that divided the two bedrooms. Apparently their breakfast had been delivered and set up on the table under silver covers. Gavin was nowhere to be seen, though the door to his room was ajar. She walked over, saw that it, too, was empty and decided she had enough time to phone her son. A cup of coffee in hand, she sat down on the couch and picked up the phone.

* * *

The Westchester's exercise equipment wasn't nearly as good as that in Templeton Towers, but it was adequate, Gavin thought as he anchored the bar weights and rose from the bench. The room was deserted this early in the morning, which suited him just fine. He'd spent half an hour working off some anger.

At himself.

He'd spent quite a few hours tossing and turning last night and he'd finally come to a harsh conclusion: Millie Crandall had somehow moved past all the barriers he'd erected through the years, attracting him despite his vow to remain detached.

He couldn't allow that, Gavin decided as he grabbed a towel from the stack on the table and wiped his sweaty face.

He was happy living alone, pleased with his life and didn't need anyone sharing it. While his brother, Trey, had said the same thing, then turned around and married his physical therapist last fall, Gavin wasn't one to change his mind readily. Practically never, as a matter of fact.

In Millie's eyes last night, he'd seen an undeniable interest, a sudden male-female awareness. In some cases that could lead to a mutually pleasant interlude, then a fond farewell. But Gavin knew himself to be a decent judge of character, and he'd pegged Millie as a woman who'd have no interest in such a temporary arrangement. If she ever got seriously involved again, she would hold out for forever. And Gavin Templeton didn't do forever.

So he'd decided that from now on he'd keep things cool, businesslike, dispassionate. From what she'd told him about her ex-husband, she might not want marriage, either, but he wasn't taking any chances. His father had made a fool of himself over a woman, his mother, who'd used him then left him. And her son. At an early age,

Gavin had sworn he'd never, ever put himself in that kind of situation where a woman would have such a hold on him, emotionally or otherwise.

No, sir, he was a free agent and intended to remain that way.

Draping the towel around his neck, he headed for the back elevators. It wouldn't be easy, he reminded himself. She was essential to his company operations for however long it took Hannah to return. They'd be working together long hours in often close quarters—and she was damnably attractive.

He stepped into the elevator and pressed the button. Riding up, he squared his shoulders. He'd known attractive women before, lots of them, and he'd always resisted. He would this time, too.

He was strong, in charge of his emotions, unlike his father and even Trey. He was immune to charm and good looks because he made up his mind to be.

Pleased with his reaffirmations, he left the elevator and walked the carpeted hallway to his door, unlocking it. Hearing a voice, he stopped.

"Oh, sweetie, that's great," Millie said, leaning back on the couch and crossing her legs. "You've always been a good speller." She paused, listening. "That request you mentioned, I'm not sure I can help you with that." She took a swallow of her coffee. "You know I'll try, but we'll have to see." Checking her watch, she set the cup down. "We'd better hang up or you'll be late for school. I love you, Joey. Be good for Grandma." She listened a moment longer, said goodbye and hung up, smiling as she pictured her son's face.

Gavin stood just inside the door, his hand on the knob. Joey was one lucky kid, he thought, to have a mother who talks to him like that. She'd told the boy that she loved him so naturally that he was certain she said it often. An errant thought crept into his mind: What would he be like if he'd had a mother like Millie?

Clearing his throat, he closed the door just as Millie stood, looking bandbox fresh.

"There you are. I rather thought you'd gone to work out." She smiled yet wondered why he seemed so deep in thought. Probably thinking about the Hudson takeover.

"I'll just grab a quick shower," Gavin said, hurrying past her. "Help yourself to breakfast."

Millie watched him leave and wondered if men knew how sexy they looked unshaven, in workout clothes, hair damp. Enough! She sat down at the table and peeked under the silver covers.

"You ordered enough for a family of four," she commented as Gavin joined her fifteen minutes later. Finished with her muffin, she picked up the silver coffeepot.

"I didn't know what you'd like," Gavin said as he accepted the coffee she poured for him. Lifting lids, he decided the three-minute eggs would be hard and cool by now, so he opted for just a bagel and cream cheese. He kept his eyes averted in keeping with his resolve to remain detached.

"Did you sleep well?" Millie asked, making small talk. He seemed a little occupied this morning.

"Yes, thanks." He took a deep breath, and that damnable cologne of hers wrapped around him. Rattled, he reached for his coffee cup and...and spilled it all over the table.

"Damn!" Rising, he used his napkin to sop up the mess, glancing at his clothes to check for stains. There was a spot on the cuff of his white shirt. Annoyed, he dabbed at it with his napkin.

"Here, let me," Millie said, dipping the corner of her clean napkin in her waterglass. "Black coffee hardly ever stains if you get it out right away." She reached for his wrist.

It would be rude to refuse, Gavin supposed, so he stood quietly while she worked on his sleeve and tried not to breathe deeply. Her head was bent over his arm, that black cloud of hair just beneath his chin, making his palms sweat. Odd how some women looked sexier in business suits than in silk lingerie. Not that he'd mind seeing her in…Gavin jerked his arm free.

Where the hell was his firm resolve?

"I think you've got it. Thanks." Deciding he wasn't hungry after all, he reached for his suit coat. "You about ready?"

"Yes. I'll just get my briefcase." Walking to her room, she wondered why Gavin was so jumpy.

The building housing Hudson Motors was even more dilapidated than Gavin's preliminary reports had indicated. The gray limo drove slowly around the perimeter. Millie had arranged for a driver who would be knowledgeable about the area.

Raymond was a black man in his early fifties and had grown up not far from Hudson, Inc. "Six members of my family worked here over the years," he told them. "In the early days, used to be real nice around here. It's called Poletown 'cause Polish people settled this section, worked hard, raised their families here. It was nice back then, clean, friendly. But young folks, second generation, started moving out and the area began going downhill fast. There was no money to fix it up. Then some politician changed all that, spruced things up for a while. But he gave up, and now, it's seedy and getting seedier."

The window between front seat and back was open and Gavin leaned forward. "Do they still make auto replacement parts in Hudson?"

"Yeah, I guess they do. My nephew, Gerard, he works here. Only one shift active these days." Raymond paused at the gate of the fence surrounding the huge factory. "Only one section open. Others been dark for years. You want me to open the gate and drive you around so you can see up close?"

There was no watchman on duty, only two men grabbing a smoke over by the double delivery doors. "I don't think so. Have you been inside?"

Raymond removed his cap, scratched his head. "Yeah, a while back. Like a ghost place. Equipment's old and dangerous. I told Gerard to get outta there, find another job. Place is an accident waiting to happen."

"Thank you, Raymond. You've been a big help. I think we're ready to go back to the Westchester."

"Wait one minute." Millie removed a small digital camera from her briefcase. "Why don't we go inside the gate and I'll take some snapshots? We can print them back at the office. Then if and when Mr. Hudson tries to sell his factory with exaggerated claims, we can pull them out and show him."

The lady was worth her weight in gold, Gavin thought as he asked Raymond to take them in. They spent the next hour photographing the old factory from every angle. While Gavin watched, Millie lined up a shot just as a tall man in jeans, a cigarette hanging from his lip, stepped out and walked over.

"Let me," she whispered to Gavin, and turned on the charm. The man wound up smiling at her, invited them inside and let her photograph what she would. When she ran out of film, Millie thanked the man and they returned to the limo.

"I think we've got some good ammunition," Millie said as she settled into the back seat.

"Incriminating information, I call it," Gavin added. "I'd be willing to wager that someone's greased a few palms and there's been no real safety inspection at that plant in a long while."

"Good leverage," Millie said as she removed the film.

Gavin edged into the corner and stretched his arm across the back of the seat. "You come up with some good ideas, Millie. How did that bank ever let you go?"

"I wanted out, to be on my own. I like being in charge of my own future."

"Amen to that." A sudden smile turned up the corners of his mouth.

"What are you thinking?"

"I'm looking forward to seeing Henry Hudson's face this afternoon at the negotiating table. He wants to *raise* the ante? I'm lowering it. It's a take-it-or-leave-it situation now."

She saw the ruthlessness just below the surface, the business face that Gavin Templeton showed the world. The one that had made him one of the most feared negotiators in the business world. Part of it was the killer instinct that Millie had noticed in many executives. The other part was a self-confidence that she would imagine rarely failed him and gave him an edge. All that money behind him, all the success. He spoke from a position of strength that could intimidate the most formidable foe.

Yet there was a soft side to Gavin, one she'd merely glimpsed. A vulnerability she'd noticed in one of his few unguarded moments. Moments when she'd spoken with him about Joey. She'd read somewhere once that we can never outrun the past, that parts of it linger with us forever. She knew only bits and pieces of Gavin's past, but she was certain some bad memories still affected him.

Gazing out the tinted windows of the limo as they sped back to the Westchester, Millie wondered why any of that should matter to her.

Chapter Three

Henry Hudson and his son, Hank, Jr., arrived at Gavin's suite at one in shirtsleeves, both puffing on cigars. The first order of business was to have them park their smelly smokes.

Gavin had never met Hudson, but he'd had Millie do some research and learned that Henry was a big, burly guy who liked fishing, hunting and sports. He was proud that his family had owned Hudson, Inc., for three generations. Hank, Jr., was a carbon copy of his father right down to the receding hairline.

"I hope you're hungry," Gavin told his guests as they sat down to lunch, which had been delivered minutes ago.

"I'm always hungry," Henry answered, patting his ample girth while Hank, Jr., smiled at Millie and moved his chair closer to hers.

"Good." Gavin had ordered steak with all the trimmings all around, figuring these men ate heartily. He watched them dig in with relish and winked at Millie. He knew she didn't consider this meal luncheon fare, but when in Rome and all that. Following his guests' lead, he cut into his steak.

"Man, this is good," Henry declared, slathering butter on his baked potato. "I don't know how you stay so slim, Gavin, eating like this all the time."

"Metabolism," Gavin said. He felt rather than saw Millie shift her chair slightly closer to his as Hank, Jr., slipped ever nearer on her other side.

Though he kept on shoveling in his food, Hank managed to ask Millie a few questions while his father chatted with Gavin. "Are you two, you know, together?" he asked in a low, conspiratorial voice, gesturing with his fork to Gavin.

Putting on her best professional expression, Millie kept her voice cool and discouraging. "Mr. Templeton and I have a business relationship."

"So then, you don't have a boyfriend, eh?" Hank persisted, cramming Caesar salad into his mouth and smiling through it all.

Millie tried to keep from looking at the junior galoot, not wanting to mess up the merger before they even started negotiating. "I have an eleven-year-old son who keeps me quite busy."

"Oh, yeah? I like kids." Hank finally remembered to wipe his mouth. "You in town long? I could show you around."

She'd thought mentioning Joey would turn him off, but it hadn't. She shot a help-me glance at Gavin, who nodded imperceptively.

Before Millie could think of an answer, Gavin zeroed in on the boorish young man while his father was busily stuffing his face. He didn't want to be insulting, so he chose the only way he could think of to defuse Hank.

Smiling intimately, he took Millie's hand in his. ''Why don't you just tell him, sweetheart?'' he asked. He saw the quick shock in her eyes, followed by an even quicker understanding.

''Oh, I'd rather you did, dear,'' she murmured, wondering exactly where he was taking this.

Gavin grasped her hand more firmly in his. ''We didn't want to break the news just yet, but the truth is, we're engaged.'' Enjoying himself, he brought her fingertips to his mouth and kissed them.

''Hey, no kidding!'' Henry was all smiles. ''Good for you, Gavin. A man needs a good woman by his side.'' He held out a hand shiny with melted butter. ''Congratulations.''

Keeping a straight face, Gavin shook hands, then turned to Hank who was staring at him, his look hostile.

''I thought you said you two were only business friends,'' he accused Millie.

''Well, I...''

''As I mentioned, we haven't broken the news to our families yet. But the cat's out of the bag now, right, sweetheart?'' Gavin slipped an arm around Millie and drew her closer, kissing her cheek possessively.

Backing off unhappily, Hank mumbled congratulations and returned to his meal. Gavin squeezed Millie's hand and she returned the pressure as they both resumed eating. Henry let out a loud burp that the other three chose to ignore.

Millie wondered if this crazy luncheon would ever end.

The negotiations were over much quicker than the meal. At the conference table, Henry stated his demands, the increased sale price which included the Mill Avenue Hudson factory. Without saying a word, Millie handed Gavin the latest financial report on the Hudson assets along with half a dozen incriminating pictures of the factory they'd visited earlier. Gavin set them in front of both men, then sat back and waited.

Henry's color drained. "Look, this here's an unaudited financial report, doesn't include everything."

"On the contrary, sir," Millie answered, "the CPA signed off on page three, stating all figures are current and accurate."

Uneasily Henry shifted in the chair. "As for these pictures, they're old. We've done renovations in there, made improvements. Isn't that right, Hank?"

"Damn straight." He glared at one photo showing a broken-down machine alongside a ripped conveyer belt. "I don't know who took these or when, but..."

"I took them," Millie said, "just this morning."

"What?" His face reddening, Hank tossed the snapshot onto the table. "No way." He shot a swift glance at his father. "I'm in charge of the Mill Avenue factory and it's in tip-top shape."

But Henry Hudson knew when to fold. He sighed heavily, hating to give in, yet knowing he had to. "All right, what's your bid?"

Gavin named what he felt was a fair price in a voice that let the Hudsons know it was his final offer.

"Are you crazy?" Hank was furious, his small eyes turning mean. "You're trying to steal our operation. We've been in business since before you were born. Who do you think you are, coming here like this? We have other offers, you know." He stood so abruptly he knocked over his chair.

Ignoring that, Gavin spoke. "You're certainly welcome to entertain those other offers, but we're leaving tonight."

Still fuming, Hank straightened his chair. "Come on, Dad, let's go."

"Sit down, Hank." Henry's voice sounded resigned as he fingered his unlit cigar. "Okay, Templeton. We'll take it."

Millie reached into her briefcase and withdrew the revised contract she'd worked up after the factory tour. She handed all three copies to Gavin, who slid them over to Henry.

"I'll need to have my legal department check these out."

Gavin checked his watch. "You have until six o'clock. After that, the offer's withdrawn, as you'll see marked on the top sheet."

Father and son left, saying they'd have the contracts delivered by six if all was correct. Hank stomped out angrily, but Henry Hudson walked slowly, like he'd just lost his best friend.

"I feel sorry for them, in a way," Millie commented as the door closed behind them.

"Why? They tried something illegal, Millie, inflating the value of their property without revealing all its flaws. They thought because my father had dealt with Henry's father, that we'd take them on good faith. Templeton Enterprises didn't get where we are by falling for deceitful offers. Our feasibility study had indicated there were problems, but I was willing to pay them a fair price for their inventory along with their customer base. Henry would have been further ahead if he hadn't tried to up the ante."

Gavin walked over to where she was sitting on the couch. "You did the rest by having their financials checked out so thoroughly. And those pictures were a really good idea. I owe you, again." He smiled at her as he sat down.

Sunshine drifted in through the windows and high-lighted her hair, turning it silky. He wanted his hands in it, on her. Remember your resolve, he told himself.

"Do you really mean it, about owing me? Because I do have a favor to ask you." Millie hated asking him, but she'd promised Joey she'd try.

"Of course I mean it." Facing her, he crossed his legs. "All right, name it."

"Friday's Joey's last day of school before summer vacation and it's career day. It's Joey's turn to get a speaker for his class to talk about their special career." She gave him a hopeful smile. "Would you talk to them on what it's like to be a business executive?"

"You're kidding, right?" Gavin shifted on the couch. "I don't know what to say to a group of kids about business." He met her eyes, saw she was serious. "Why doesn't he ask you?"

"Because one of his friends corraled me last year. As to what to say, just talk about how you got started, the education a person needs to work in business, some of the pluses and minuses."

Gavin leaned forward, bracing his elbows on his knees. He didn't want to turn her down, but talking to kids? Of all the things she could have asked him, he'd never considered this. "I'm not really good with kids, you know. Never been around them much."

"They're just people, only younger and smaller."

He caught her smiling at his discomfort. "Very funny."

"Would you at least think about it? It's really important to Joey. And to me."

That last one got him. "I'll think about it."

How in hell did he get himself into this trap?

* * *

At a quarter to six a messenger arrived at their suite with the signed Hudson contracts, and waited until Gavin signed and Millie witnessed, then left.

Gavin handed her the contracts to put into her briefcase. "Okay, now, you have two options. We can choose a really good restaurant and go out for a celebratory dinner, leave afterward and still get home at a reasonable hour because of the time change. Or we can leave now, eat on the plane and get home early. Your choice since you've been such a big help."

"It's not that I don't appreciate the offer of a lovely dinner, but to tell you the truth, that huge lunch was a lot to handle."

"You didn't eat much of it."

"Oh, I ate plenty. I would like to get home earlier." She looked at her watch and calculated. Hopefully in time to make Joey's game.

Gavin studied her, almost saw the wheels turning. "The mother in you wants to get home, right?"

She looked up at him, surprised he had her figured out after such a short time. "Yes, that's right. Joey..."

"Has a game." He'd wanted to delay departure for some reason he couldn't name. Wanted to wind down by having a leisurely meal with a lovely woman, some wine, some conversation. Then fly home through the starry night, getting home in time to go to bed. That way he didn't have the whole evening stretching out before him with nothing planned.

Of course, he could call any number of people who'd be glad to dine with him or catch a movie or whatever. Then why was he feeling so alone suddenly? It wasn't like him, Gavin reminded himself.

"Yes, as a matter of fact, he does have a game scheduled. However, if you need me for something..." After all, she had promised to be available.

"No, that's all right. I'll call the pilot." He walked to the phone, his back to her.

Funny how this man, with all the money in the world, had looked forlorn for a minute there. She must have read him wrong. But maybe not. She waited until he hung up the phone.

"Gavin, this is probably a silly invitation for a man like you, but would you like to come with me to Joey's game? You were in Little League and you told me you love baseball."

Wouldn't Trey or any of his friends laugh to think of Gavin Templeton at a child's Little League game? So out of character.

He cleared his throat. "Thanks, but I've got a million things to do at the office. You go, have a good time." Walking toward his room, he spoke over his shoulder. "Better get packed. Limo will be here in half an hour."

A million things to do at the office, Millie thought as she went into her room. Did the man do anything besides work? Even his meals were business luncheons. He was handsome and charming when he wanted to be, and though he was very nearly ruthless in business, there was a human sadness in him she couldn't define.

Oh, well, none of her business, she decided as she placed her case on the bed.

Gavin crumpled up the third piece of paper and tossed it into the wastebasket. What had he been thinking, agreeing to talk to a sixth-grade class of children? What could he have to say that would be of interest to eleven-year-olds? He was used to speaking to adults, business people, giving seminars. But kids? What if they dozed off or booed him?

Now he was getting paranoid. They were young people who might one day go into business. He could do this. Only, Millie was going to be there to introduce him. To listen along with the kids. *Oh, Lord!*

He left his desk and began pacing and thinking. What had he been like at eleven? His mother had taken off the year before. He'd been confused, angry, scared. His father had been no help to two frightened boys. Cindy hadn't been much of a mother, but at least she'd been around some of the time. Gavin remembered that both he and his brother had blamed themselves for her leaving, especially after Dad had begun drinking, locking himself in his room, rarely around. It had taken them years to realize that Cindy's departure was no one's fault but hers. She'd never wanted to be a wife and mother. She'd only wanted the good life that a wealthy husband could give her. Some women were like that, getting what they could, then taking off.

Hands in his pocket, Gavin stared out the window at the lights of downtown San Diego. He was supposed to be writing a speech, not recalling his less-than-perfect childhood. Joey Crandall had it far better than he had, growing up with a mother who obviously loved him a great deal. All right, so the kid's father was a jerk, but his mother more than made up for the man's absence. Probably his grandmother cared a lot, too.

Focus, he told himself. On business, on wanting to succeed, on education and discipline. That's most likely what Joey's teacher and even Millie was expecting to hear. The trouble was, he'd never had this great ambition to be the head of a huge corporation. He'd inherited it, along with Trey, who'd left him with the whole enchilada when the spirit moved him. Now that he was married, his brother was making noises about possibly returning, to work again side by side with Gavin. He would welcome the help, someone to share the work load and the worries. Someone to talk with who shared his interest in making Templeton Enterprises the best it could be.

Neither he nor Trey had been given much of a choice. After their father died, the company had been run by executives appointed in the will until the boys had finished college. No one had ever asked if that was what they wanted to do. They'd told them instead that they must take over. So Gavin had, like the good doobie he'd been since childhood. Trey had rebelled early on and later even more. But not Gavin. Gavin had always been there—reliable, dependable, stable, capable.

And dull, most likely.

Not that anyone had ever told him that, but he'd felt it. At first the company had been a challenge, to do better than his father had, even though Dad would never know. Afterward, he'd gotten caught up in it and even enjoyed most of it. But the truth was that all work and no play had undoubtedly made Gavin Templeton a dull man. He had no outside interests to speak of, no friends outside the business, no weekend getaways with pals from the past.

A small plane, wing lights blinking, eased past the window in a cloudless sky. Why was he suddenly so introspective? Gavin wondered. Maybe because the other evening, when he and Millie had returned from Detroit, she'd hurried off to her son's ball game while he'd gone home to his empty apartment. For the most part he was happy with his living quarters, had even decorated the rooms himself. But there were days, and nights lately, when he'd felt lonely. He didn't mind being alone, often preferred it. But loneliness was something new.

Millie. This restlessness, this searching for answers to questions he'd never before asked himself, had started since meeting her. Naturally, her efficiency and intelligence had impressed him from the start. But there was more to her, so much more. She was warm and kind and funny and beautiful. Her maternal instincts guided her every move, securing her son's financial future as well as his emotional development. Every time she spoke to Joey on the phone she told him she loved him. Amazing.

Gavin scraped a hand over his face as he turned from the window. To hell with writing a speech. He'd wing it.

Millie watched Gavin walk toward her wearing a pinstriped gray suit and a shaky smile. He was impeccably groomed as always, but as he came nearer, she noticed a slight tic in his left eye. Could this CEO who'd spoken to hundreds of successful executives be nervous about a small group of eleven-year-olds?

"Hello." She greeted him warmly, trying to put him at ease. "I'm glad you could make it."

He'd almost called to back out at the last minute, but then he pictured Millie's disappointed face and couldn't go through with it. His gaze took in her white linen dress with a red paper flower pinned to her shoulder. "You're looking very festive."

She touched the flower. "Joey gave it to me to thank me for talking you into coming."

He took her hands in his. "So now, after this, you owe me, right?"

"Absolutely." His fingers were cool, almost cold. He *was* nervous. Why she found that charming she couldn't say.

The nearest door opened and a pleasant-faced woman with tightly curled gray hair smiled at them. "Are you both ready?"

"I think so," Millie said, then introduced Gavin to Mrs. Lomach, the sixth-grade teacher.

"So glad to have you with us, Mr. Templeton. Earlier today we heard a clown tell us all about life in the circus. The children are looking forward to your talk."

I'll just bet they are, Gavin thought. He was following a clown act. How appropriate.

"Mrs. Crandall, if you'll introduce him to the children, please," the teacher said, stepping back so they could enter.

Gavin followed Millie to the front of the room, but he hardly heard a word of her introduction. Thirty-two fresh-faced kids sat staring at him, daring him to inform or entertain. Or fall flat on his face. Why had he ever agreed to this? he asked himself as he stepped up to the podium to scattered applause.

Swallowing, Gavin took his time looking at each and every one's face. Finally he spoke.

"When I was growing up, I wanted to be a ballplayer. Not just any ballplayer, but a professional on a winning team. Anyone here feel the same?" Half a dozen boys raised their hands and even two girls. Gavin smiled his all-American smile and nodded. "That's good. Now, how many want to be astronauts?" More hands. "How about firemen, policemen, singers or dancers?" A few more hands went up.

"The point I'm trying to make here is that whatever it is you want to do with your life, you need to set goals. Then you need to find out what you have to learn to reach those goals, and then comes lots of hard work to attain those goals."

He paused, noticing them watching him intently. He also spotted Joey from the picture Millie had taken on the trip, surprised to see that he was a towhead. "I didn't have to make a goal. My father owned this big company and when he died, my brother and I were left to run it. No questions asked, we had to do it. Lots of times when a parent dies or leaves, the children have to adjust, to change their goals to fit the needs of the family. No one asked me if I'd rather be a baseball player or run my dad's company. Maybe you or someone you know has had to make adjustments like that."

Several kids looked around and a few nodded. "But you know, a funny thing happened after I started working at my dad's company. I studied and watched experienced people and learned. And I got good at it. Next thing you know, I began to like what I was doing. Sometimes our goals change and it's important to recognize that and not fight it. I'm not sure what would have happened if I'd insisted on being a baseball player and to heck with the company. That would have been really selfish, to let all those people down. And how many guys who try out for the majors ever make it anyhow?"

Gavin shifted from one foot to the other, his hands on the podium growing damp. Was he talking over their heads? "Working in the business world is fascinating. You get to travel, to meet with others and compete, hopefully turning out a better product or service as a result. The company hires a lot of people who meet their goals by working with you. You get satisfaction, pleasure and money. Oh, not the kind of money a top-notch ballplayer makes, but enough. Certainly enough to go watch the Padres play."

Reaching into the inside pocket of his jacket, he brought out an envelope. "That reminds me, how many of you like baseball?'' As he'd expected, every hand went up. ''That's good because, with your teacher's permission, I've got two tickets for each of you to Saturday afternoon's game.''

A big cheer went up, and Gavin finally smiled. Mrs. Lomach came to take the envelope from him, beaming a big smile as she shook his hand.

''How about it, children,'' the teacher said, ''how do we feel about Mr. Templeton's fine speech and generosity?'' Another big cheer followed by applause.

Wanting nothing more than to get out of there, Gavin thanked the teacher for having him and made his way to the door, where Millie was waiting. Out in the hall finally, he let out a relieved breath. ''Don't say it, I know. I told them very little about business. But honestly, Millie, what do eleven-year-olds want to know about business? It's dull and boring and...''

''Stop it. You were a hit.''

''You really think so?''

''Mom?'' Joey came through the door, hesitant.

Millie introduced the two, then turned to her son. ''So what did you think of the talk, Joey?''

He glanced at Gavin. ''The best one we've heard so far.''

''You're just saying that because I'm standing here,'' Gavin remarked. ''And because of the baseball tickets.''

''No, honest.'' Tall for his age, the boy had his mother's sharp blue eyes and sincere manner. ''I liked what you said about families pulling together when there's changes. Like, my mom had to go to work and we had to change some goals. But we made new ones.''

A smart kid. ''So what are your current goals, if you don't mind me asking?''

Millie slipped an arm about his shoulders encouragingly. "Short-term goal, I'm saving for a PlayStation 2 and a gift for Mom's birthday next Friday. I do odd jobs for Mom and Grandma and the neighbors. Long-term goal, college, but I don't know what I want to study yet."

Gavin was impressed. "You've got plenty of time to decide."

Joey looked up at his mother. "Do you think Mr. Templeton would like to come for dinner tonight? Grandma said to ask. She's making pot roast." He smiled at Gavin. "It's the best."

She should have known, Millie thought. Her mother and her matchmaking. "Joey, I don't think Mr. Templeton has time to—"

"What time, Joey?" Gavin asked. He hadn't had home-made pot roast since before he left for college.

"Six o'clock."

Gavin nodded. "I'll be there."

"Great." Joey grinned before returning to the class-room.

Gavin swung his gaze to a surprised and slightly em-barrassed Millie. "Unless you don't want me there?"

"No. I mean, yes, of course I do. I just feel you were sort of forced into coming." She started walking down the hallway to the door leading to the parking lot.

He fell in step beside her. "I love pot roast. Our house-keeper, Connie, used to make it often."

"All right, then. I'm heading over to Blair Industries to pick up some tax papers. I'll see you at six." She opened her car door, then turned back. "Oh, you don't have the address."

"Sure I do. See you later."

Of course, the personnel files. "Dress casual," she called after him.

Gavin waved as he got behind the wheel of his BMW and watched her drive off.

What in hell had he gotten himself into now? Not that he was a snob, but pot roast in suburbia? Sure, he loved pot roast, but he was careening out of control again. Getting snared in, not only by his attraction for the mother but by the downright smart little kid right out of central casting.

Gavin had wondered how many kids in the class would get his message about goal setting and being flexible enough to change, but Joey certainly had. The kid reminded him of himself as a youngster, quick-witted, wanting to please. He'd allowed his mother to put her arm around him in the hallway in front of a stranger, not the least embarrassed. That showed maturity and a strong, affectionate bond between the two of them. Which he'd guessed earlier.

Starting the engine, he shifted into gear and drove slowly out of the parking lot. He'd half expected Millie to say he'd overdone it with the ballgame tickets. One short phone call and he had them. He'd write them off as a donation. Templeton had a box at the park. He could really impress Joey by taking him and his mother there tomorrow. Funny how it gave him pleasure just thinking about being able to share an experience that he usually took for granted. Often as not, he gave the box seats away to one of the executives and their wives.

But that really might be overkill. Besides, Joey would probably rather sit with his friends. Maybe another time.

Whoa! Gavin braked at a light. What other time? Now he was already taking this arrangement into the future? Usually a man of strong resolve, he was annoyed with himself.

He'd go to dinner, enjoy the pot roast and leave early.

No payback invitations. No box seat ball games. From now on, strictly business.

Turning the corner, Gavin wondered when he'd gotten so good at lying to himself.

Chapter Four

"That was the best pot roast I've ever had, Mrs. Donovan, bar none." Gavin carried his empty plate to the kitchen.

"I'm sure you're used to eating much more gourmet food than my pot roast," Lois told him, taking the plate from him. "Now, you go sit down. Guests don't help with dishes where I come from."

"I'm not just giving out compliments. That was delicious." He passed Millie coming from the small dining room, her hands full.

"You old flatterer," she whispered.

"Why won't anyone believe me?" he asked, sitting back down. "If you ate out in as many restaurants as I do, you'd know I was telling the truth." He picked up the basket of fluffy rolls with only two left and considered having another, then passed it to Joey to take away. "I'm stuffed. How about you?" he asked the boy.

"I still have room for chocolate cake," Joey answered. "Want me to set out the dessert plates, Grandma?"

One look at Gavin rolling his eyes and Millie caught on. "Why don't we go out back for a while and have our cake later?"

Joey made a face, but he went. Lois welcomed the suggestion. "Yes, go out on the swing. It's a lovely evening."

"You come, too, Mom," Millie said. "We'll do dishes later."

"All right, honey. Just let me put away the leftovers."

The stucco fenced yard was spacious with a big oak tree near the back, a chain-link swing hanging from a thick branch. Muted ground lanterns around the perimeter lent a soft glow. In the dusk of twilight, fireflies flitted about and one lonely cricket sang a mournful tune. Joey tossed a ball against the side of the house, catching it in a mitt that seemed to swallow his small hand. A warm breeze brought the scent of hibiscus from a bordering flower bed.

Millie led the way to a two-seater swing at the far end of the patio under a canvass awning. Gavin sat down beside her, gazing around. A nice yard and nice people.

"Smells like the neighbors are cooking steaks next door," Millie commented, watching the smoke spiral up. "Next you'll hear Jim swear, then his wife, Evelyn, will yell that he's burned them again."

"Life in the suburbs, eh?" He kept the swing gently moving with his foot as he stretched one arm along the back. "Nice out here."

"Tell me, did you really want to play pro ball when you were in your teens?" she asked, wondering if he'd made up the story for the benefit of the kids.

"Yeah, I did. I even tried out for the baseball team at

college, but I've got a bum knee from a childhood accident. I made the team mostly because the coach felt sorry
for me, but I spent all season on the bench. I never would
have lasted in the majors.''

''Another dream bites the dust.'' She let the swing rock
them for a while, very aware of his warm thigh touching
hers. ''What else did you want to be?'' she finally asked,
to distract them both.

''You'll laugh if I tell you.'' His fingers found their
way to her shoulder, then gently threaded through the hair
at her nape.

''No, I won't.'' Millie felt a shiver slide up her spine.

''I wanted to be a rancher.''

''You mean cows?''

''No, not a cattle ranch. More like a horse ranch. I was
about eight or nine when Dad took us to visit a friend
who raised quarter horses on his ranch in western Arizona.
One of the few times we ever went anywhere as a family.
I remember my mother was bored to tears, but Trey and
I loved it.''

''Do you ride?''

''Sure. Dad got us lessons in everything, though he
never joined us in anything. In my teens I spent two sum-
mers at a ranch in New Mexico, learning how to work
with horses, overseeing the breeding. Last year I found
this ranch for sale with great stock and even a stable for
riding lessons, plus a small lake on the property. I almost
bought it, then I thought, when would I have time to work
it?'' His fingers wandered, caressing her neck.

''So you let it go,'' she said, finding her voice a little
trembly. What was he doing and why? She couldn't move
over since there was no room. Did he know that he was
playing havoc with her concentration?

"Yes, I let it go, but I still think about it now and then."

Millie shifted, angling her body, effectively blocking his hand out of reach. It was still light enough to see his eyes, the way the chocolate brown deepened. "Do you think you'd be happy running a horse ranch after running a multimillion-dollar corporation?"

Gavin took his time answering, gazing out to the middle distance, a place only he could see. "Yes, given the right circumstances, I think I would be."

"It can be a lonely life."

"So can running Templeton." He felt her eyes on him, knew she was trying to read between the lines. "What about you? Is owning a secretarial service your lifelong dream?"

Millie smiled at that. "No, not really. I sort of gravitated to it. I started college, then dropped out to get married. Joel never made much money, so I got a job when Joey was about three, doing the only thing I was good at, the typing and shorthand I'd learned in high school. A year later my dad died and I got divorced. Mom sold their big house, and together we bought this place. After a while I got tired of working for others, so I started my company, training my employees personally. It's a good living, but no, it's hardly my dream job."

He had a habit of listening intently, of sitting very still as if hearing what the other person had to say was of the utmost interest to him. That was probably one of the reasons he did so well in business, Millie thought.

"It's a shame, isn't it, that circumstances often dictate how we live our lives. I wonder how many people are truly doing exactly what they want to do. Like Thoreau said, most people live lives of quiet frustration or desperation, something like that." Not to be thwarted, Gavin put his hand on her shoulder, stroking through the soft cotton of her top, the gesture seemingly casual.

"Do you believe that?"

"Yeah, I think I do. Take my brother, Trey. He inherited half of our father's assets along with me. He's three years older, so after college he took the reins of Templeton alone until I graduated and joined him. We worked well together, but there's always been a restlessness about Trey. Then he got this notion that there was a family curse and he was going to die." Gavin shook his head as if he thought the idea absurd.

"A family curse? What kind of curse?"

"A nutty one, if you ask me. He researched and found that most if not all the Templeton males died in their thirty-eighth year. All from different causes. So, at thirty-six, fast moving up on the curse, he took a leave from the company, saying his life would soon be over and he didn't want to die at a desk."

Millie found the story interesting, despite the way Gavin's hand stroking her back now was making her feel. Warm, fidgety, aware. "So what did he do?" Apparently Hannah didn't know about this or never got around to telling her.

"He started doing all the things he'd never done, reckless and dangerous things, searching for new indulgences so he could experience everything worth doing before the curse would take him." Gavin's lips twitched, finding Trey's obsession humorous still.

"You're making this up," she accused.

"No, I swear I'm not. He raced cars and sailboats, bungee jumped, went on an African safari, tried climbing the highest mountain, went deep-sea diving, kayaking in Alaska. You name it, he did it."

"Obviously he came through it all because he's still alive, right?"

"Oh, yes, mostly because of modern medicine. He broke a whole bunch of bones, ruptured his spleen, nearly lost a kidney."

"But he's given all that up now?" She really hadn't heard much about the other brother's antics, but then, she rarely glanced at the sports section of the paper.

"Sort of. See, he fell in love with his physical therapist, a terrific lady named Cilla. She didn't believe in curses and told him so. I think she also said he could keep up his adventure seeking or he could have her, but not both. He finally realized he wanted her more than the dubious thrills. They got married last year. Trey turned thirty-seven recently and the heavens didn't swallow him up."

Joey's ball hit the wall and bounced, then rolled to a stop by Gavin's shoe. He tossed it back to the boy.

Still caught up in Trey's life, Millie was curious. "But he hasn't gone back to work at Templeton?"

"No, not yet. See, as the eldest son, he also inherited this huge mausoleum of a house where we grew up. After my mother left him and all but cleaned it out, Dad neglected the house, but Trey still lived there with our old housekeeper, Connie, mostly because he was gone a lot and so busy outrunning the curse that he didn't find time to fix things. But Cilla wasn't about to live like that so, since his marriage, they've been renovating the place. Once that's finished, Trey says he'd like to come back."

"How do you feel about that?"

"Great. I'd love to have him back. He's smart, innovative and works hard, when he wants to." Gavin paused, suddenly aware that he hadn't talked this much about his family in…well, he couldn't recall *ever* talking about all that to anyone. "You're awfully easy to talk with, you know that?'' His hand moved to cup her chin. Maybe too easy. Why was he confiding all this personal stuff? Hadn't he learned that the more someone knew about you, the more ammunition they had against you if push ever came to shove?

''You are, too.'' This close, she thought she saw hints of concern in his eyes. Was it about their subject matter or his feelings?

Recovering, Gavin reluctantly let go of her and shifted the focus of the conversation. ''But enough about me and my family. What about you? If you gave up your company, what would your dream job be?''

''Oh, that's a hard one.'' Millie leaned back into the corner of the swing. ''I've been so focused on making a go of this, of paying the bills and making sure there'd be money for Joey's college, that I rarely give thought to anything else.'' Such as a man in her life who suddenly made her feel very much like a woman.

He watched the evening breeze ruffle her hair and almost sat on his hands to keep from touching her. ''I understand, but what if you had the option to choose a dream job? What would it be?''

''If I didn't have responsibilities, like Joey and my mother, I'd choose something in travel. That trip to Detroit was the first time I'd been out of California since I was a teenager and Dad drove us to the Grand Canyon one summer. I'd especially love to see Ireland where my father's family came from.'' She laughed at herself. ''Nothing petty about my dreams, eh?''

''I've always thought if you dream, you might as well dream big. Who knows, maybe one day…''

''No, I don't think so. It's fun to dream, but I live in the real world where bills come due every month and Joey will need braces soon, and college tuition by the time he turns eighteen will probably be through the roof. I'm certainly not unhappy with my life.'' Her eyes drifted to her son, still plugging away, working on catching the ball. ''I have more than many people.''

Gavin followed her gaze. ''I agree. You do.'' He felt an unusual sensation, one that could be best described as a sadness twinge and a bit of envy. She had Joey who obviously adored her. He'd never planned to marry or to have children. The fine examples of his parents haunted him still. But watching the boy, he felt an uncharacteristic longing.

When the ball Joey had been tossing about landed at Gavin's feet again, he welcomed the intrusion to his troubling thoughts.

Scooping it up, he stood. ''Want to hit a few with me?'' he asked.

Joey was hesitant. ''I'm not very good. Coach says I don't track the ball well.''

''Is that so?'' Gavin walked out a ways on the grass as Joey picked up the bat. ''Walk over there and let's see how it goes.''

Sizing him up, Gavin threw the first pitch. And Joey missed, swinging too early. Embarrassed, his head down, the boy ran to get the ball.

Millie, watching from the swing, was more than a little surprised. Who would believe Gavin Templeton, San Diego Business Man of the Year two years running, would be here on her lawn playing ball? Would wonders never cease?

She saw Gavin walk over to her son and confer with him, correcting his grip, explaining, encouraging. She didn't know what he said, but Joey was nodding as if he understood. Gavin returned to the makeshift pitcher's mound and threw another ball. Joey hesitated, then let the ball go on by. He tossed it back to Gavin and Millie saw his face take on a determination she hadn't seen often enough.

This time when Gavin threw the ball, Joey managed to bunt it out of bounds. Millie heard Gavin say that that was all right, then a few more instructions. To everyone's surprise, including Joey, he hit the next pitch over Gavin's head into the stucco fence on the opposite wall. She couldn't help herself. Millie stood up and cheered.

Grinning, Joey got in position again. Gavin warned him to stay focused, to not swing unless he thought he had a chance to connect. Joey let two balls go by, then hit the next one square down the middle. The fact that Gavin caught it with a high jump didn't diminish Joey's pleasure one bit. The two guys went into a huddle again as Millie sat back on the swing, her thoughts in a turmoil.

She couldn't help wondering how Hannah would view this scene in her backyard. A mere ten days working with Gavin and the uptight executive had loosened up considerably. Maybe too much, she thought, remembering his hands stroking her neck.

She mustn't get involved. This had nowhere to go. Millionaires didn't fall for their substitute secretaries, even if she owned the secretarial company. Not in the real world. If she allowed this to continue, she'd be the one hurt, while he would move on with his life after Hannah returned. She wasn't young and starry-eyed this time around, she reminded herself.

Millie watched as Joey and Gavin laughed about something, then separated to resume the practice. She hadn't even told Gavin that Joey needed help with his hitting. He'd told her he loved baseball, but he hadn't planned on giving some pointers to Joey, she was certain. Then why was he doing it?

She'd have to be careful, because more than her feelings were involved here. As a mature woman, she'd manage somehow, but what about her son? She couldn't allow him to get too attached to Gavin. She'd so rarely dated since her divorce that Joey wasn't used to a man around. She hadn't wanted to expose him to a series of men who might try to get to her by charming her son. In so doing, she'd sacrificed her own need for male companionship, but it had been her choice and, she was certain, the right choice.

But still, looking at Gavin relaxed today, the breeze shifting his always perfect hair, laughing with the young boy who owned her heart, Millie felt a longing that was almost physical. After her break with Joel, she'd never allowed herself to think about normal domestic situations like this, certain she wasn't meant to have them. And that was still probably true.

But, although she couldn't tell Gavin, more than wanting her dream of traveling to faraway places, she wanted a love of her own with a man who would share a strong commitment with her and be a father to Joey, to live in a house they would turn into a home. Millie sighed, unaware how forlorn she sounded.

"Penny for your thoughts," Lois Donovan said, joining her daughter on the swing.

Startled out of her reverie, Millie pointed to where Joey was hitting more pitches than he was missing. "Look at that." She hoped her mother hadn't noticed the glisten of tears in her eyes.

"Just like I've said, the boy needs a man to teach him some things we can't." Lois shouted encouragement to her grandson as he beamed a smile in their direction.

"Mom," Millie said, lowering her voice, "I want none of your matchmaking comments in front of Gavin. I work for him, and that's all. Hannah will be back soon and that will be that. He's a millionaire, for heaven's sake. What would he want with a middle-class woman with a son?''

''Don't underestimate yourself, Millie. You have a lot to offer.''

''Not to a man who's sophisticated and worldly. Please, don't embarrass me.''

Lois waved a dismissing hand, her eyes on Joey. ''Have I ever?'' she asked, slightly offended.

Millie almost laughed. Almost.

A few more pitches and the ball players walked back to where Millie and her mother sat on the swing, Gavin's arm around Joey's shoulders.

''Thanks for the workout, sport,'' she heard Gavin say as he smiled at the boy.

''No. Thank you.'' Joey was all shy smiles. ''Did you see, Mom? I'm getting better, right?''

''You sure are.'' She hugged him and drew him close, brushing back his damp hair.

''What do you say we all go inside and have some cake?'' Lois asked, rising.

The cake was wonderfully gooey and the milk cold. Gavin had two pieces, declaring he'd have to work out twice as hard all week after such a great meal. He checked his watch and rose to thank Lois, who offered to send some cake home with him.

''Thanks, but I'd better pass.''

Joey trailed after Millie as she walked Gavin to the door. ''Are you going to be at the game tomorrow afternoon? All the kids are going, you know. Mom and I'll be there.''

Gavin looked regretful as he shook his head. ''Not this

time, but I'll tell you what. My company's got some box seats and I'll take you and your mom real soon.''

Joey's eyes widened. ''Honest? You promise?''

''You bet. I promise.''

Gavin saw Millie's back stiffen as she told her son to thank Mr. Templeton for working with him on his hitting, then to go take his shower. Following her outside, Gavin wondered what he'd said to cause her cool reaction.

On the porch she turned to him. ''Don't do that, please. Don't promise my son things. Kids take adults at their word and then when you can't make it, they get hurt.''

He stood looking down at her, at the moonlight streaking her dark hair, turning it silver. ''I'm not your ex-husband, Millie,'' he said softly.

Turning slightly, she crossed her arms over her chest in a defensive gesture. ''I know that. I also know you're a busy man. I'll go with him tomorrow, and we thank you for those tickets. You don't need to take him later.''

Gavin felt a rush of annoyance bordering on anger. Yet he understood all too well where she was coming from. He put his hands on her shoulders and turned her to face him. ''I know why you're saying that. Remember, I grew up with a father like Joel. Oh, he lived under the same roof but he wasn't really there. He also made all kinds of promises that he never kept. Trey and I were disappointed over and over, until we stopped believing in promises.''

Her eyes were downcast, so he cupped her chin and forced her to look at him. ''Having gone through that, I wouldn't *ever* do the same thing to Joey. Or anyone else. If I promise something, I will do it. I know you don't believe me, but you could give me a chance to prove it. You're judging me by the yardstick of your ex-husband and that isn't really fair, now, is it?'' He saw her eyes soften as she blinked several times.

''I suppose not. You'll have to forgive me. I've had years of not trusting.''

''Me, too, Millie.'' Mindful of the open door, he guided her into the shadows and saw a question move into her luminous eyes.

''What...what are we doing here?'' she asked, her voice a shaky whisper.

He wasn't sure, he only knew that he had to remove that anxious look from her, and that he had to taste her. His mouth took hers as he edged her back until she was flat against the bricks of the house. Arms crushing her to him, he drank from her.

Heat rushed through Millie's system, heat like she'd never known. Surprise had her gripping the cotton of his shirt at his back. Her lips parted of their own accord to allow his tongue to enter, to dance with hers. She felt off balance, on a roller coaster of desire that drove her to give as good as she got.

Needs he'd not acknowledged, lust he'd put on the back burner far too long, frustration at war with propriety—all those emotions and more skidded through Gavin's system as he angled his mouth and took her deeper. She'd been so cool and confident in those smart little business suits while they worked together, yet with that enticing scent sending his imagination soaring. He knew this way lay madness, yet he wanted more. So much more.

But he knew he should stop.

Breathing hard, he pulled back from her. They stared at each other, her hands still tangled in his shirt, his fingers buried in her hair. To hell with what he *should* do, Gavin decided, and dragged her mouth back to his. The kiss was explosive, fiery, churning with new passion. He couldn't get close enough, inwardly cursing the barrier of their clothes. Her hands burrowed under his shirt to trail along the hard flesh of his back.

Peripherally he heard the screen door open, then quickly bang shut. Stepping back, he lowered his head, trying to pull himself together while waves of desire refused to recede.

Millie leaned against the brick wall and closed her eyes, her breath coming in labored puffs. Whoever had opened the screen door had thankfully gone back in. She'd likely have some questions to fend off, whether it had been Joey or her mother. That was the least of her concerns.

Slowly she opened her eyes and saw Gavin standing there disheveled looking, studying her.

"Are you all right?" he asked, fairly sure he wasn't.

She let out a trembling breath. "What...what just happened?"

"Damned if I know." Turning, he ran a hand through his hair. "I hope you don't want me to apologize."

"I'd be insulted if you did." She tested her legs and took a step, grateful they'd stopped shaking.

"I think I'd better go," Gavin said, sending her a sideways look. And wished he hadn't when he saw her mouth swollen from his kisses, her eyes a dark blue and still hazy with desire. He hurried down the porch steps. "I'll see you Monday at the office."

Millie leaned against the porch pillar and watched him drive away until the lights of his car were just red dots on the road. So that was how it felt to be in the eye of a storm, she thought as she slowly went inside.

"I'm so glad they let me take Emma home," Hannah said into the phone. "She's much better, but she has to stay in bed awhile yet."

"What went wrong? Do you know?" Millie asked.

She'd naively thought that giving birth was a simple, uncomplicated procedure in these days of modern medicine. Apparently not.

"She had to have a Cesarean, of course, since the babies were so big and something ruptured. I'm not sure exactly what, but it was touch-and-go for days. Lord, I was scared, Millie." Hannah's usually calm and confident voice was still ragged with worry.

"Of course you were. But she's out of the woods now. What about the babies?"

"They'll have to stay in the hospital a few more days. But, Millie, they're so adorable. Two tiny, perfect little girls. I'm itching to get my hands on them. But I'm a little nervous, too. It's been a long time since I took care of newborns."

Poor Hannah. She did sound frazzled. "Well, at least you can relax about things at this end. The two mergers are a done deal. I filed the final papers this morning." It was four o'clock and Millie was stretched out on the living room couch, having left the office early for a change. Gavin had said he had some errands to run and he didn't have anything for her right now. Joey was at a friend's house and her mother was shopping. Millie was grateful for some quiet alone time.

"You're still getting along with Gavin? I know he can be difficult, even obstinate at times. And if you don't stop him, he'll work you around the clock. The man never seems to get tired. But down deep inside he's really a pushover." Hannah paused, but when Millie didn't respond, she went on, a note of concern in her voice. "You're not having problems, are you?"

Problems. Oh, no, not if you don't count a couple of kisses that blew off the top of her head and the memory that kept her awake nights. They'd worked together this morning and it had been a bit strained. She'd caught him looking at her, his eyes narrowed and contemplative, when he didn't think she was watching him. She knew Gavin had been as stunned as she at his reaction to those kisses. It was inconceivable to ignore them and impossible to dismiss the incident lightly.

Therein lay her dilemma.

"Millie? Are you there?" Hannah sounded ever more strained.

"I'm here and no, we're not having problems. I'm just a little preoccupied." Thinking fast, she grasped at a likely straw. "Do you know a Donna Warwick from Accounting?"

"Sure. Short, dark-haired, average looking, midthirties. She dressed kind of cheap. Arrived with glowing credentials, having been with the IRS, I believe, but her work didn't back up her experience. George Walters isn't too happy with Donna," she added, naming the head CPA. "Is there a problem with her?"

Millie tried to remember the details. "George let her go last week because her work, as you mentioned, wasn't up to par and her errors were getting costly. He gave her a good severance package but she's filed a discrimination suit against Templeton."

"Discrimination?" Hannah sounded indignant. "What's she citing?"

"You're going to love this. She's got dark hair, as you said. She claims that only blond women get promoted at Templeton because both George and Gavin have a thing about blondes."

Hannah made a rude noise. "That's ridiculous. The court will throw it out as a nuisance suit."

"I'm not so sure. She's compiled a fairly long list of names, all blond women, who've moved ahead in the company, plus a list of brunettes who are still at their present jobs after years.'' Millie sighed. ''We can't just dismiss her. We have to answer her claims. Gavin and I've been in a huddle with Legal, but so far we don't have a clear defense.''

''Is Gavin upset?''

''Actually, he's cool as a cucumber, but I know he's concerned. As I'm sure you're aware, he hates lawsuits.''

''What do you think Donna Warwick is after, money or attention?''

''Oh, probably both. George offered to reinstate her with an increase, contingent on how she does on a trial basis, but she turned him down. I think she smells more money. Or her attorney does.''

''We had a discrimination suit brought against us a couple of years ago, dragged on for months. One of the managers in our Dallas office apparently didn't like women, kept hiring men over better-qualified women. We lost and it cost a bundle, I can tell you.'' Hannah let out a huff of air. ''Everybody's sue-happy these days.''

''They sure are.'' The doorbell sounded, interrupting. ''Hannah, someone's at my door. You take care, and I'll be in touch.''

''Okay, honey. Say hi to your mom for me.''

Millie opened the door to find a delivery man standing on the porch holding a vase of yellow roses and a wrapped package. ''Crandall residence?'' he asked.

''Yes.'' She took the flowers and package from him and placed them on the end table, then signed the delivery sheet. He waited while she found her purse and gave him a tip with her thanks. Closing the door, she wondered who'd be sending her a gift.

But the card with the roses was addressed to Lois Donovan, thanking her for a lovely dinner, and was signed by

Gavin. Millie smiled as she set the vase on the dining room table, knowing her mother would be pleased.

Picking up the package, she saw it was addressed to Joey Crandall. A frown creased her brow. What was he sending Joey and more important, why was he sending it? Millie wished she wasn't such a naturally suspicious person, but she was. Setting the gift on the coffee table, she sat down and speculated, but couldn't come up with a single good guess. Joey was due home soon, and she could hardly wait.

"A brand-new baseball mitt, Mom, and look! It fits." Joey was ecstatic. "Boy, I'll bet this will help me catch better."

"It's very nice," she said without enthusiasm, but she was sure Joey didn't notice.

"Can I go show Todd?" His best friend lived three doors down. "Maybe we'll toss a few, okay?"

She let him go, then sat back, thinking. What exactly did Gavin Templeton think he was doing?

He was already seated at his desk when Millie walked into his office through the connecting door. "Good morning," she said as she took a seat opposite him.

Gavin looked up, having noticed the lack of warmth in her voice. "Good morning. Want some coffee?"

"No, thanks. I've got the file on Donna Warwick, thought you might want to go over it. I've already talked with George and…"

"Wait." He spoke softly but firmly as he picked up his pen and leaned back. Something was definitely wrong, and he hadn't a clue what. He swallowed a sigh, thinking he never had these kinds of problems when Hannah was here. But then, he'd never kissed Hannah the way he'd kissed Millie that night. She'd seemed all right yesterday, though she'd avoided meeting his eyes and had sat as far away from him as possible. Was that it, the memory of those kisses suddenly bothering her?

Like they bothered him.

"What's wrong, and don't tell me it's nothing." Finally she raised her eyes to his.

"The flowers you sent my mother are lovely."

"She already called and left a message thanking me." Was she upset he hadn't sent her flowers? No, he didn't think that was it.

Millie drew in a steadying breath. "The baseball glove fits Joey just fine. He's crazy about it."

"Uh-huh. He called, too." Gavin almost smiled at the breathless message on his answering machine. Such a small gift, yet it had made such a big impression on the boy. "I thought his other glove was way too big and that a smaller one might help him catch better."

"How very thoughtful of you." She dropped her gaze to the file on her lap, tracing its edge with a finger.

Gavin studied her a long moment, and it finally came to him. "You think I'm thoughtful and you also think I'm deceitful, that I'm trying to get to you by sending your mother flowers and giving your son a glove." He leaned forward and threw down his pen. "Does that about cover it?"

Again she raised those wide blue eyes filled with questions and a trace of hurt mingled with temper. "Are you?"

"Damn it, Millie, why is everything I do suspicious to you? I sent your mother flowers to thank her for dinner, since I thought it was very gracious of her to invite me on such short notice. I've sent others flowers for dinner invitations countless times. I sent Joey the glove because…well, because that hand-me-down glove was part of his problem and…and I like the kid.'' Anger simmering, he got up and moved closer, leaning against his desk. ''Maybe I do want to get closer to you, but I draw the line at using your mother and son to do it. When are you going to stop comparing me to your ex-husband or other men you've known?''

Millie felt heat move into her face because he was right. She had been thinking exactly what he'd accused her of. And she'd been wrong.

''I'm sorry. I apologize.'' Her lower lip trembled just a fraction. ''I reacted before thinking it through.''

''Apology accepted.'' He drew her up to face him. ''I'm not going to deny wanting you in my bed, but I'm not going to travel a devious route to get you there.''

Her eyes widening, Millie struggled to grasp his words. ''I'm not going to sleep with you. I'm not going to get involved with you. I don't want you…''

''Are you absolutely sure you don't want me?'' His hand at her back, he eased her closer until she was hard up against him. Her breasts pressed into his chest and that damn cologne attacked his senses. ''Because the way you kissed me the other night tells a different story.''

She stiffened her spine, tried moving back, but he held her firmly. ''That was a fluke, a mistake, one I won't repeat again.''

Enjoying himself, Gavin smiled slow and sexy. ''Is that a fact?'' He bent his head, and his mouth took possession of hers.

Absolute possession, Millie thought, as if he knew ahead of time how she'd react. She'd seen the kiss coming, had told herself she'd resist, stand firm, not respond. But her traitorous body betrayed her so-called strong will by pressing against him, her hands snaking up over his shoulders and tangling in his hair. Lost in sensation in a matter of moments, she clung to him, afraid of losing her balance.

He'd wanted to send a message, to prove her wrong, but he found himself wanting her more than he'd anticipated. She had his head spinning, his thoughts whirling, his own admonitions to stay uninvolved flying out the window. Now that he'd proved his point, he should pull away, back off, let her go.

And he would, in just another minute. As soon as his lips tasted hers more thoroughly, and his hands explored down along her rib cage and inched forward to settle over her breasts. He swallowed her moan as her lips parted and his tongue slid inside to plunge and plunder, to know more of her.

She wanted him, Millie thought with the tiny part of her brain still functioning. Oh, how she wanted him, alone in some quiet place with candles burning and soft music playing, where they would be free to caress and be caressed. She'd heard that there were men who could turn a woman's knees to water, but she'd never met one. Until now.

The intercom buzzed loudly and they pulled apart like guilty children who'd been caught dipping into the forbidden cookie jar. Millie's silk blouse was wrinkled from his damp hands and pulled out of the waistband of her linen slacks. Gavin's hair was mussed from her hands, and his tie was hanging crookedly. The sound of their heavy breathing filled the room.

Again, the intercom buzzed, longer this time. Slowly, like a man who'd just awakened from a hard sleep, Gavin made his way around the desk and hit the button. "Yes, Tara?" he managed, hoping she wouldn't notice his ragged breathing.

"Donald Watkins from Legal here to see you, sir," Tara said.

He'd totally forgotten. "Please, have him take a seat. I've got to finish something. I need about ten minutes."

"Certainly, sir."

He clicked off, straightened and looked over at Millie, finger combing her hair with shaky hands.

"I'm going to my office to splash water on my face," she said, picking up her things. "I'll be back shortly."

"Millie?" he said as she walked away. He waited until she stopped and turned to face him. "Have you ever heard the saying 'You can run but you can't hide'?"

She didn't know how to answer that, so she left, closing the door between their offices.

Gavin got out his pocket comb. What in hell was he getting into? he asked himself.

Chapter Five

Gavin stood in the marble foyer of the house he'd grown up in, and his mouth nearly dropped open. Standing beside him, Cilla Kovacs Templeton gave a short laugh.

"Quite a shock, I take it," she said, wiping a smudge of paint from her hand.

"You can say that again." The old wallpaper he'd always hated was gone, replaced by a soft white-on-white subtle design, and the carpeting leading up the stairs was a plush pale blue. The carved railing had been sanded down, waxed and polished to bring out the sheen of the solid oak. Through the archway, he could see the living room had been gutted and redone in sea green, almond and pale coral, the furniture looking comfortable and inviting. "You two have really been working hard."

Cilla gave him her easy smile. "I cannot tell a lie. We had help. Plasterers, plumbers, carpenters. But Trey and I picked out all the colors together and we're doing the painting.''

"And where is my big brother?" Gavin asked.

"Come on upstairs and I'll show you." Her feet were bare and she was wearing white shorts and a loose yellow top, her auburn hair caught up in a ponytail and tied with yellow ribbon. There was a happy glow about her that had Gavin smiling as he followed her up. "Marriage seems to agree with you. You look great, Cilla."

"Thanks." She turned right and headed for the open door. "Connie's going to be sorry she missed you. She's at the market."

"Give her a hug for me, will you?"

"Sure." Cilla stopped at the third door and motioned for Gavin to go in. "Your brother, the artist," she announced.

Doubly surprised, Gavin just stared. There was Trey sitting on a stool drawing a freehand blue bunny on the wall above the maple wainscotting that matched a rather large crib in the corner. "Well, now I've seen everything," he said, admiring the baby chick, the little white duckling, the long-necked goose and a mouse wearing glasses. "I had no idea you were so talented, bro." And no idea they were expecting.

Carefully setting his brush atop his paint can, Trey grinned. "Didn't know I had it in me, either, to tell you the truth." His eyes found his wife, who moved to stand alongside him as he slipped an arm around her waist. "This woman can get me to do just about anything."

Hands on his hips, Gavin turned about, checking out all the various animals. "You're damn good, you know."

"He used to doodle these drawings and I kept telling him he was really good." Cilla squeezed his arm. "See, I told you."

"Yeah, you told me a lot of things." He kissed her lightly.

"So, when's the baby due?" Gavin wanted to know.

"Six months, right around Christmas," the proud father said.

"Why don't I get us some iced tea?" Cilla suggested. "We have the air off and the windows open because of the paint smell so it's kind of warm in here."

"That would be great, honey." Trey got up, wiping his hands on a rag he'd pulled from the back pocket of his jeans. Gazing around, he stretched his neck this way and that to get the kinks out. "You really think it looks okay?" he asked Gavin. "I wouldn't want to scare the kid."

Gavin shook his head in wonder. "You, a father. Hard to believe." He strolled over and sat down in a bentwood rocker. "A lot of changes and not just in the house." His brother was different, calmer, happier.

"You can say that again," Trey answered, dropping down on the floor by the window. "Never say never, I've learned." He motioned toward the door with his chin. "I couldn't have done it without Cilla, and I don't mean the domestic changes. I'd probably be dead or, at the very least, crippled for life if it weren't for her."

"I tried to tell you that curse was silly and that you'd maim yourself trying to outrun it." Trey had celebrated his thirty-seventh birthday last November right before the wedding. Lo and behold, he was still standing.

"I know. I wouldn't listen. Hard head, you know. Inherited." He grinned. "We both have one." Trey saw his brother nod in agreement. "So, what brings you here at long last?"

"I came to see what you've been doing. You've been after me to visit and here I am."

"Mmm-hmm. What else?"

Gavin frowned, rocking. "What do you mean, what else?"

Trey pretended to consider the question deeply. "Let's see. Either you want to take four or five years off like I did, which I think you have coming, or you want to sell everything, which I wouldn't be opposed to, either. Or there's some woman who finally got to you." Watching closely, he noticed Gavin's mouth twitch. "Aha! A woman. I told Cilla that was probably it when she told me you were coming over."

"I didn't say there was a woman," Gavin protested without heat.

"You didn't have to. Come on, little brother. Talk to me like we used to years ago."

They had confided in each other years ago, Gavin remembered. After all, they had had only each other. "She's not just some woman. She's smart and clever and beautiful. She had a bad marriage and has an eleven-year-old son. A really great kid."

"Uh-oh. A cute kid. Now I know you're hooked."

Gavin leaned forward. "No, no, I'm not. I mean, I wouldn't mind if she wound up in my bed, but you know me. What do I know about kids? Besides, I'm not the forever type. Marriage is out."

"That's what *I* said and that's what I meant. Until I found I wanted Cilla more than my so-called free lifestyle. You know those guys I used to pal around with? I took a good look at them, and they're not really happy. They keep busy with all their frantic activity, telling themselves they're on top of the world. But inside, they're lonely as hell."

Lonely. A word Gavin hadn't thought about much until recently. He didn't especially want to think about it now.

But there it was, staring him in the face. Maybe he'd kept himself so busy with Templeton Enterprises so he wouldn't have to face the facts.

"Does she care about you?" Trey asked, draping his arms on his raised knees.

"Who knows? We're very…attracted, but we haven't really talked about how we feel." Gavin scraped a hand across his unshaven face. He'd been driving around, trying to sort things out, when he'd impulsively called and told Cilla he'd like to drop by.

"Okay, you're attracted. Is sex all you have together?"

Gavin gave a short laugh. "We haven't actually gone to bed yet."

Trey's green eyes bore into his. "Why not?"

"Because if we do, we'll definitely be involved and you know how I feel about that. I'd make a lousy husband. And father. That boy deserves a real father, a good one."

"What makes you think that man isn't you? Why do you think you'd be a lousy husband and father? You're not Dad, you know. Just like I found out I wasn't. We don't have to let history repeat itself."

Gavin leaned forward, his face earnest. "You honestly think we can be different, better?"

"I wouldn't have gotten married if I didn't. As for fatherhood, I'm going to be the best damn father you've ever seen. My son or daughter is going to know without a shadow of a doubt how much I love her. Or him. At least we know how *not* to act, as a parent."

Gavin was quiet, thoughtful.

"I'll bet I know what's holding you back." When his brother looked up, he went on. "You're afraid of disappointing her and her son, right?"

There was some truth to that. "Pretty much, yeah."

"Don't be. If you care enough, you'll do fine. One day at a time, bro." Rising, he clamped a hand on Gavin's shoulder. "You'll see." Walking to the doorway, he heard glasses clinking. "Here comes our tea."

Gavin watched his brother take the tray from his wife, saw the look that passed between them and felt a jolt of envy so sharp it nearly staggered him. Was it possible for him to change as much as Trey had, to overcome his long-held beliefs that marriage and fatherhood wasn't for him?

"Wow, did you see that, Gavin? He jumped right up into the air about twenty feet and caught that ball!" Joey wiggled and squirmed in the front-row seat of the glassed-in Templeton box at Jack Murphy Stadium.

Seated behind him, Millie ruffled his hair. "I don't think it was quite twenty feet," she said, enjoying her son's enthusiasm.

"Okay, maybe fifteen. What do you think, Gavin?"

"It sure was a high jump," Gavin said, winking at Millie. She'd wanted her son to address him as Mr. Templeton, but he'd insisted the boy should call him Gavin. It was friendlier. She finally gave in.

Just as she'd given in on letting him take all three of them to the company box seats to watch the game. He'd even asked Mrs. Donovan, but Lois had said that baseball bored her to tears.

That last out had been number three, so the Padres were up to bat. Joey was on the edge of his seat, watching through the glass high over third base. He'd brought his new glove along and kept it on, punching his other fist into it often. Gavin had shown him how to oil it and break it in. Millie had told him Joey even slept with it. The kid was something else.

A knock on the door brought the waiter in with cold

drinks and all sorts of snacks that Gavin had ordered. He tipped the man before turning to his guests. "Anyone hungry or thirsty?"

Joey, who was always both hungry and thirsty, took a minute to grab a soft drink and a bag of chips, then quickly returned to his front-row seat, not wanting to miss even one minute.

"Did I forget to thank you for inviting us today?" Millie asked, adding lemon to her iced tea. "Joey will be big man on campus when he tells his friends about this."

"My pleasure." Gavin lifted a few lids, checking his order. Cold shrimp with sauce, noodle salad, crackers, chips, hot dogs, huge chocolate-chip cookies. "I wasn't sure what eleven-year-olds eat."

"You did fine." But her eyes were concerned as she carried her drink to the third and last row of seats. This was lovely, a carefree afternoon watching a big-league game in a plush box with anything you wanted to eat or drink. Your private rest room, no waiting in line with the riffraff. Valet parking, no walking miles through a crowded lot. Easy to get used to. Too easy.

"Something wrong?" Gavin asked, sliding into the seat next to her, stretching his arm across the back of her chair.

Millie took a sip of her tea. Raspberry flavored. No ordinary orange pekoe up here. "It's a beautiful day, my son is having the time of his life. What could be wrong?"

He wasn't buying it. "Something is. Look at me."

Slowly she turned her head, wondering what he would see of her feelings. She'd gotten rather good at masking them.

"Are you angry with me because I brought you both here and proved that I keep my promises?"

"Now, how could I be angry with someone who kept a promise?"

He took her hand, lowered his voice even though Joey, three rows down from them, was on his feet, his face almost pressed to the glass, wrapped up in the game. "You forget that I'm used to reading people, gauging them as to which way they're leaning in business situations. That carries over into my personal life."

"Does it? What exactly do you read in me?"

He studied her eyes, but the blue depths didn't reveal much. "You're upset with something I did, but you're too polite to take me to task for it. Let's take the gloves off, Millie. You can say anything you want to me. I can take it. I'm a big boy." He gave her his winning smile, but she didn't return it, only turned to gaze thoughtfully out at the field.

"Mom, Tony Gwynn's up to bat. Number 19. He's our best guy." Stuffing chips into his mouth, Joey couldn't take his eyes off the game.

"That's great, sweetie." She knew Gavin was waiting for an answer, knew also that he was anything if not persistent. "All right, Gavin." She swung to meet his gaze, her voice barely a whisper. "I don't want my son to get used to this life. He has to live in the real world, not this one." *After you leave us.* "I don't want him to be hurt by longing for things he can't have." There, she'd said it.

Instead of getting annoyed or upset, Gavin placed his hand on her shoulder. "You worry too much."

"Parents have a tendency to do that."

"Listen, Millie. Suppose Joey won a contest, a trip to Disneyland, all expenses paid. He could go on every ride, buy every souvenir he wanted, stay at their hotel and have lunch with Mickey. Do you feel that he'd think that was the way things would go for him from then on, that he'd be able to go to Knotts Berry Farm and Sea World or anywhere else and get the same treatment?''

"No, of course not. A prize is a one-time thing. But after experiencing something like this, it's not that easy going back to sitting in the hot sun in the bleachers. Am I right?''

Trey had told him he had a hard head, but Millie was a hard sell, even for him. "I don't think you give your son enough credit. Look at him. He's watching the game, involved in every aspect of it. He's not even sitting on the nicely upholstered seat or eating the expensive snacks. He could care less. He just wants to watch baseball.''

"If that's true, and you knew that, why didn't you get us seats up in the nosebleed section?''

"Are you so against enjoying the things money can buy? Do you think every time Joey is exposed to something special that he'll then be disenchanted with his current situation? Hell, no. Why? Because you and your mother keep him grounded. It's not things that impress kids most. It's people. If anyone can attest to that, it's me.''

Remembering what he'd told her about his family, how he and his brother had been raised by a housekeeper, basically abandoned by both parents, she understood what he meant. "Maybe you're right. I just don't want him to be disappointed that I can't give him everything his heart desires.''

"*Things* aren't what this is about. Trey and I grew up in a mansion. Our father would get us whatever we asked for because that way he could go about his business and we'd leave him alone. After a while it was no pleasure to ask for a new bike or even a convertible. We had no one who unconditionally cared for us. Except maybe Connie, the housekeeper.'' Hearing himself say those words aloud jolted Gavin. But then, the truth often did that to a person.

Millie could see on his face that he hadn't meant to blurt that out and that the realization bothered him. She'd read somewhere that if a child grows up without even one person loving him, he becomes terribly needy for love. Yet he's afraid of love, afraid to trust it when it comes along. Did that apply to both Trey and Gavin? she wondered.

He was staring out at the game, but Millie doubted he was actually seeing it. She touched his arm. ''I don't mean to be ungrateful. I really do appreciate you bringing us here.''

But Gavin was still caught up in their discussion. ''Do you know what Joey and I talked about when you were in the rest room a while ago? He asked me if I knew any dragons? I told him I didn't think dragons were real, and he said that they were to some people. I mentioned that I'd seen dragons in movies, read about them in books but I didn't personally know one. Then I asked him why he wanted to know.''

He saw that he had her full attention now. ''He told me that his friend, Timmy, saw dragons once in a while, but it was okay because his father was a dragon slayer. See, a parent can slay dragons because he loves you, Joey said. I asked him if seeing a dragon, say in your bedroom at night, was just like seeing something else you might be afraid of, like ghosts and the like. He smiled and said yes, that was right. He seemed pleased that I caught on.''

''I'm not sure what all that means,'' Millie said, puzzled.

''I believe it means that you're his dragon slayer, the one who chases away the bad dreams, those nighttime fears that every kid has now and then.'' Because he couldn't resist, his hand wandered up and toyed with her hair.

Maybe that's what Joey meant, Millie thought. Or maybe he was looking for a male dragon slayer like Timmy's father. This was getting too complicated. Standing up, she called down to her son. "How about a hot dog, Joey?" She would think about all this later.

The conference room at Templeton Enterprises was a rectangular room paneled in rich mahogany. One entire wall consisted of windows that offered a spectacular view of downtown San Diego. A highly polished table dominated, with eight chairs on each side plus a large armchair at the head.

Gavin was aware that in business as well as in life, positioning was important. He sat at the head with Millie to his immediate right and next to her was Donald Watkins representing their legal department, then George Walters, the head CPA. To Gavin's left was Aaron Armstrong, attorney for Donna Warwick who sat next to him. Kay Sutherland, one of the secretaries, sat off to the side, ready to take the notes of the meeting.

As Gavin's assistant, Millie introduced everyone, then sat back, resting her hands on a manila folder. She had a feeling just how this meeting would go, and that it could get ugly.

"If you'd care to begin, Mr. Armstrong," Gavin invited.

Donna's attorney was a short man with a wiry build and thick black-rimmed glasses. He wore a loud plaid sports coat that would have been more appropriate at the racetrack, where it was rumored the man spent quite a bit of time. Gavin knew Armstrong only by reputation, and while he wasn't quite sleazy, he wasn't highly respected, either.

Shuffling through his papers, Armstrong finally found what he was looking for and handed the report to Gavin before distributing a copy to everyone at the table. "As you can see, Mr. Templeton, listed on the top sheet are the names of your female employees from your San Diego office who are blond. The next page lists all the brunettes. You'll see a five-to-one ratio in favor of blond women. In subsequent pages you'll find a similar comparison for all of your offices in the various locations, just in the United States. I didn't think it necessary to involve your overseas operations but I can if you feel that information is necessary for comparative purposes, showing a decided trend." He paused, peering through thick lenses, noticing that Gavin was flipping through the sheets. Since no comment was forthcoming, he chose to continue by passing out a second report to one and all.

"This second comparison shows promotions within your firm going back ten years. If you'll check them with the corresponding sheets listing blondes and brunettes, you'll see there's a marked similarity. Blondes not only get hired by Templeton more frequently, but they get promoted much more often." Sitting back, he pushed up his glasses. "I take it by calling this meeting you'd like to avoid going to court, as would my client. Naturally, that would involve you agreeing to a settlement."

Gavin kept his eyes on Armstrong. "What kind of settlement did your client have in mind?" He didn't bother looking at Donna. He'd seen her come in wearing a demure little black suit set off by a white blouse with a sweet little Peter Pan collar. She had on medium-heeled pumps and her hair—her dark hair—was curled softly around her face. She had applied a minimum of makeup and sat with her hands folded in her lap.

He hardly recognized her. Obviously, she'd been coached by Aaron or someone as to what to wear and how to act. Too bad someone didn't coach him on how to dress, Gavin thought, flinching at his garish tie. The Donna Warwick he remembered had worn low-cut blouses and skirts so tight he wondered how she managed to sit down. She'd preferred stiletto heels and used a heavy hand applying makeup. He hadn't bothered to mention her attire to George as head of accounting because the public had no access to that department.

However, Gavin had mentioned her behavior not long ago to Donna herself one evening when she'd managed to trap him alone in an elevator as he was leaving for the day. She'd hit the stall button, dropped her raincoat to the floor and all but attacked him, heaving her large bosom into his chest and thrusting her tongue into his ear. He'd calmly disengaged her and told her if she wanted to keep her job, she should never, ever touch him again. He should have fired her right then, Gavin now thought, but she'd gotten all teary-eyed, claiming she didn't know what had come over her. Also, it would turn out to be his word against hers, and he'd had the feeling she'd go to the EEOC if she was discharged.

Two weeks later George had severed her and soon after that, she'd filed her discrimination suit.

Sliding his myopic gaze to his client, Armstrong pointed to something on a paper in front of Donna and she nodded. He named a figure. "I believe if we come to terms on that, my client will drop her discrimination suit."

"Is that so?" Gavin's face gave nothing away. "Ms. Crandall, do you have anything you want to add to this?"

Millie opened her file and began to read. "In 1998, Ms.

Warwick was with Meredith and Jones Insurance Agency in San Francisco. She filed a discrimination suit against her employers saying she wasn't treated fairly because she was *short*. The case was thrown out of court for lack of evidence. In 1999, she was in Los Angeles working for the IRS, or so she claimed. When we checked with her immediate supervisor, he gave her a glowing report, which was instrumental in Templeton hiring her. A recent recheck with IRS revealed that that supervisor had been her lover and had made up most of her qualifications.''

Glancing up at Aaron Armstrong and noticing him looking uncomfortably warm, Millie picked up her final report. ''Just last year, Ms. Warwick was party in a lawsuit against Ames & Ames Accounting in Monterey. This time she claimed sexual harrassment by the elder Mr. Ames, who was seventy-two at the time.''

There was silence all around as Millie finished.

''That old coot,'' Donna said, speaking for the first time and rising out of her chair, ''he pawed me every chance he got. I would've won that case if his son hadn't been close friends with the district attorney.'' She switched her attention to Gavin, looking ready to cry. ''Mr. Templeton, you know me. I'm not like she's making me out to be. You're not going to believe her, are you?''

Gavin just stared at her until finally Aaron Armstrong touched her arm and all but pulled her back into her chair.

Aaron cleared his throat, determined to take one more stab at it. ''Even if all those things are true, the discrimination proof I've shown you is also true. If the media got ahold of those figures, Mr. Templeton, they'd have a field day.''

Donald Watkins, from legal, took over. ''Oh, I don't think you want to involve the media, Mr. Armstrong.

Your client shows a pattern of attempted extortion, thinly disguised, in her accusations.''

"I wonder if the courts would feel the same," Aaron threw out.

Watkins rose, closing his briefcase. "I truly don't think it's in your best interest to take this case to court, sir. But if you do, I welcome the opportunity to go up against you." Pushing back his chair, he nodded to Gavin and the rest of them, then walked out.

Her eyes shooting daggers, Donna headed for the door, as well. "Give me a cigarette, Aaron," she ordered over her shoulder.

Armstrong picked up his papers, stuffed them in his briefcase. "Sorry we took up your time," he mumbled, then hurried after her.

"Quite a show," George said, also rising. "Who found all that info on her? Makes us look like fools for not checking into her background more thoroughly."

"Millie researched the information," Gavin said quietly.

"Good work," the CPA said to Millie, his eyes downcast.

"George," Gavin began, "I want to implement a thorough background check on *everyone* who works for us now and in the future. I'm going to instruct Luther in personnel to get on it right away."

"Good idea." He stood. "If you don't need me…" He gathered his papers and left.

Millie rolled her shoulders. She'd been putting data together and talking on the phone since seven this morning, and it was already four.

"You did a hell of a job, as always. Thanks." Gavin rose, noticing that she looked uncomfortable. "Your neck muscles are tense." He placed his hands on her shoulders, gently massaging. His strong fingers moved up to the muscles of her neck, kneading, stroking.

"Mmm, that does feel good," Millie said, letting her head fall forward. His hands were large and powerful, working loose the knots. She felt herself relaxing, closing her eyes, going with the flow.

Standing this close behind her, Gavin inhaled her special scent as his hands shifted position and concentrated on her shoulders, the ridge of muscles between them. He could tell just when she began to trust him, when she let go and turned her body over to him. She was wearing a cocoa-brown silk blouse with a scoop neck so he had easy access to her skin. It was golden from the sun, he assumed, although when she had time to catch some rays he couldn't imagine. She worked long hours without complaint and always did a great job for him. He'd never imagined that Hannah's replacement would be better than the woman who'd worked by his side since he'd come to the company straight from college. Yet Millie *was* better.

He heard a soft sound escape her lips as he struggled to unknot a particularly stubborn bunched muscle. "Am I hurting you?"

"No, you're doing just fine." Only, she wasn't doing just fine, becoming increasingly aware of his touch, which had changed from impersonal to almost intimate as his hands engulfed her, sliding to the front, caressing her throat, her breastbone.

She was getting in over her head here, Millie decided, and moved forward, out of his reach. "Thank you. That was wonderful." She began straightening her papers, placing files in her briefcase.

"You're still a bit tense," Gavin insisted, as he himself was. The way she'd turned into his touch and almost melted had made him more aware of her as a woman. The rapid way his heart was beating was a direct result of having his hands on her the way he'd been dreaming of. And he wasn't ready to stop.

Millie clicked shut the lock on her briefcase and stood, thinking it best that she get out of here, because the way she was feeling, it wouldn't take much to get her to do something she might later regret. But when Gavin turned her to face him, when those hot, hungry eyes looked at her as only he could, she found herself trembling.

She guessed what was coming now and tried to deflect him as he shifted her into his arms. "Gavin, I don't think this is wise."

"Wisdom is overrated." Gathering her close, his lips brushed her hair. "You smell so damn good." He slipped around and kissed her cheek, then raised her face to his and found her mouth.

What harm could one little kiss do? Millie asked herself, even as she realized the folly of that question. She'd thought his mouth hard when she'd first met him, but she'd been wrong. His lips were the softest thing about him as he drew her in, his hard arms circling her so that she was wrapped around him. She sighed and decided to enjoy the kiss because, boy, could he kiss!

Must have taken lessons from some older, very lucky woman, she thought somewhat inanely. Then he shifted and deepened the kiss, and her mind went blank and she could no longer think. Just feel. And, oh, all the things she felt. Swept away, carried off on a cloud of desire, blocking out the real world.

When Gavin finally lifted his head, she blinked and swayed, though his arms held her upright. Catching her breath, she knew she should end this right now. "I should go. I *have* to go. I haven't seen Joey all day and..."

"He's with your mother and they're both fine." Gavin

placed small teasing kisses on her temple, her forehead, her eyes. He was through fighting this, through denying his feelings. He wanted her with an ache that surprised him with its intensity.

"This isn't smart. We work together. We shouldn't..."

"I know. You're probably right." Unable to resist, he kissed her again, slowly, sweetly, and heard her soft moan. He felt her shiver as he eased back and gazed into blue eyes hazy with passion. "I'm tired of always doing the right thing. I want you, Millie, and it's driving me crazy."

Her hands bunched in the soft material of his jacket, she searched his eyes, trying to think of a reason to refuse him. She could find none. She knew as well as she knew her own name that Gavin Templeton wasn't a forever man. But she, too, was tired of always passing by life's pleasures, of always being the proper lady. There comes a time when you have to reach out with both hands and take what is offered, for it may never come your way again.

Gavin watched through her expressive eyes her internal battle and also saw the moment he felt she'd finally won the battle. "Stay with me tonight, Millie?" he asked softly.

"Yes."

Chapter Six

His living quarters were a surprise. She'd been expecting lots of chrome and glass, modern designer furniture, a great view, very *House Beautiful*. The only thing she'd been right about was the great view.

The area was built on the wide so that nearly every room had floor-to-ceiling windows. His taste oddly ran to the rustic rather than the classic. The great room had polished oak flooring with a huge area rug in rich tones of emerald green and gold with streaks of rust. A long couch in butter-yellow leather faced the windows, and a comfortable easy chair and ottoman with a reading lamp sat beside a wall of bookcases filled to overflowing. A red-brick fireplace was on the opposite wall with ashes in the grate, as if it had been used recently. The whole room had a cozy feel, a warmth, a lived-in look that appealed to her enormously.

"This is nice," Millie commented, knowing he was watching her. "Did you do it yourself?"

"Yes." Gavin took her briefcase and his, parked them on the floor, then removed his suit coat and tie and draped them over the back of the couch along with her jacket. "It took me a while, but I like it." His blood humming, he didn't want to talk about decorating, yet he didn't want to rush things, either.

He walked her through the kitchen and dining area, red-tiled flooring, copper pots hung over a large black marble counter, country charm alongside state-of-the-art appliances. Millie moved slowly, needing a little time, her nerves on edge. She'd read that you could learn a lot about someone from the way they decorate their home, so she looked around and made mental notes.

Gavin all but tugged her into the bedroom through louvered, walnut double doors. She could tell he liked natural things—warm woods, bright copper, rich leathers.

The huge wrought-iron bed with its deep-red coverlet and wheat-colored carpeting suited him, she thought. But the candles on his dresser, his two nightstands, even his desk was another surprise. She hadn't pegged Gavin as a romantic. In the corner was a beehive fireplace also looking recently used.

She turned to him as he stood leaning against the archway, watching her learn the secrets of his most private place. "I see you actually use your fireplaces, even in the summer in California?"

"I do. Nights get cool." He walked over to the windows and looked down. "We're right on the ocean and we lose a lot of heat through all this glass. But I think the view is worth it."

She strolled over to join him, but not too close. Not yet. Late afternoon and the sun was playing hide-and-seek with several gray clouds. As so often happened in June in San Diego, a cool spell was in progress with rain in the forecast. Looking straight down, Millie saw a few people walking on the beach but no boats in the water and no one swimming. She wondered what it would be like to be up here twenty-seven stories high, watching the sun set or experiencing an electrical storm. Exciting.

"This is a spectacular view. How can you tear yourself away from it and get anything done?"

Gavin took her hand and turned to face her. "Some things take precedence over the view." He drew her close so she could hear his pounding heart. And felt her answering response.

But he had to know something before they went any further. "Millie, are you sure?" he asked. He wanted no regrets, no morning-after remorse.

She felt the flutter of his pulse as she held his hand and decided that he was a little nervous, too. The realization had an oddly calming effect on her. "Yes, I'm very sure."

He wanted to reassure her and himself. "You should know, it's been a while for me. I've never brought a woman here."

She'd wondered about that and was enormously pleased she was not one of a long line of women in his bed. "A long time for me, too," she confessed.

Though she'd not been one to take the initiative as a rule, now she did, stretching to place her hands on both sides of his face, his handsome face. She let her fingers do some exploring, daring to touch his brows, the corners of his eyes, his strong chin. Then, rising on tiptoe, she reached to kiss him. It was a slow, lingering, delicious kiss, so unlike the others they'd experienced, where it had seemed a raging fire of passion had instantly ignited and consumed them both. This was easy, lazy, tender.

Gavin eased back and began unfastening the long row of buttons down the front of her blouse, his fingers none too steady. ''You don't know how often I've wanted to undo these prim little blouses you wear, how often I've wanted to rip them right down the middle.'' Working intently, he found the going slow, for the buttons were covered in material and the buttonholes too small for his big fingers to maneuver easily.

Her eyes were downcast, watching his progress, so still and patient, her hands resting on his forearms. She didn't help him, just waited. When at last he finished, parted the silk and slipped the blouse from her, he gazed at the satin of her bra. Millie heard him pull in a deep breath as he trailed his fingers over the soft mounds of her flesh, and she felt her skin quiver at his touch.

''My turn,'' she said, her voice throaty as she pulled his shirt from the waistband of his slacks and went to work on his buttons. He wasn't nearly as patient, undoing his cuffs and all but ripping the shirt off before she'd finished. Millie closed her eyes as he eased her close, her breasts pressing against the hard wall of his chest. The feeling was exquisite.

But Gavin needed more, so his fingers fumbled with the clasp of her bra, finally freeing her and dropping the silken barrier. Pulling her close again, he rubbed her full breasts against the soft hair of his chest and closed his eyes at the incredible sensation.

Millie had never known a man who took such care in making love, who took each step to a new height. Her breathing was growing labored in anticipation, her heart beating wildly. She touched the side zipper of her skirt, but he stopped her, taking matters into his own hands. In minutes he had the rest of her clothes off, his eyes dark and wide with wonder as he gazed at her.

"You're perfect," he murmured as his hands slid down her rib cage and along her thighs.

"Not really. I've had a child."

"Mmm, yes, which makes your body more womanly." Finally his hands closed over her breasts, and he heard her sigh of pleasure. He caressed and skimmed, then lowered his head to taste the hard nipples. Millie shifted restlessly, wondering how long her legs would continue to hold her upright. Her shaky hands moved to his waistband, but he stopped her. Too soon.

Gavin felt her sway and walked them both over to his bed, laying her down on the soft coverlet. Quickly he removed socks and shoes and followed her down. The kiss was slow and gentle, meant to settle nerves already jumpy—delaying on purpose to prolong the pleasure. Whisper soft, his mouth moved over hers, and his tongue worked his own brand of magic on her.

As he made love to every secret part of her, Millie found herself floating on a wave of desire. Love was born inside her just that quickly, just that easily. She hadn't invited it, had in fact run from it. But no matter. It bloomed within her and made everything he did achingly beautiful.

She was slender, almost willowy, yet every inch female. His head exploded as his senses came alive. Her taste, her scent, the feel of her satin-smooth skin, the sight of her lovely face as she struggled with sensations of passion, the soft sounds she made for his ears only. Never in all his years had he known a woman who could capture him so thoroughly, who could enrapture him so completely. As he sought to give her more and still more, he found his own enjoyment increasing.

She was moving now, under his ministrations, restive, trembling her response to each new delight. With lips and tongue and teeth he moved over her, down her. She tensed a long moment, then shuddered her release and whispered his name. To give her that, to answer her need, gave him a wild burst of pleasure.

As she came back to herself, Millie's hands again roamed to his waistband where she tugged open his slacks. She wanted him, all of him, right now.

Knowing her desperation matched his own, Gavin stood and shoved off his slacks and briefs.

His body was beautiful, Millie decided, lean and strong, tanned and fit. But it was her last coherent thought as he lay back down, kissing her mouth, then sliding lower to suckle her breasts. Her restless hands roamed over his back, his strong shoulders.

At last he rose above her and with one long stroke, entered her. He paused, bracing his weight on his arms, enjoying the moment as he savored the feeling. He watched her chest heave as she breathed deeply, getting used to the feel of him. Then she lifted slightly and he began moving. Eyes on each other, they climbed together, damp slippery hands clasped together, their breathing more and more ragged.

As the climax engulfed her, Millie closed her eyes and felt her whole world change forever as Gavin pressed his mouth to hers.

Millie stood at the tall wall of windows in Gavin's bedroom looking out at the rain coming down in snaking rivulets against the glass. It was a lonely scene outside, and she felt lonely inside. Funny how you needn't be alone to feel lonely.

She turned and moved quietly to the bed where Gavin slept on his side, one arm stretched out toward the empty space she'd occupied a short while ago. So much had happened tonight.

The first time they'd made love, she'd felt a high such as she'd never experienced before. Gavin had been so attentive, so warm and caring afterward. He'd talked her into calling her mother to say that something important had come up and they'd be working all night, no easy sell to a woman as suspicious as Lois Donovan. If she'd been skeptical, Lois hadn't let on, had merely said to be careful and not to worry, that both she and Joey were just fine.

They'd made love again, and he'd wrapped her in one of his robes and himself in another. They'd padded barefoot into the kitchen where he'd fixed scrambled eggs, sausage and toast. She'd eaten but scarcely remembered tasting anything. They'd smiled and laughed and touched a lot.

She was in love.

He'd coaxed her back to bed, not that she'd needed much prodding. But the glow hadn't lasted long. There'd been no talk of love and certainly none of a future together. The longer she stayed, the more she berated herself. Yes, she'd reached out for something she wanted and had thought she could handle the aftermath. Thought she could be a "modern woman," one who took her pleasure with someone she cared about but expected nothing in the way of future commitments.

She'd found out she wasn't cut out for casual sex.

Oh, she had no doubt that Gavin would invite her back to his place and his bed while she substituted for Hannah, for he seemed insatiable. However, she also had no doubt that when the older woman returned, he would thank Millie for filling in and doing such a great job, and that would be that.

What else had she expected, fool that she was? She

couldn't blame it on youth and stupidity the way she'd been with Joel. No, this time around she was merely stupid. When she thought of having to work with Gavin every day until Hannah's return, she cringed. How could she handle that, loving him and yet knowing that to him she was just one of those things?

Well, she'd have to, that's all. Slipping her feet in her pumps while she shrugged into her jacket, she stopped for a final look at Gavin. It wasn't yet midnight, but he was sound asleep. Apparently, she'd tired him out. If only she could turn off her mind, not worry about tomorrow and a son who deserved to be loved by a man who loved his mother, as well. That man wasn't Gavin, never had been. Not his fault. He hadn't lied to her, hadn't led her on. She'd merely followed her heart and lost it. Now she would have to pay the piper.

In the kitchen she found a notepad and pen. She tried to think of what to write, what words would be appropriate. In the end, she didn't leave a note, just picked up her briefcase and took the elevator down to the garage level.

Driving home through the nearly deserted streets, she decided she couldn't break her promise to Hannah. She would see this assignment through by being her usual efficient self and not alluding to anything personal that happened between them. She'd play the game same as guys did—cool, detached, just one of those things. She'd let him off the hook that way, in case he was worried she'd become clinging. No, sir, not stiff-upper-lip Millie Crandall.

If only she could carry it off.

Gavin arrived at his office at seven the next morning, anxious to see Millie. He couldn't imagine why she'd left like that without a word. He'd awakened around one, reached out for her and was shocked to see the bed empty. Jumping up, he'd hurried through his apartment, but there wasn't a trace of her.

Except that maddening cologne clinging to the pillow-case next to his.

He couldn't very well call her house at that hour nor even at five when he'd finally given up trying to sleep and gone down to work out. Even the shower that followed hadn't washed away his anxiety. As he left his private elevator, he saw that Tara was already at her desk, setting up work for the day. Office doors were open and business machines were humming. Everyone who worked for Templeton Enterprises knew that Gavin began his days early and expected them to do the same. But today it wasn't business that was on his mind.

"Good morning, Tara. Is Ms. Crandall in?"

"No, sir. Her mother called about ten minutes ago, said that Millie wasn't feeling well. Flu-like symptoms. Said she would call in later." Tara gave him her practiced smile.

Sick? She hadn't been sick last night. "All right. When she calls, let me know right away, please." He went into his office, closing the door.

Thoughtfully Gavin poured himself a cup of coffee from the sidebar where Tara always kept the brew hot and fresh. Sitting down at his desk, he wondered what was wrong with Millie. Perhaps he should call.

He checked his Rolodex and dialed her number. Mrs. Donovan answered and he could hear the yipping of a dog in the background.

"Hello, Mrs. Donovan. It's Gavin Templeton. I'm sorry to hear Millie isn't up to par."

"That's nice of you." More background chatter and Joey's voice, then his grandmother's. "Put the dish over there, Joey, not on the rug.'' Lois Donovan sighed. ''I'm sorry. Joey's dog-sitting his friend's terrier, and the busy little pup gets into everything.''

''How's Millie feeling now?'' he asked, picturing the chaos in the kitchen.

''Not so good. I'm sure she'll be better in a day or two.'' Lois sounded distracted. ''That's too much dog food, Joey.''

''I don't suppose she could come to the phone,'' he suggested, getting exasperated.

''I don't think so.''

''All right. Tell her I called, will you? And ask her to call me as soon as she's better.''

''Sure, sure, Mr. Templeton.'' Lois hung up.

Gavin sat staring at the phone for a long while. It wasn't that he didn't have lots of things to do, because he did. It was that he didn't feel like doing any of them. Not without Millie.

Leaning back, he recalled their night together, and a smile formed. It was magical, wonderful. *She* was wonderful. Not just for the sex, which admittedly was great, but as a person. She was loving and sweet, charming and funny, which was why he was…was…no! No, not in love. Couldn't be.

Could it?

A light tap on the door had him glancing up, hope surging. Unexpectedly Trey walked in.

''Never fear, Trey is here,'' his brother said, grinning.

''You're back? You mean, to work? To stay?''

''That's right, little brother. I just hauled all my stuff back into my office, and I was hoping you had time today to bring me up to speed.'' Wearing a tan summer suit with a deep navy-blue shirt open at the throat, Trey sat down across from his brother.

"Yeah, sure." Maybe Millie would feel better and come in this afternoon. Together they could brief Trey.

Trey's eyes narrowed. Gavin was distracted and, more important, he wasn't working like mad with three phones ringing and four people waiting to see him. What was wrong with this picture?

"Anything going on I should know about?" he asked.

"What?" Gavin jerked his attention back to his brother. "No, nothing."

Trey gazed about, saw the connecting door closed. "Is Little Miss Perfect Assistant in?" Gavin had told him how Millie Crandall had scored big in both the Blair merger and the Hudson takeover. He claimed she was even better than the ultraefficient Hannah.

"No, she's out sick with the flu." His voice sounded disbelieving even to his own ears.

"The flu? In June in San Diego? Really? Or is something else going on?"

"Damned if I know." Gavin hesitated only a moment, then decided he just might need some advice. So he told Trey about last night, just how wonderful it had been, without going into intimate details, and that they'd fallen asleep in each other's arms. Then he'd awakened to find her gone, and now her mother said she was sick with the flu. "It sounds fishy to me."

Trey moved his right ankle to rest on his left knee, his injuries finally healed, and considered his brother. Funny thing was that not since their college days had they discussed the female sex as applied to women they were dating. And here was Gavin looking uncharacteristically upset. Over a woman.

"Do you think maybe she had second thoughts and regretted spending the night with you?"

"No." Gavin leaned back in his chair. "I've been with

enough women to know when one is responding 100 percent. I know I haven't known Millie long, but you know me—when I make up my mind, it's usually quickly. I didn't mean for this to happen, but I think I've fallen in love with her.'' He pushed a nervous hand through his hair. "And now she pulls this."

"Let's slow down, here. We don't know for a fact that she has pulled anything. Maybe she really is sick and she's staying home because of that." Trey pondered the situation a minute or so. "Did you tell her how you feel about her, during all this tangling in the sheets?"

"No. I was going to see how she felt this morning and discuss it with her then. I had it all planned, but she left before we could talk." He paused, wondering if he'd blown it. "She's had one less-than-perfect marriage, so maybe that's what frightens her. Damn but I miss her."

"Take it from someone who's been there, you never really miss someone until they're no longer around."

"Yeah, thanks."

"Do you think she cares about you, *really* cares?"

"I sure thought so last night. Today I'm not so positive."

"If she does care—and we have every reason to believe she does because I don't think, from what you've told me, that she's the kind of woman who'd go to bed with you unless she has deep feelings—then she's got to be afraid of something. Such as maybe you don't care as much as she does. Or that you aren't the marrying kind, which I imagine she's heard, maybe even from you."

His chin resting in his hand, Gavin looked up. "Probably."

"What about her son? A woman with a child comes as a package deal, you know. Maybe she's afraid you don't care enough about the boy."

"I haven't been with him much, but, yeah, I like the kid. I'd like to do more with him, be the father image he needs. Even have more children with her."

"But you never mentioned any of this to Millie?"

"Damn it, Trey, I didn't have time. I've only known her a few weeks, and I really didn't realize I was in love with her until...well, until this morning."

Trey nodded his head, looking thoughtful. Finally he leaned forward, looking straight into his brother's eyes. "Okay, I have a solution. But you're going to have to do exactly as I say."

Gavin was skeptical. "Are you going to make me look like a fool?"

"No, but no more questions. I need to know a couple of things from you, then I'll tell you my plan. Are you game?"

There was no question that Trey had had more experience with the opposite sex than he had, Gavin thought. He was certainly not getting anywhere sitting and brooding. "All right, let's hear it."

With a conspiratorial grin Trey pulled his chair closer to Gavin's desk.

"This is the silliest thing I've ever heard of," Millie said, protesting in vain as Lois tied a black kerchief over her eyes. "Mom, why are you doing this?"

"You'll see soon enough, honey. Don't be obstinate. You're going to love the surprise, I promise you." Carefully Lois walked her daughter down the porch steps, just as the big black limo drove up.

"Yeah, Mom, be cool," Joey added. "Surprises are fun."

"I think I'm a little old for these games," Millie insisted. She wasn't in the best of moods, having slept very little and having cried a great deal. Then this morning her mother and son, heads together whispering, told her what clothes to put on and that she was going on a fun escapade. Offhand, Millie couldn't think of a single escapade that would cheer her.

She stopped in her tracks. "If you two don't tell me who's behind all this *fun,* I'm going to pull off this blindfold and..."

"Oh, now, honey," her mother interrupted. "Don't be like that. Someone's gone to a great deal of trouble to surprise you."

Millie could think of only one person who'd dream up something like this, but why wasn't he here in person to invite her along? "I want to know who it is," she demanded stubbornly.

"The dragon slayer, Mom," Joey said, grinning.

"Why won't you give me a name?"

"Because that would spoil the surprise," her son answered.

Trey Templeton got out of the driver's seat and hurried to open the door of the limo. As Mrs. Donovan led a blindfolded Millie to him, he took her arm. "This way, Ms. Crandall." And he deposited her inside the plush grey leather interior.

"You know my name? Who are you?" Millie was losing patience. Fun was fun but this was too much.

"Your driver, ma'am," Trey said, then closed the door and winked at Lois and Joey. "Don't worry. I'll take good care of her." Getting behind the wheel, he pulled away from the curb.

"Where are we going?" Millie asked, raising a hand to the blindfold.

"Don't touch that and you'll find out soon enough," Trey told her, watching in the rearview mirror. "Just a short ride and we'll be there. Now, relax and enjoy yourself.''

Relax, indeed. Fuming and fidgeting, Millie sat back, trying to listen hard so she'd figure out where the mysterious driver was heading. But the street noises didn't reach the car's interior. She heard only smooth jazz coming from the speakers behind her.

Gavin had to be behind this, though she'd not thought of him as even marginally silly or prone to pranks. Quite the contrary. But he was...such a great lover, kind and thoughtful. He was everything she'd dreamed of, once upon a time. At least she'd had one night of marvelous pleasure that she would remember all her life.

Toward morning, by the time she'd beaten her pillow to a pulp, she'd decided she simply couldn't go back and work alongside Gavin after last night. At eight, she'd phoned Hannah and learned the woman would be returning to work next Monday. She'd called Gavin's home phone around ten and left a message of resignation, giving her health as the major reason she had to quit so abruptly and telling him that Hannah would be back in four days. That done, she'd gone in to shower and had another crying jag. Her mother and Joey had accosted her when she'd come out, hurriedly preparing her for she knew not what.

The way she'd walked out on Gavin after a night of making love, she'd have thought he'd want nothing more to do with her. If he was whisking her off to demand an explanation, he was certainly going to a lot of trouble. A tiny bubble of hope deep inside had her thinking he might have decided that he cared for her and wanted a future with her. But that bubble burst when she remembered that he wasn't a man given to long-term commitments.

Face it, she couldn't readily imagine why he was doing this.

She felt the limo stop, heard the driver mumble a few words to someone, then the big car moved forward. And she still didn't know what those two coconspirators she lived with had gotten her into.

Moments later the car stopped again, and the driver helped her out. She could hear noisy engines and what sounded like planes taking off. "Are we at an airport?" she asked as he took her arm and led her straight ahead.

"Just a little farther," he answered and kept her walking. Suddenly he stopped. "We're going up about a dozen steps now." He put her right hand on the railing. "Hold on."

Somewhat clumsily Millie climbed, wondering why she hadn't yanked that silly blindfold off in the car. Just wait until she got ahold of Gavin or whoever initiated this ridiculous prank that she was certainly not in the mood for.

The driver's arm, intertwined with hers, guided her to the top landing where they stopped. "Your package, sir, delivered as directed," the man said.

"Package? That does it." Millie yanked the blindfold down and...and found herself standing in front of Gavin, who was smiling down at her. "What is this?"

"Millie, I want you to meet my brother, Trey." He indicated the man who still held her arm, a man as blond as Gavin if a little windblown, casually dressed and grinning. "Bro, this is my lady, Millie Crandall."

Too stunned to speak, Millie felt Trey take her hand and kiss it in a courtly gesture.

"*Your lady?*" she finally managed, turning to Gavin.

"Have a good flight, kids," Trey said, then skipped back down the stairs. "Don't worry about a thing."

Still puzzling over what he'd called her, Millie allowed Gavin to escort her into the same plane they'd flown in to Detroit. "Will you tell me what this is all about?"

Pushing her gently into her seat, Gavin bent to fasten her seat belt. "I'm kidnapping you, that's what." Straightening, he looked toward the cockpit. "All set to go, Emil." Sitting down alongside her, he worked on his own seat belt, aware she was staring at him as if he'd lost his mind.

Well, maybe he had. And his heart, as well.

Taking her hand as the plane began to taxi, Gavin began. "I owe you an explanation."

"At the very least. Where are we going? Let's start with that."

"In a minute." So he told her about how he'd awoken to find her gone, how he'd paced and worried, then heard she had the flu, though he didn't believe it. After Trey had come to his office, they'd considered several possibilities as to why she'd left him in the middle of the night without even a note.

"I said you were scared, and Trey said you didn't trust me." He looked into her eyes, but they revealed nothing. "Then Trey asked me what I wanted to happen next. And I told him that I'd fallen in love with you, though it had taken me a while to realize it. That I'm nuts about your son, and that I want you to marry me so we can be a family."

Now Gavin saw tears form in those gorgeous blue eyes, but he pressed on. "Trey asked if I thought you'd believe me and I said I doubted it. So he came up with this plan." He waved his arm to include the plane. "The kidnapping, the trip to Vegas and…"

"Vegas?" Things were suddenly moving awfully fast.

"Yes, because we can get married there rather quickly. I'll make it up to you later with a big wedding, I promise."

Millie pulled in a big breath. "Back up a little here. What did you say about love?"

As the plane left the ground and headed for open sky, he shifted closer. "I said I love you, Millie Crandall. I'm sorry it took me so long to realize it."

Finally she smiled and reached to caress his cheek, too moved to speak.

"How...how do you feel about me?" his voice sounding hopeful but shaded with uncertainty.

"I love you, too, you big dope." And she leaned into his kiss, dreamily, happily. "And Mom and Joey were in on this?"

"Absolutely. I talked to them this morning while you were upstairs." He couldn't help smiling. "Joey said that he was really happy that I'd be his dad, and he wants to know if I want to coach his Little League team."

"Oh, my, this is a lot to take in."

"I haven't told you the best part. Trey's back at the office for good, and Hannah will be back Monday. I arranged for one of our office managers to oversee your company in your absence. And Lois will take care of Joey while you and I go on our honeymoon."

"Vegas, you mean?"

"Oh, no." He removed an itinerary from his pocket. "Read this. We're touring Ireland."

Blinking through her tears of joy, Millie grabbed hold of him and hugged hard. "Am I dreaming?" she whispered.

"If you are, so am I." Gavin shifted and gave her a kiss filled with promise.

Epilogue

"He's awfully little," Joey declared. "Was I that little, Mom?"

Millie smiled at her son as he stood by the couch where Cilla was holding Terrence Templeton IV, who was one week old on this Christmas Eve. "You sure were."

"What do you think of your new cousin, Joey?" Trey asked, sitting down beside his wife and son.

"He's okay, I guess, but he sure doesn't do much besides eat and sleep and yawn."

Walking in, Gavin laughed out loud. "Yeah, guys, what good is he if he doesn't play ball, right, Joey?"

"He will one day," Trey assured them, touching the small fist of his son, the wonder still so brand-new and exciting. Looking into Cilla's eyes, he decided he was the happiest guy on the face of the earth right now.

"I think I'll take him up and put him in his crib," Cilla said, rising.

''Then can we open the presents?'' Joey wanted to know.

''We sure can,'' Millie assured him, gazing up at the huge tree they'd all decorated together a few nights ago. It dominated the living room of the Templeton mansion.

''Patience, patience, little fellow,'' Connie said, carrying in a tray of glasses filled with eggnog and a plate of decorated cookies. She set the tray on the glass-topped coffee table and began passing around the eggnog.

Gavin leaned over and picked up a cookie—a Christmas tree with colored candy balls on green icing. ''I hear you helped Connie with these, Joey. They look great.'' He took a big bite. ''Mmm, good.''

''Mom helped, too.'' He wiggled between Millie and Gavin, snuggling into them, but his eyes were on the gaily wrapped packages under the tree that he'd been told not to touch quite yet. ''See that long one, Dad, in the snowman paper? I think it's a new bat, and it's got my name on it.''

Gavin felt a warmth every time the boy called him Dad and wondered if it would always be like that. ''Are you sure it's not for the new baby?'' he asked, winking at Millie over Joey's head.

''Nah, he's too little.''

''What would you say if we had a little baby like that at our house?'' he asked the son he'd adopted soon after marrying his mother. Joel Crandall hadn't fought the adoption, couldn't have legally because he'd already signed off on his parental rights some time ago. Gazing into the boy's eyes, Gavin knew that Joel didn't deserve to have Joey in his life.

Joey's gaze went immediately to his mother's flat stomach and he frowned. He'd watched with fascination as his aunt Cilla had grown bigger and bigger before his cousin was born, but his mother didn't look like that. "Are you going to have a baby, Mom?"

"Would you like that?" she asked, studying his face. With his blond hair and blue eyes, he was often mistaken for Gavin's biological son, which pleased her husband no end. And Joey hadn't mentioned Joel in months.

"I don't know," Joey said hesitantly. "Will I have to share my room? Babies cry a lot, you know." The new ranch house Gavin was having built was almost complete, and from the start Joey had had input into where his room would be. A baby, he reasoned, might spoil everything.

Entering the room after putting her son down, Cilla caught the conversation. "What's this about more babies?" she asked, looking Millie over with a practiced eye. "Are you...?" She let the question hang.

Millie shook her head. "Just considering future possibilities."

But it was Gavin who answered Joey. "You absolutely would not have to share your room. Remember when we were first looking at the house plans and we said that one day our family might grow, so we included a couple of extra bedrooms? That's where the new baby would go, when the time comes, so that when he cried, he wouldn't bother you. Okay?"

"Yeah, I guess so. But I thought one of those rooms was for Grandma?"

Lois Donovan was spending Christmas with a close friend recently widowed in Florida, and Joey missed her, Millie knew. "We have a room set aside for Grandma to visit anytime she wants, but she's happy in the house where we used to live."

Millie could hardly wait until they could move to the ranch Gavin had purchased in Arizona about an hour and a half away by plane. At last he'd have a chance to try his hand at ranching, something he'd dreamed of for too long. The sale package included eighty acres, some two dozen quarter horses, a breeding and birthing barn, stables, paddocks and lots of grazing land. There was also an inviting pond in back. The only thing they were waiting for was for the builder to finish their home in the spot where the old one had been torn down.

Babies and grandmothers forgotten, Joey wanted to get on with the main event. "Now can we open presents?"

"In a minute." Trey lifted his glass as he slipped his arm around his wife. "To the best Christmas ever and to my lovely wife, who turned this empty shell of a house into a home. I love you." Now, at thirty-eight, Trey no longer worried about a curse.

"I love you, too," Cilla answered.

"I'll second that," Gavin said, and hugged both Millie and Joey, who was still seated between them. "I never used to like this holiday." He turned to Connie, whose eyes were suspiciously damp. "Trey and I both remember that you were the only one who tried to make Christmas happy for us. Thank you, Connie."

"From me, too," Trey added.

"I should be thanking all of you for including me in this holiday." Connie swiped a tear away.

"Hey, you're family, Connie," Trey said. "And now you're helping with another generation of Templetons."

"Like me," Joey said, jumping up and going to Connie, hugging her. "I'm a Templeton now, too."

She held him close, kissed his cheek. "You sure are, and it is my very deep pleasure to be with you all." Lifting her glass, she toasted them, then sipped her eggnog.

"Mmm, this is good, Connie." Cilla told her.

"I told you she makes the best eggnog," Trey said. "And tomorrow, Christmas Day, when we all go over to

Mama and Papa Kovacs's, Gavin, you all can try Papa's homemade wine. It really separates the men from the boys, I can tell you.''

"Do they have a Christmas tree up, too?" Joey asked Cilla.

"They sure do. And all the cousins you met at the wedding will be there. Of course, there'll be presents under the tree for all of us, too.''

Suddenly serious, Trey gazed around the lovely room so beautifully decorated for the holidays and at his family, thinking of his son sleeping upstairs. "I have all the presents I need right here.'' Again he drew Cilla close and kissed her.

"I'm so happy for all of you, for finding each other,'' Connie said.

"Yeah, me, too. *Now* can we please open the presents before Santa takes them all back?'' Joey asked hopefully.

They all laughed. "We wouldn't want that,'' Trey said as he went to sit alongside the tree to pass out gifts.

On the couch, his arm around his wife, Gavin watched his son take each gift to the person named on the tag, and let out a happy sigh. "Merry Christmas,'' he whispered, and Millie answered with a kiss.

* * * * *

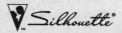

Award-winning author
SHARON DE VITA
brings her special brand of romance to

✦ Silhouette

SPECIAL EDITION™
and

SILHOUETTE *Romance*™

in her new cross-line miniseries

SADDLE

FALLS

This small Western town was rocked by scandal when the youngest son of the prominent Ryan family was kidnapped. Watch as new clues about the mysterious disappearance are unveiled—and meet the sexy Ryan brothers…and the women destined to lasso their hearts.

Don't miss:

Available at your favorite retail outlet.

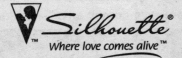

✦ Silhouette®

Where love comes alive™

If you enjoyed what you just read,
then we've got an offer you can't resist!

Take 2 bestselling love stories FREE!

Plus get a FREE surprise gift!

Clip this page and mail it to Silhouette Reader Service™

IN U.S.A.	IN CANADA
3010 Walden Ave.	P.O. Box 609
P.O. Box 1867	Fort Erie, Ontario
Buffalo, N.Y. 14240-1867	L2A 5X3

YES! Please send me 2 free Silhouette Special Edition® novels and my free surprise gift. After receiving them, if I don't wish to receive anymore, I can return the shipping statement marked cancel. If I don't cancel, I will receive 6 brand-new novels every month, before they're available in stores! In the U.S.A., bill me at the bargain price of $3.80 plus 25¢ shipping and handling per book and applicable sales tax, if any*. In Canada, bill me at the bargain price of $4.21 plus 25¢ shipping and handling per book and applicable taxes**. That's the complete price and a savings of at least 10% off the cover prices—what a great deal! I understand that accepting the 2 free books and gift places me under no obligation ever to buy any books. I can always return a shipment and cancel at any time. Even if I never buy another book from Silhouette, the 2 free books and gift are mine to keep forever.

235 SEN DFNN
335 SEN DFNP

Name	(PLEASE PRINT)	
Address	Apt.#	
City	State/Prov.	Zip/Postal Code

* Terms and prices subject to change without notice. Sales tax applicable in N.Y.
** Canadian residents will be charged applicable provincial taxes and GST.
All orders subject to approval. Offer limited to one per household and not valid to current Silhouette Special Edition® subscribers.
® are registered trademarks of Harlequin Enterprises Limited.

SPED01   ©1998 Harlequin Enterprises Limited

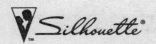

COMING NEXT MONTH

#1459 THE PRINCESS IS PREGNANT!—Laurie Paige
Crown and Glory

A shared drink—and a shared night of passion. That's what happened the night Princess Megan Penwyck met her family rival, bad boy Earl Jean-Paul Augustave. Then shy Megan learned she was pregnant, and the tabloids splashed the royal scoop on every front page....

#1460 THE GROOM'S STAND-IN—Gina Wilkins

Bodyguard Donovan Chance was supposed to escort his best friend's fiancée-to-be, Chloe Pennington—not fall in love with her! But when the two were abducted, they had to fight for survival...and fight their growing desire for each other. When they finally made it home safely, would Chloe choose a marriage of convenience...or true love with Donovan?

#1461 FORCE OF NATURE—Peggy Webb
The Westmoreland Diaries

A gorgeous man who had been raised by wolves? Photojournalist Hannah Westmoreland couldn't believe her eyes—or the primal urges that Hunter Wolfe stirred within her. When Hannah brought the lone wolf to civilization, she tamed him...then let him go. Would attraction between these opposites prove stronger than the call of the wild?

#1462 THE MAN IN CHARGE—Judith Lyons

Love 'em and leave 'em. Major Griffon Tyler had burned her before, and Juliana Bondevik didn't want to trust the rugged mercenary with her heart again. But then Juliana's sneaky father forced the two lovers to reunite by hiring Griffon to kidnap his daughter. Passions flared all over again, but this time Juliana was hiding a small secret—their baby!

#1463 DAKOTA BRIDE—Wendy Warren

Young widow Nettie Owens had just lost everything...so how could she possibly be interested in Chase Reynolds, the mysterious bachelor who'd just landed in town? Then Chase learned that he was a father, and he asked Nettie to marry him to provide a home for his child. Would a union for the baby's sake help these two wounded souls find true love again?

#1464 TROUBLE IN TOURMALINE—Jane Toombs

To forget his painful past...that's why lawyer David Severin escaped to his aunt's small Nevada town. Then psychologist Amy Simon showed up for a new job and decided to make David her new patient—without telling David! Would Amy's secret scheme help David face his inner demons...and give the doctor an unexpected taste of her own medicine? SSECNM0302